THE GUIDAL
DISCOVERING PURACORDIS

✿

BY ROXY ELOISE

CONTENTS

To my mum for being my number one fan.

To my dad for teaching me to never give up.

To Carrie for always believing.

To Hannah for greeting me over the park with "Serve, Honour, Protect, and Defend."

To Jack for looking after me.

And to Kabir for teaching me that everyone deserves a tail wag.

CHAPTER ONE

TRI-DA DADINAY

Tears rolled past my temples, dampening my pillow. *It's not real. It's not real. It's not real.* I had the dream about my parents again—the one with the young boy who couldn't save me. It always made me wonder how my parents died. But that topic of conversation was considered disrespectful and never discussed between Young Enforcers. We were in training now and we should be grateful for it. Our past? Irrelevant.

I lay still, stealing a few more minutes in bed, before dread engulfed my body. I twisted onto my front, pushing my face deep into my damp pillow. The day was finally here.

"Up now, Little Lady." Nanny Kimly Luminosa came bursting through my bedroom door.

I responded with a long involuntary groan, holding the pillow tight around my head.

"It's an important day for you," she continued, ignoring my muffled moaning. "You're going on to bigger and better things."

"Better things?" I mumbled into the pillow. "I just want to stay in Mustard forever."

"You want to stay in the children's quarter forever? Hmm?" She hummed after I stayed quiet. "How silly would you look in Mustard when all others your age will be in Navy?" She perched on the edge of my bed and stroked the loose white hair out of my eyes. She looked almost the same as she did in my dream. Perhaps slightly curvier

1

now, and silver strands laced in her red bun. "And, my dear," she said, still stroking my hair, "it's Unity. You could *match*. That'd be nice, wouldn't it?"

"No, Nanny Kimly, it wouldn't. I don't want to match. I'm going to answer the questions so honestly and ensure I won't. I don't want to get married." I sat up in bed hoping to convey my seriousness. "I'm only *sixteen*."

Nanny Kimly hid a subtle smile, as she sometimes did when I pushed my luck. "Unity only matches you. Look at it like an engagement. The wedding will only take place the year you or your partner turns thirty."

"Yeah, but if I match with a Thirteenth-year then that will be next year. He will be thirty *next year*."

"Such an age gap seldom happens, Aurora. It is scientific. If you *are* matched," she gave my hand a squeeze, "you *will* like it."

I huffed. "I don't understand why we can't choose to be omitted."

"Seioh Boulderfell just wants what's best for his children."

"This is the *Boulderfell Institute for Young Enforcers*, not the Boulderfell Asylum for Arranged Marriages."

"Enough," Nanny Kimly said simply, reminding me to stop overstepping my boundaries.

"I'm going to miss you." I respectfully changed my tune.

"Come on, get ready," she said, fidgeting with the thin silver buttons on her tunic's side split. She reached towards the end of my bed. "Your new uniform," she added, handing me a navy jacket, a pair of navy combat trousers, and a new pair of black boots.

My eyebrows pulled together. "Won't my uniform already be in my new room?"

"It will, but what do you suppose you will wear to get to your new room? Do you want to be walking around Navy Quartz in your Mustard uniform?"

"Ah. I didn't think about that."

"Hmm," she hummed in her usual, all-knowing way. "It will be so strange seeing you in blue instead of yellow. You're going to look so grown up." She smiled, and then the hazel of her eyes glazed over.

I figured she was reminiscing about our past, and I seized my opportunity. "Nanny Kimly, did I come in with a young boy the first time I met you?" I asked about the boy from my dream, needing clarification it was just that, a dream.

But Nanny Kimly frowned. "I said that's enough, Little Lady." She gave me a stern look before standing up and brushing off her black tunic. "Now, don't concern yourself with such things. You're in the adults' quarter now, and you have a busy day ahead of you."

I kept my mouth shut and faked a small smile. Nanny Kimly gave me an approving nod for holding my tongue.

"And, Aurora, please stay on the right side of Seioh Jennson. He won't be so lenient on you now you're in Navy. Please keep yourself out of trouble…for me?"

I nodded, and she left my room. The automatic door closed softly behind her. I sighed, kicking the duvet off me and swinging my legs off the bed. The display screen beside me showed a sunny beach, so I asked Soami, the Digital Assistant, to play a scene better fitting to my mood. "Soami, play a stormy rainforest, please."

"Yes, Miss Aviary," replied the soft female voice. "Good luck in moving over to Navy today."

"Yeah, thanks."

Rain began to hammer at the fake window, and all around my room I heard the gushing of torrential downpour, and chirping of exotic birds. I instantly felt my shoulders drop, and I began carefully folding the yellow uniform I wore yesterday. I carried the neat pile to the far side of my room and held it over the laundry chute. My room, my Nanny Kimly, and my uniform were the three things I could always rely on to be there. Today, I was losing them and leaving all I'd ever known behind. I closed my eyes and let the uniform go.

After a small sigh, I glanced over at my new Navy uniform. It waited for me on my bed in its protective wrapping. *Guess I should get this over and done with.* It wasn't that I was not ready to grow up, or that I wanted to remain a child forever, it was just that I didn't like all these changes happening so suddenly. For thirteen years of my life, every day and everything remained the same, day in, day out. Now it was all being taken away in a single day.

I tore off the plastic wrapping, separated the blue combats, blue vest, and slim-fitted jacket, and changed quickly. I straightened out my jacket, brushing it down, and touching the familiar institute logo above my hip. It was the same as on my Mustard jumper: a smooth metal ring overlaying a sharp 'X.'

Unable to delay things any longer, I tied my long white hair in a high ponytail, picked up my trunk by the handle, and wheeled it towards the door. I glanced around the empty room, the rumpled bed sheets, the empty wardrobe, the clear desk. *Goodbye room.* I inhaled deeply, crushing the feeling inside my chest, and I walked out of my bedroom backwards.

This building had been my home for as long as I could remember. Children under fourteen were taken here whenever the authorities issued a care order. Neglect or simply not having biological parents were all grounds for adoption here, and preventing children from being raised here at the *Boulderfell Institute for Young Enforcers* was considered dishonourable.

The institute was a massive circular building, probably the biggest in Vencen, the capital city of Venair. It was a simple building to navigate and had four colour co-ordinated quarters: Mustard Quartz, a place for children under the age of sixteen; Khaki Quartz, for the Khakidemy where we all went to study and train; Navy Quartz, the section for adults between the ages of sixteen and twenty-nine; and finally, Claret Quartz, the place our prisoners, known as Juvies, were detained. The residential corridors were long, monotonous, but slightly mesmerising. Especially with the hypnotic rumbling from my trunk's wheels running over the joints in the floor panels. I was on my way out of Mustard Quartz, following dull-yellow strip lights along the walls.

"Hello, Aurora," greeted a Navy boy as we passed each other. He, too, towed a plastic trunk.

"Hello," I returned, the obvious absence of his name tugging at my insides. I quickened my pace until I turned into a larger corridor, yellow lights on one side and green the other. These main corridors could take me to the Food Hall or to the outskirts of the building where the receptions were. Children stayed inside the institute most of their childhood, so glass doors and glass walls around the building gave us the closest feeling to being outside. I turned right into Khaki Quartz, seeing it was still dark out in the city and the streets were deserted. Curfew didn't end for another ten minutes.

Arriving at the Navy reception, I stood in front of a large curved reception desk, dark-blue lights reflecting on these white surfaces. "Good morning," I said quietly. "I need to check into my room, please."

A plump receptionist straightened up to see me over the top of the wide counter. Her wild, crispy, dark-brown hair blocked out most of the holographic broadcast playing on the back wall. "Good morning, *ma'am*," she corrected me.

"Good morning, *ma'am*, I need to check in to my room." I intentionally exaggerated the 'ma'am,' hoping to move things along.

Her eyes flared along with her nostrils. "Would you like me to call for Seioh Jennson?" she asked, her blue eyes bulging. "He will not stand for your rudeness and neither will I."

We used the word 'Seioh' as a sign of respect for high-ranking officials, and I *in no way* wanted another encounter with Seioh Jennson again, so I sucked it up. "No, I'm sorry, ma'am. I have just advanced from Mustard Quartz. I am Aurora Aviary, and I need to check in…ma'am…please?"

"I know who you are, and your insolence may have been tolerated in Mustard, but it will not be tolerated here." She thrust a large brown envelope towards me. I reached over to take it, but she held it down with her chubby finger.

"Yes, ma'am. I am very sorry, ma'am. I will behave, ma'am," I replied, holding back a laugh after amusing myself. *Sarcasm gets you nowhere, Aurora.* I swallowed, anticipating the backlash, but the ogre lifted her hand. Unable to believe my luck, I took my envelope quickly and fled from the receptionist before she cooked me up for breakfast.

I was pleased to find my new room was *exactly* the same as my old one. It had the same plain panelled walls, the same window display by the bed, the same laundry chute by the wardrobe, and the same ensuite by the desk. The only way of knowing I hadn't walked back into my old room was the blue duvet cover on the bed. I rolled my belongings into their designated place alongside the ensuite, and opened my welcome pack. It enclosed a huge stack of paperwork, which included a temporary daily schedule and a welcome letter. A cold shiver ran down from the top of my head, waking up the hair on my neck. My eyes focused on a sentence in the letter. The posh font didn't make the content any more attractive.

'*Successful candidates of the Unity assessment will be allocated new bedrooms next to their betrothed.*'

I had momentarily forgotten all about the Unity assessment, and the letter reminded me like a wet fish to the face. Now the fish felt like it was swimming around in my stomach. I studied the sentence again—'*next to.*' Well, at least that was something. Sod sharing a room with a *boy.*

From the moment I read the letter, I couldn't cope with the overwhelming anxiety. I needed to get rid of the fish, so I decided to head to the Khakidemy to sit the test without meeting up with my best friend, Silliah, first. I was sure she would be in there anyway. She'd probably be already eagerly completing her test; she loved Unity. It was supposed to find our perfect partners, someone we would be expected to spend all our time with, and someone we would eventually be expected to have children with. For what reason? I had no idea. I always heard the same thing, 'Unity is a privilege, a rare prequisite.'

The Old Library was busy with enthusiastic Navies, all quietly completing their assessments. After a failed scan for Silliah, I searched for a free booth, finding one nestled between two girls who didn't even notice me take a seat. Whilst settled on my stool, conscious of the cameras pointing at my face, detecting my blood flow, temperature, and muscle movements, I touched 'Begin.' My heart rate displayed onscreen. I assumed that had something to do with the picoplant under the skin in my wrist, and this whole setup gave me the impression these assessments were impossible to cheat.

I read through the introduction briefly, avoiding another explanation as to why this test was so great. Trying to keep my heart rate steady, I wondered what my vital stats were identifying. Could they tell I was irritated?

Yeah, betrothed to marry, I know. Yes, I'm honoured to be given this privilege. Okay, here we go, question one, let's see.

"Cats or dogs?" I read the question aloud. "What has that got to do with finding my soulmate? I thought this test was supposed to be scientific."

Amused eyes looked over in my direction.

"Aurora, that's enough," said Lady Joanne Maxhin, supervising the candidates this hour. "If you want me to call for Seioh Jennson again, you are going the right way about it. You're a Navy now, not a child. Keep your head down and start thinking before you speak."

"Yes, ma'am."

"You know this is a confidential assessment. So I mean it— silence; not another word from you."

Grrr. What kind of test was this? I rubbed my face so hard it hurt. How could I be matched on the basis of liking cats or dogs? *It's so stupid.* I hated this Unity week already.

Tea or Coffee—*neither, thanks.*

Hot or Cold—*what?*

Up or Down—*are they serious?*

A few more questions passed like that before asking me questions as to whether I agreed or disagreed.

I experience my emotions intensely—*strongly agree.*

I am easily intimidated—*just disagree.* I almost strongly disagreed, but I was slightly intimidated by Seioh Jennson, the head of the institute. I'd had too many run-ins with him to not be. *So...I'll just disagree on this one.*

I trust others—*strongly disagree.*

Once I'd completed all one hundred questions, I jumped from my stool feeling better about my chances of matching; I highly doubted it. I couldn't imagine anyone else hating this farce as much as I did. Surely the results would detect that. The two girls I sat between were still at their booths, thinking through their answers thoroughly and making their decisions carefully. I almost rolled my eyes but I caught Lady Maxhin watching me through her holographic display. I pushed in my stool, patted the backrest awkwardly, and fled from the room.

Leaving the Khakidemy, I left any thoughts about the test behind and headed to the Food Hall for breakfast. I entered a hall with the majority of tables reset in their default table-of-four position. Only one group had their table set up as a bench for twelve. I breathed in the near empty room, grateful I'd missed the mid-morning rush. Although the room was cleverly designed—with circular rows upon rows of tables—it was hard to find a single table during busier times.

Situated in the very centre of the building like the bullseye on a target, the Food Hall was the only room that inhabited all four quarters of the institute. I chose a table in Claret Quartz, the section with polished, purply-red floor tiles. Sitting down, I glanced over at a few Musties huddled together, whispering, and turning to look at a Navy standing in the centre by the meal dispenser. Curly blond-brown hair reflecting his chilled-out demeanour, he seemed blissfully unaware of the attention he was being given. From the sound of things, the bench full of Navies also appeared to be talking about him.

"Quickly. Pax is on his own. What should I order?" asked a slender girl with a giggle, looking down at her tabletop screen. "OK, I ordered a fresh green juice; that will do." She floated up out of her chair and wafted over—in what seemed like slow motion—flicking her glossy, cocoa-brown hair. Her friends watched eagerly. I, too, couldn't help myself; I needed to see how this one played out.

"Hey, Pax," she said in a sickly tone, brushing her fingers across the length of his broad back.

"Hey, Pipila." He didn't seem to mind the invasion of his personal space, yet didn't encourage it either.

She played with her hair, tossing her head from side to side. I personally thought she looked demented, but I supposed she was going for cute.

"Order ready for Miss Darlington," prompted Soami, the Digital Assistant, indicating food had arrived in the hatch.

"Oh, that's mine," said Pipila. "Can I just get my—" She leant over Pax, using his arm as support, scanned her picoplant to open the hatch, and reached for her juice. "Hmm, best way to start the day, eh, Pax?" Pipila tipped her head back and sipped the juice delicately. "Well, good luck with Unity this year. Third time lucky for us; I hope we match. Oh, I mean, I hope we *find* a match," she 'corrected' herself before swanning back to her table. *Right...*

Slightly bemused, it was about time I ordered my breakfast. I double-tapped the table to activate my screen and chose a platter of chopped mango, pineapple, and bananas. A four-minute counter filled my screen, so I headed over.

"Order ready for Miss Aviary," called Soami from the meal dispenser.

Offering the back of my wrist to release my food, I took the tray and sat back down. As I did, I caught the eye of a freckly boy sitting over with Pipila. I snapped my eyes back down to my breakfast. A dull thud made me look back up.

A lizard-faced Navy had slapped the freckly boy across the back hard. Both of the boys' eyes were on me.

"She's mine, Brindan!" said Lizard-face to the boy whose eye I caught sitting down—Brindan. "Isn't that right, lovely?" Lizard-face winked at me with creepy beetle-black eyes.

The muscles in my stomach tightened, and with it, a loss of appetite. I didn't know either of the two boys and didn't wish to know them either. My eyes flicked back over at Brindan. He looked as uncomfortable as I felt, his freckly face now a shade of red closely matching the floor tiles beneath my feet.

"We will be married before you know it," Lizard-face continued to taunt me, his black eyes still burning into the side of my head.

Pipila whipped her neck round to see what all the fuss was about. "*Her*?" she cried, placing strong emphasis on the H. "Why would you want to match with *that*? Have you seen her hair?"

My fists pounded the table as I sprung up from my chair. I found myself heading her way. My vision tunnelled on her and a pounding sounded in my ears. Then my whole body jarred back the way I came, someone's fingers gripping firmly around my bicep, snapping me out from my rage. *Oh no.* I acknowledged self-control was not my strong suit—but what was I doing?

"I wouldn't do that," said the boy Pipila had spoken to earlier, Pax. He kept hold of my arm, assessing my current emotional state.

"Ah, my hero, Pax," said Pipila, laughing.

"Stupid girl," added another, amidst a noisy bombardment of insults. "What is wrong with her?"

"Ooh, you're going to be in trouble," sang Lizard-face.

"I'm fine," I said to Pax, freeing my jittering arm from his hold. I left my tray on the table and withdrew from the hall.

Fighting and bullying of any kind was strictly forbidden here. I had never known what it felt like to be picked on. The children were kept in line; why weren't the adults? I was starting to think being in Navy was like being in a prison with no guards.

CHAPTER TWO

SEIOH

After embarrassing myself, I went straight to bed, claiming I didn't feel well. That didn't normally work for me, but somehow, I was left undisturbed, hiding under my duvet all day. Nanny Kimly's words floated around inside my head incessantly, 'Please keep yourself out of trouble…for me?' How could I have been so stupid? I clenched my fists at the 'stupid girl' comment knocking about inside my brain. Soon, I tired of the mental chatter and fell into a restless sleep until the alarm woke me up the next morning.

It's not real. It's not real. It's not real. I covered my eyes with my forearm to block out the lights before they switched themselves on. The young boy's eyes from my dream remained behind my eyelids. They glistened, wet from his tears, guilt swimming in their piercing blue. My own tears rolled down my face, and I'd woken up to a damp pillow once again.

My crying settled, but the ache throbbing in my chest didn't. *Stop it,* I told myself, *it's only a dream.* There was no way it could be real. I felt things I shouldn't have, and I heard things I couldn't have. *You can't know how the boy was feeling, let alone what he was thinking. It's a dream.*

Eyes closed under the weight of my arm, it replayed vividly in my mind. It always started the same way every time…with that young boy, Tayo. He would be standing under the stars, head tilted back, gazing up at a tall glass fountain. The falling stream glowed with a

11

white mystical hue reflecting the moonlight. He stood soothed by the song of flowing water, focusing in on it until he heard something else behind the trickle. I felt the panic drench his veins.

The rhythmic marching of Young Enforcers disturbed the sleeping city. Tayo watched them in the distance flooding out of the institute. Taser guns clutched against their chests, they strode in formation towards the woodlands near Tayo's home. He was breaking Curfew, and risked being taken away from his parents if he got caught. He had to get home before the woodlands were littered with Enforcers. If they got there first, the chances of getting caught were high. Without a second thought, he began running for the woods.

Reaching the border, he lost sight of the battalion through the expanse of trees. *I can't see anything,* he thought, slowing down. A click sent his neck twisting to the right. He crouched, trying to attune his senses to his surroundings, but he couldn't see further than a few shadowed tree trunks. A rustle in the other direction and his eyes searched the sheet of black, his ears pricked, listening closely.

Still creeping in the direction of his home, he kept searching for signs of movement. His fear made the woodlands look unfamiliar. Blinding darkness and demonic shadows followed him. A crack split the air and he jumped. Rubbing his face, he shook his head at the broken stick under his own slipper. *Come on, Tayo. Be brave. You can do this.*

But Tayo froze. He strained his ears for a faint scraping noise. Someone was close. His heart felt as though it had leaped into his throat. Pinned to the spot, he squinted, looking for movement between the trunks. Suddenly, the ground lurched underneath him and he met the ground with a shooting pain in his lower back.

Tayo suppressed a gasp and kept still. He'd spotted my dad coming up through a hole in the ground.

"Averlynn?" Dad whispered down the hole for my mum. He'd emerged up through a peculiar trapdoor concealed in the woodland floor. In one hand, my dad held on to the hinged door responsible for Tayo's fall, but in the other, he held on to me.

I was only a toddler in this dream. Pillow creases marked my cheek. One unicorn-speckled pyjama leg was hitched up around my knee. Both of these, and my messy ice-white hair, all suggested I'd been sleeping and we left in a hurry.

"Averlynn?" came another of my dad's urgent whispers. He searched under the trapdoor for my mum. His glassy pale-blue eyes darted frantically around in the darkness. The call was met by silence. A sudden deathlike pallor overcame his face—a wife in danger down below, but a child who needed protecting. He scanned around, seemingly lost, but probably unsure what to do.

"Tayo?" My dad saw Tayo on the dry, hard ground. "What are you—never mind. I'll talk to you later about your law breaking. Please, take Aurora, run and hide. Keep her safe. Don't let anyone take her. Do you think you can do that for me?"

Tayo took his first full breath in a while. Still sitting back on his hands, fingers splayed through the loose earth, he immediately jumped to his feet and dusted off his hands. "Yuh-yes, sir."

"Go with him, Ra-ra." He gave my hand to Tayo.

"Daddy." I shook my head, trying to pull away from the young boy.

"Shh. I have to go help Mummy." He brushed my tears away with both thumbs. "Go with Tayo. Mummy and Daddy will be right behind you." He kissed my head, holding there a moment as he inhaled me, eyes closed. Pulling back he hesitated, looking at me, conflict clearly seen behind his eyes. Was he making the right decision? He swallowed, changed his expression to a smile, nodded, and disappeared under the trapdoor.

Tayo and I stood alone in the dark, holding on to each other's hands.

"Come, Aurora, this way," said Tayo, coming back to his senses. "We can hide at mine."

Tightening his hold on my tiny hand, he led the way through the overgrown foliage. We stumbled together over the uneven surface, huge ferns hitting me in the face, whipping across my sensitive skin and leaving a sting in their wake. I made no attempt to cry out, being away from my parents my only concern.

I squinted, unable to see through the mass of attacking ferns. I tried to look back for my parents when suddenly Tayo yanked me into his chest and covered my mouth. He pulled me closer, slowly lowering to his knees and hiding in the ferns. I was tucked into his lap, folded until my knees almost touched my chin. There were ten or fifteen of them—civilians, not Enforcers—all slim and of different heights, travelling stealthily on foot. Their silhouettes crossed up ahead, baggy trousers clinging to their shins and hoods flapping with their movement. They were too quiet; this was not their first time creeping about during Curfew. What were they hunting for?

My eyes were squeezed tightly shut when I felt Tayo's breath becoming slow and even against my ear. He got up, encouraging me to stand. The lithe figures gone, he took my hand, and we set off running again.

"We're almost there," Tayo reassured me. It was almost enough to calm me, but the real relief came from the sound of two sets of footsteps catching up behind us. Certain my mum and dad had finally caught up with us, our staggering feet slowed right down.

"Hold it there, you two," demanded a bleak voice.

My heart sank to the soil. That was not the familiar voice of my loving dad. Tayo knew it, too. He brought me in closer, shielding me from the two Enforcers standing before us. I wrapped my arms around Tayo's legs. The Enforcers towered over us, resembling robots in their intimidating navy-blue body armour, the tinted helmets hiding their faces. We stumbled backwards as the Enforcers reached out to get us.

"No! Get your hands off her," shouted Tayo, trying to keep hold of me after I was grabbed by an Enforcer. "I have to look after her. Let go!"

The other Enforcer pulled at Tayo's shoulders. Two hands on my wrist, Tayo refused to let me go. I fixed onto his helpless eyes as our grips slipped from the strength of the two grownups separating us. Sensing defeat, Tayo writhed aggressively. "Get off." He lashed out, managing to kick the Enforcer's ankle.

"You little sh—" The Enforcer stopped himself.

I didn't imagine the kick hurt all that much because the plastic-like armour was too thick. If anything, Tayo's attempt made the Enforcer even more determined, and with one last hard yank, my hand slipped from Tayo's. At the same time, the golden bracelet looped around my wrist broke, but Tayo managed to reel it in. The disgruntled Enforcer held out Tayo's closed fist, took out a wand-like reader, and scanned the picoplant in the back of Tayo's wrist.

Nothing happened.

The Enforcer tried again, waving the wand-like reader and watching the screen. "Why isn't this working?"

"Oh, look what we have here," said the female Enforcer, scanning my picoplant, "Aurora Aviary, aged three, parents *deceased*."

Tayo's insides wrung, draining blood from his face. "No, that's not right."

The Enforcer yanked Tayo by the arm. "Shut up, boy." He hammered a few buttons on the reader and tried for Tayo's information again. "What is wrong with this thing? You will be going to the institute, too, if I can't get this flipping picoplant to scan."

"But she's not an orphan," Tayo muttered weakly, sensing he was only making things worse for himself. "I just saw her father."

The Enforcer dug his taser gun into Tayo's back and began walking him towards the city centre. My Enforcer picked me up and followed after them. Head down, Tayo kicked at old leaves and twigs as he went, hands clenched in his pyjama bottom pockets. Tears soaked my cheeks as I searched the darkness for my mum and dad.

After twenty minutes or so, we arrived at glass doors to the enormous dome-shaped institute building. The Enforcer removed his gun from Tayo's back and grabbed him by the wrist, waiting to enter the reception.

Inside, miserable dull-red lights only worsened our inner angst. This was no place for children. An echo of heels tapping on the sterile white surface grew louder until my Nanny Kimly showed up on my left, reaching a hand to my face. "Now, now, stop those tears." She gently wiped my cheek with her thumb.

Tayo snatched his wrist away from his captor and held on to Nanny Kimly's hand. "We are not orphans, ma'am," Tayo spluttered. "We shouldn't be—"

"The boy's picoplant is defective," interrupted the male Enforcer. "That's if he even has one."

"OK, my sweet boy, let me see here." Nanny Kimly took her reader and hovered it over Tayo's wrist. Then she raised her eyebrows from underneath her trim fringe and shot a look over at the Enforcer. "Tayo Tessan, aged six, parents Mr. Jarl Tessan and Mrs. Tora Tessan. What is this young man doing here? Take him home immediately." Nanny Kimly lifted my arm and waved the reader over me. "Sometimes," she said, giving the Enforcers a quick glance, "you Young Enforcers do worry me. Come now, Little Lady." And with that, she took me into her arms and carried me away.

I reached out for Tayo from over Nanny Kimly's shoulder. He reached out for me. Held back by an Enforcer, Tayo's outstretched fingers slowly lost hope as I slipped further away. A tear fell down his young face. Watching me disappear, he lowered his hand and touched at the dull ache in his chest. I heard the thoughts plaguing his head: *I couldn't save her. I was told to keep her safe, and I couldn't save her.*

It's not real. It's not real. It's not real, I continued to tell myself. It felt realer than any dream I'd ever had, but it was far too strange to ever be a memory. Firstly, I felt the young boy's emotions, and secondly, I heard his thoughts. *It's clearly a dream!*

Before I had finished convincing myself of that fact, my bedroom door slid open. I removed my arm from my eyes, expecting to see Nanny Kimly, albeit confused since Navies didn't have caregivers, but I couldn't imagine who else would be storming in my room so early. In the past, Nanny Kimly was the only one who did that.

"Up, Miss Aviary, now," ordered a serious, deep voice.

My guts left my body through my mouth, and I fell out of bed as if it were on fire. Scrambling to my feet, I straightened up to attention, heels touching, chin up, and hands hidden behind my back. "Yes, Seioh." Sleep still blurring my vision, I blinked the outline of his black suit and the harsh edges of his greying military haircut into focus.

Seioh Jennson stepped towards me, holding a yellow garment against his old-fashioned suit, a suit I'd only seen Bricks-'n-Mortar men wear from the 1900s. "Put this on," he said, proffering a Mustard uniform.

My eyes scanned the yellow crew-neck jumper, the black shoulder patches, the ribbed detailing. *Put it...on?* I brought my gaze back up to meet his. *Surely, he didn't mean—*

He did. Apparently, word spread about my outburst in the Food Hall.

"You wouldn't be waiting for me to repeat myself, would you, Miss Aviary?" he asked almost casually, turning me to face the ensuite, and holding the uniform to my chest.

"No, Seioh." I stepped off, Mustard uniform in hand.

The door shut behind me and I began to change, my outburst from the day before playing out in my head. This was all because of *her*. I was born with white hair. Granted, I'd never seen anyone else with my hair colour but I liked that. *She must be jealous.* Forcing myself to stop reliving the moment, I returned to stand in front of Jennson, looking no different than I did two days ago. It was unlikely anyone would even notice my punishment.

"If you are going to behave like a child," started Jennson, "then you can dress like a child."

"But she was the one wh—" I stopped myself, briefly closing my mouth and eyes. *What am I doing? Shut up.*

He lifted a dark eyebrow. "I'm sorry? Is yellow not to your liking? Perhaps you would prefer claret?"

"No, Seioh," I said without hesitation. If I thought walking around in my old uniform was humiliating, it had nothing on wearing Juvie overalls. *That* had to be the most degrading punishment imaginable for a Young Enforcer.

"One moment." He ignored me, reaching for his Fellcorp Slate from the inside pocket of his black jacket. "I will just get that arranged."

A sharp inhale rushed my throat, making my airy voice shake. "No, Seioh, *please.*"

"Perhaps you should start engaging your brain before you open your mouth, Miss Aviary," he advised, leaving his Slate where it was and taking the Navy uniform slung over the back of the chair.

A weight lifted off me. "Yes, Seioh."

"Collect this from me at the end of the day."

"Yes, Seioh."

He left without another word.

I slumped down on my bed, tucking my head between my knees. *My second day and I'm wearing this! Calm down*, I thought, trying to reason with myself. *Nobody will even notice.* I had no idea why he had taken my Navy uniform; I had plenty more hanging in my wardrobe. I stared at the closed wardrobe door, weighing up the consequences of putting one on. It probably wasn't worth my life.

⚹⚹

As predicted, my unusual attire didn't attract any attention at breakfast. There were too many Musties and Navies around for anyone to notice. A constant buzzing of chatter filled the air, and it was clear people were still excited about Unity; looking around, lowered heads and animated faces confirmed it. I overheard a group of girls gossiping behind me. They had the number nine displayed on their arms. They were Ninth-years, so this would be their ninth Unity week.

"Celeste and Thorn are bound to be matched this year. They have been inseparable since First-year," said one.

"No way. If they were going to be matched they would have done so already," argued another.

My eavesdropping stopped when I caught sight of Silliah approaching from the corridor. Even though the bright lights cast a shine over her narrow, rectangular glasses, her lenses were so strong, I could still make out her dazzling green eyes, and saw she looked rather baffled as she headed my way.

"Not feeling your new uniform?" she asked with a smirk, taking a seat in front of me and ruffling up her long, thick side fringe. "Go on, what happened? I missed you yesterday."

"Seioh Jennson happened," I answered, giving a heavy sigh.

"*No?*" Silliah's already magnified eyes widened.

"Yes. I had a pleasant wake-up call from him this morning."

"Why? What did you do this time?"

"I flipped out at some stupid Third-year," I replied, rubbing my head, trying to push the memory from it. Silliah's jaw dropped. "I didn't touch her," I quickly added to clear the distorted picture she was building. "No, but I think I would have done if it wasn't for some guy, Pax, stopping me."

"Pax?" Silliah perked up like a little meerkat.

"Yes."

She crinkled her small nose and gave me a new look. "He's quite nice, isn't he?"

"I don't think he was doing it to be nice."

"No, *nice*. As in," she glanced around, fixed back on to my eyes, and mouthed, "fit," with the same eager expression as most others in the room.

"I guess he works out—we all do." I shrugged, clueless as to why we were still talking about him. She rolled her long-lashed eyes, flapped a hand at me, and started scrolling through the breakfast items on her tabletop screen.

I ordered the same platter—which I didn't get to eat—as yesterday, but I mostly pushed the moist chunks of fruit around on my plate. Silliah sat nibbling on some perfectly golden toast. We both ate our breakfast in quiet, our minds on Unity.

Once I saw she was on her last piece, I signalled towards the exit. She stuffed the toast into her mouth all in one go, giving me a wide grin through bursting lips. "Let's go," she mumbled with her cheeks bulging like a greedy hamster, and she led the way to a Juvie on duty. "You," Silliah started, chewing her mouthful quickly, "missed our first training session with Navies yesterday."

"I know," I replied, handing my tray to the Juvie waiting by a chute. "Thanks."

"Thank you, ma'am," he said, taking both our trays. He assembled them into racks before continuing to look sorry for himself, sweeping his white plimsole backwards and forwards in rhythm. Silliah and I headed to the Khakidemy.

"How was it yesterday?" I asked Silliah about her training session. "I'm looking forward to seeing how good everyone is."

"It was fun," she answered. "There're a lot more of them than when we were in Mustard, so there's a little more queueing for our favourite machines. But they are pretty impressive and good to watch. I saw Theodred and Saulwyn training yesterday. You wait until you see them. It is no wonder they hold most of the leaderboard top spots."

Silliah pushed through into the girls' changing room. We navigated the crowd and found our lockers. But it was only when

I opened my locker that it finally dawned on me. "I don't know if I'm allowed to get changed," I said, looking around at the undressing crowd of grownups.

Silliah gave an awkward nose laugh. "I doubt it, Aurora."

I groaned. *She's probably right.* I collapsed onto the hollow plastic bench studying my garish yellow combats. *This can't be happening.* Everyone in the Colosseum was going to be wearing their training clothes, a khaki-green vest; black, lightweight, stretchy trousers with padded knees; and black fingerless gloves. I was going to be as inconspicuous as undigested sweetcorn—the only yellow in a sea of green.

The changing room was full, and I noticed I kept catching the eyes of curious grownups. My shoulders tensed as the self-consciousness set in.

"This is a Navies' class, darlin'," said a Ninth-year, sitting by my side and observing me under tightly curled black hair. "Do you know where you are supposed to be?"

"I know, I…" *Oh no, how do I explain this one? I'm being punished by Jennson like a child. Because that's not embarrassing.* I leant closer to her. "Jennson is making me train like this."

"*Seioh* Jennson," she whispered back. "OK, how about you take your jumper off? Otherwise you'll be very warm. And I'll get Lady Maxhin to announce it. That way, no one else will bother you. How does that sound?"

I nodded. I supposed that wouldn't be so bad; like ripping off a plaster, better to get it over and done with quickly. I took off my jumper and held it in my lap, folding down the collar on my yellow polo shirt.

"Come on, it'll be fine." She stood and offered her hand. "What's your name?"

"Aurora," I said, being helped to my feet.

Her eyes flicked to a birthmark on my wrist briefly, but then, not wanting to stare, they quickly came back up to meet mine. "I'm Celeste. If anyone bothers you, you tell me, okay?"

"Thank you."

Celeste smiled and made her way back to her friends. I glanced down at my big black boots and decided for myself to change into my black running trainers, knowing I wouldn't do well on anything if I didn't. Then, after stuffing my jumper into my locker, I pressed my forehead onto the cool metal door, and closed it shut with my face.

"You'll be alright," said Silliah as we left the bustling changing room.

I only nodded. My enthusiasm from earlier had slowly diminished because of the garishness of my yellow uniform. When we reached the Colosseum's wide frosted-glass door, I paused and took a minute to ready myself. Then I walked in with my chin up.

Chills softly brushed over my skin. This was the only room with dark-green panels from floor to ceiling. It was such a contrast from the floods of white everywhere else that it always gave me a rush. I instantly checked the scoreboards bordering the edges of the room. They kept scores of the most popular machines in the Colosseum. Yet again, Theodred Dorchil and Saulwyn Field held most, if not all, the top spots.

In the distance, Lady Joanne Maxhin stood out in her all-black training attire. It was the same as ours but with a black vest instead of khaki. Celeste stood with her, no doubt informing her about my unfortunate situation. Moments later, Lady Maxhin glanced over in my direction and shook her head disapprovingly, her naturally hard face looking even sterner than usual. I felt a weird pang of guilt, like I had just disrespected her by stepping foot into her domain dressed like an idiot, as if I didn't take her training seriously. I dropped my eyes and chewed the inside of my cheek.

"Want to wait by the Flexon Pro?" asked Silliah, pointing to a machine in the centre of the room.

I eyed her, trying to read her face. "Are you enjoying this?"

"What?" She couldn't speak without smiling. "It's in the middle of the room: the best place for everyone to see you when Lady Maxhin makes her announcement."

My returning smile dropped when the reality sank in. I peeled my eyes off the Flexon and grimaced at Silliah. "Maybe I can hide up there." I pointed to the observer platform suspended from the ceiling. "Or under the slope?" I added, turning towards the platform's ramp.

"Or maybe you would just look ridiculous because the platform is transparent and everyone will still see you."

"The tiered seating?"

Silliah made a sweeping glance at the seating all around the room. Then she looked at me and shrugged.

"Oh, what the hell. Come on." I accepted my fate and navigated the busy room. Ignoring the whispering and stares, I came to stand by the Flexon Pro, my feet crossed and fingers twisting together.

"You know we get to play in the Parkour Games this year if we match," said Silliah, readjusting her fingerless gloves and then running her fingers along the clean-cut shaved lines in her hair. The sides had not long been freshly shaved, leaving a ruffled, long top sweeping across one eye.

"I do," I answered, folding my arms, and shifting my weight onto one leg. "Basically, we'll get a painful electric shock, and then lose hours of our life lying there unconscious until there's a winner."

"That's if you make it to round two."

"Alright, if not, then get a painful electric shock and lie there until round two. It's the exact same thing."

"True." Silliah's eyes followed someone behind me. She looked back at me with a cheeky glint in her eye. "So, did you get a chance to do the Unity thing yesterday before you lost your head?"

"Ye—"

"Of course she did!" That lizard-faced boy from yesterday butted in. He squeezed between us, slinging his arm around my shoulder. "Brindan wanted her, but he thinks she's too immature now, but *I'm* still happy for the match."

I wriggled to free myself from his hold, but he tightened his grip, placing his bicep right under my throat.

"Leave *it* alone, Ryker," said Pipila, passing me with an up and down glance.

"Oh, Pipila, you're just bitter you had a run-in with Jennson," Ryker replied. "He *almost* had you in your musties!"

Ryker pressed his lips to my ear and fake laughed. I turned my face away sharply, avoiding his warm breath. He let go of me, quickly dodging and ducking towards Pipila as if he were boxing. Reaching her, he tugged at her khaki vest and then hopped around, still pretending to spar her.

"Ignore him, Aurora. I don't think you're immature." Brindan excused Ryker, his face a familiar beetroot red. Brindan separated from the gang and stood with Pax, who already waited by the machine alongside us.

"How have you managed to attract the attention of that crowd?" Silliah asked, her expression a mix between concern and surprise.

"That's the Third-year I told you about."

"Pipila Darlington? Oh." She pulled at her lip as she watched Pipila's crowd walk away.

"*Serve, Honour, Protect, and Defend,*" Lady Maxhin called for our attention from mid-way up the tiered seating.

"*Serve, Honour, Protect, and Defend,*" we all chanted back obediently with a closed fist over our hearts.

"OK, listen up," Lady Maxhin's amplified voice filled the room. "I want another good session from you today. I know you are all excited about the Unity celebrations, but I want focus from all of you. You are still Youngens, and it's important to keep training. Plus, for all you betrothed couples, the Parkour Games are coming up. As you know, the pain is very real, so you need to train hard to give yourselves the best chance. Everyone, please support the First-years—and the young lady in the yellow isn't lost."

Heads turned in all directions, trying to work out what she meant. Once people began pointing at me, it was understood. My face burned. Playing with my trainers, I tried to avoid the three-hundred-odd nosey eyes staring at me. Thankfully, it didn't take long before they lost interest, and within a minute, everyone scattered like ants around the Colosseum.

For our first bout of training, Silliah and I queued up behind two First-years for the Flexon Pro, an appliance used to improve reflexes.

"Here, watch this," said Silliah, gesturing to the far side of the room, towards Celeste about to take her turn on the Ascendant. Celeste set off running up a black, thirty-foot, vertical wall. The wall lit up green, detecting her highest touch, and then a mechanical platform brought her safely back down to the ground.

"What did she get?" I couldn't hear Celeste's score from here, but I swore she reached double what I could.

"I didn't hear, but you know that's high. I can't imagine ever being able to wall-run that high."

My lip pulled up at one corner. "Maybe if you grew taller than a ten-year-old?"

"Hey! We can't all be super tall like you."

"I'm only five-foot-ni—"

"Look." Silliah pointed over by the Ascendant.

A big guy high-fived Celeste and then readied himself at the Ascendant II. He placed his hands and feet on two thirty-foot walls. A timer started and he rapidly scaled the vertical walls. At the top he pounded a big red button, and then a platform brought him back down to the ground.

Silliah spun to face me, her long fringe catching air and uncovering her wide green eyes. "Stupidly quick. I told you. They are so good."

The Flexon Pro's game-over drone sounded, and we turned to see a blonde girl gracefully hop off the pads, landing feet together.

"Thirty-seven," announced Soami from the machine. "Good job, Miss Lafern."

She smiled at her friend, pleased with her score, and then the friend eagerly took his turn.

"Thirty-four. Great improvement, Mr. T Cicero," said Soami.

He gave the blonde girl a solemn shrug, not so pleased with his score. She bumped into his shoulder lightly and they headed for another machine. Then Silliah jumped on the Flexon Pro, taking her turn and finishing with a score of forty-one.

On my go, I stepped up onto the black foam mat. The sensors adjusted themselves to my body dimensions, and I took my stance, shifting my weight from toe to toe. The first lighted pad appeared directly in front of me and I jabbed it out. My face muscles tensed as I waited for the next one; behind me—I spun and dug it with my elbow; bottom right—tapped it with my toe; top left—jumped, smashing it with an uppercut. I continued dancing effortlessly around on the spot, punching and kicking the soft pads, my frustration being released with every one. I was in the zone. Right up until the electronic drone sounded, implying I had missed one. Annoyed I didn't see it, I waited for my score from Soami.

"Ninety-two. A personal best. Nice work, Miss Aviary."

Applause and cheering erupted around the Colosseum. My performance on the machine—or perhaps more accurately my performance looking like a Mustard—had attracted everyone's attention. Lady Maxhin stood waiting at the edge for me to step down.

"Wow, Aurora, you are a natural," she said, her grey eyes glittering from under spikes of short black hair. "That's the highest score I've ever seen from a First-year. It starts getting harder at sixty, and not many First-years make it far past. Keep that up, and I'm sure we'll be seeing your name on the scoreboards in no time. I'm awarding you one hundred Worths." She patted me on the back as she walked away.

Worths were the credit system the whole country of Venair used. When Fiat currencies like the Euro, Dollar, and Pound became unreliable—all resulting in eventual collapse—we started using time as money, and Worths were stored and tracked on our picoplants. All civilians completed compulsory schooling, and once graduated, they were graded into Bands: one Worth per hour for Band D, and four Worths per hour for Band A. All Young Enforcers were automatically awarded Band A at the start of First-year, clocking up forty-eight Worths a day until compulsory retirement (at the end of Thirteenth-year), and we lived very comfortable lives upon leaving the institute. In the meantime, instructors had permission to give and take Worths as they pleased.

"*One hundred* Worths." Silliah jumped on me once the cheering faded. "How are you so good?"

"I don't really think about what I'm doing—"

At that moment, Pipila barged past me to jump up on the Flexon. She swished her long cocoa-brown ponytail, and took a similar stance to me, dancing on the balls of her feet. Silliah and I looked at each other sideways. *What a loser.*

We gave the machine some distance before, "One hundred and forty-eight. Excellent, Miss Darlington," was declared by Soami. We didn't give her the satisfaction and pretended not to hear.

※

Dinner started at nineteen hundred hours, but before I went to the Food Hall, I walked sheepishly to Seioh Jennson's office, hopeful to get my Navy uniform back. I hesitated before knocking on the door, remembering the first time I ever entered this room…

…I was eight years old and allowed to eat in the Food Hall unsupervised for the first time. I was feeling, let's say, a little overconfident whilst waiting at the meal dispenser with Silliah. This happened to be when I, not long before, had discovered Seioh

Jennson's first name was Kiwick. On that morning, he rushed past us, and I, thinking he was far enough away to not hear, smugly said, "Quick, Kiwick," to Silliah.

How wrong I was to think he'd made it out of earshot. Jennson changed direction so quickly. My word, did I panic, and it was that I'm-never-going-to-make-it-out-of-this-alive panic you have when you get in trouble as a child. He ripped back in my direction and, without saying a word, placed a thumb and a finger firmly on the back of my small neck, leading me out of the Food Hall. Marching me through the Navy Quartz corridors to the door I stood outside now, he pushed me into his office, sat me in a chair by the desk, and then…left. Jennson walked out, leaving me glued to the spot, gripping on to the chair until my fingers turned white, waiting. Waiting…*all day*. I dared not move from my seat because I expected him to return any minute. But he didn't come back until eighteen hundred hours, almost twelve hours later. I sat in the chair, reduced to tears not knowing when he was coming back, trapped in my own head '*nightmaring*' about all the different methods of punishment I was going to be subjected to. He returned after what felt like an eternity, guided me out of the office, and shut the door, leaving me standing in the empty corridor, wondering if I could go. With my muscles aching, throat dry, eyes bloodshot, and my face wet and blotchy, I was exhausted. All that, and without even saying *one word*. The punishment had been very effective, leaving me on edge for days after.

I pinched the bridge of my nose, dissolving the residual emotions from my memory, and braced myself, fist poised, ready to knock on the door.

"Come in," Seioh Jennson responded to my tapping.

I took a long inhale for encouragement before pushing the shining, ice-blue access button. Inside the office was just as I remembered it: weird. The same black wheelie chair I sat on all those years ago still lived in front of Jennson's old oak desk. Feeling like a child again, I stood behind it and waited for Jennson to speak.

The fact Jennson still used a wooden desk was weird but the desk's craftmanship made up for it. Intricate carvings covered the front and side panels, and I imagined someone quite important used to sit behind it. I had traced my feet over the carving in the centre panel many times whilst waiting to hear of my punishment from Jennson. The carving was of an eagle holding arrows in its talon. It was quite impressive and a good distraction when I needed to control my nerves.

"Good evening, Seioh," I croaked after a while of standing to attention.

My attempt at instigating a conversation fell flat, and he continued to leave me standing in the heavy silence. In my boredom, I reacquainted myself with the strange room. The wall-length wooden bookcase hadn't changed one bit. I always thought it looked odd and out of place. Nobody owned real books these days. That was what our Fellcorp tablets were for.

Seioh Jennson still didn't look up. He continued to work on his computer, tapping away at a foldable touchscreen. He could have a 3D holographic display, but due to the confidential nature of his work, he chose an older version. Go figure—if his office and dress sense were anything to go by, anyway.

Finally, without looking at me, Jennson pointed a finger past my arm. I turned to see my Navy uniform folded in a bag on a side table. The table was part of a seating area with a black leather sofa and two matching arm chairs, all with small silver feet. I wasn't sure if he wanted me to sit or take my uniform. Well, I knew what I was going to try first. I crept backwards and slowly leant over to take the bag. When he didn't speak, I lifted my uniform, keeping him in my peripherals just in case. Standing back up straight, I waited for further instruction, but I may as well have been invisible.

"Thank you, Seioh," I said after an uncomfortably long time.

Nothing.

I took a tiny step backwards, advancing towards the door. *Should I just leave?* I decided I would, so I took another step back, still keeping my eyes on him. The door opened automatically with my next step.

"And, Aurora," he eventually spoke. "I'm taking one hundred Worths from your account."

My palms opened up to the ceiling in protest. He was taking away the first Worths I had ever been awarded. Lady Joanne Maxhin gave them to me for my ability on the Flexon. It took every ounce of control I had not to curse at him.

Jennson shot me a look with his soulless blue eyes, sending my insides screaming. I remembered myself and threw my hands behind my back. In the hope he hadn't noticed my slip up, I pretended nothing happened, and kept my mouth from spilling an incriminating 'Sorry, Seioh.' When he looked away, I gradually backed out of the office, holding my breath. The sliding door closed me out in the deserted corridor, and I filled my lungs with air. I tiptoed away, hugging my uniform to my chest.

CHAPTER THREE
IN LONG, IT COULDN'T BE MORE WRONG

After my close call with Jennson, I headed straight to dinner. The Food Hall was not so busy by the time I got there because it was the time a number of Navies were out in the city on Curfew Duty.

Venair had a compulsory curfew forbidding civilians from being out of their homes between twenty hundred hours and zero six hundred hours. So, at the start of Curfew, Young Enforcers were sent out to catch the few who didn't make it home in time. Often law-abiding adults, these people became the perfect targets for our training. They were considered low-risk and easily detainable, no matter our age or ability. I hadn't had the pleasure of this duty yet because Navies always worked in pairs, and without knowing if we were betrothed, Unity was completed first. If I matched, my fiancé would become my working partner, but if I didn't match, another Navy would be assigned. Neither option appealed to me, unless, of course, Silliah became my working partner, but I highly doubted two First-years would be paired up to fend for themselves.

My mouth began watering at the warm aroma filling the Food Hall. The delicious infusion of garlic and sage influenced my choice of dinner this evening, and I scoffed it so fast I had a pain in my chest. I couldn't help it. The fluffy roasted potatoes melted in my mouth, and the skin had a crisp, satisfying bite. Rich gravy dripped off my broccoli and dribbled down my chin numerous times. *I don't want to know what I look like.* To stop myself from looking any more ridiculous, I controlled the urge to lick my plate, and used my last roasted potato to wipe it clean of gravy instead.

After giving my tray to a Juvie on duty, I took the long way round to my room and wandered the outer corridors. A thick carpet of grey clouds foretold the small dusting of snow settled on the flowerbeds. Snow-speckled Enforcers returned from Curfew Duty, and I watched them, envious of their night time excursion. The Khaki receptionist stood up at her counter, and pushed the access button, letting the party in. An icy evening breeze swirled through the open doors, tousling my white hair. I inhaled deeply, allowing the refreshing air to tingle my nostrils. I couldn't wait for my Curfew Duty to start.

"Nice work on the Flexon today, Aurora," said a deep, silky-smooth voice from behind a sleek navy helmet. I couldn't see his face, only my startled reflection in the tinted visor. This guy was huge, built like a tank, way over six feet tall.

"Thanks," I said to my own reflection.

"Good to see you have your Navy uniform back, too." He gestured down at the bag hanging by my side.

I smiled and held the bag up under my chin. "Yep."

What am I doing? I was acting like a child with a paper lunch bag, responding to an attentive mother's 'have you got your lunch' question. I put the bag down and held it like a normal person. The Tank (my new nickname for the faceless terminator) patted me on the shoulder lightly with his massive armoured glove, then continued on his way to catch up with the Enforcers he came in with. Looking at the sheer mass of plasticky material the guy sported, I half expected him to clank noisily as he strode away, but the EU he wore was surprisingly silent.

※

Determined to not be caught off guard this morning, I leapt out of bed as soon as the beeping alarm hit my eardrums. I carefully watched the door.

Elated nobody came in to ruin my morning, I happily threw on my Navy uniform and admired my new grown-up self in the mirror. I practically skipped down to breakfast, taking the outer corridors just to see the moonlight glistening on the surface of the snow. The ogre at the Navy reception looked down her bulbous nose at me, but I was determined to not let anything get me down today. I was going to have an uneventful day, a good day, and a day *not* dressed like an idiot.

"Oooh, look at you," said Silliah, meeting me in a Food Hall filled to the brim with Young Enforcers. She ruffled her walnut-brown fringe and sat in her chair.

"I know." I boastfully opened up my arms, showing off my Navy uniform. "It's funny, I was so sad to let my Mustard uniform go down the chute on Monday that the gods gave me another chance to wear it."

"Seeing the funny side today, then?" Silliah gazed up at me under messy hair, only one large green eye showing through her strong rectangular lenses.

"Hey." My tone dropped with my arms. "I can joke about it, but I dare anyone else to try it." I lowered down in my seat opposite Silliah, and, after a small smile to each other, we scrolled through the menu on our tabletop screens.

On our way back from the meal dispenser, I saw Nanny Kimly over in Mustard Quartz supervising a large group of children. She floated around handing out napkins; double-tapping tabletop screens for kids who couldn't manage the precise finger gesture; picking up Mustard jumpers which had fallen on the floor; and catching beakers before their contents soaked the table. She looked like a super woman—so effortless and elegant. The heavy feeling in my stomach from seeing her felt like I swallowed an ankle trap—a device worn by Juvies. I didn't realise I missed her until just then.

"Aurora. Silliah. Do you want to sit with us?" asked a porcelain-faced First-year. I hesitated for two reasons: one, I couldn't think where I had seen her face from; and two, I didn't want to sit there.

"Sure." Silliah turned and shrugged at me.

Sure? SURE?

"I don't think we can because we've already signed on to the table over there." I scrambled for an excuse.

"No, that doesn't matter, you have already collected your food," the First-year corrected me.

Well, that's it then; looks like we are sitting here today.

The beautiful First-year whipped her long sun-kissed-blonde hair behind her back and programmed another table beside her, creating a long bench. The table rose out of the floor in a compact block, unfolded its components like something out of a horror movie, and revealed a matching glass-topped bench with four white chairs.

"I'm Hilly, and that's Tyga, Shola, and Hyas," she explained, pointing at her friends in turn.

Tyga gave us an upwards head nod; Shola lifted her slender fingers off the table giving a casual wave; and lastly, Hyas smiled shyly then quickly looked away. I recognised him. He was the boy I had seen in the corridor on my first day, the one who knew my name but I had no idea of his. *Hyas,* I repeated to myself, transferring it to my long-term memory. Wait a minute. I looked at Hyas and then back at Tyga. They had exactly the same boyishly good-looking face. Tyga had black hair swept back in a quiff, but Hyas had gingerbread-brown moppy hair.

"Yes. We're twins," said Tyga, reading my mind.

I flashed a smile and took the empty seat next to Shola. This was one good-looking group of friends. Even Shola was pretty. She had a naturally beautiful face with smooth olive skin and dark-brown eyes.

"Are you albino?" asked Hilly.

I looked up after a moment of silence to find her intently eyeing my hair. "Oh, no," I reacted, realising she was speaking to me. "Not that I know of, anyway."

"I suppose you do have dark eyebrows, and your eyes are really blue."

All four of them turned to look at my eyes. I didn't know where to look, and if I didn't already regret taking a seat at this table, I sure as hell started to now.

"We saw you on the Flexon yesterday, Aurora," broke in Tyga. "You were incredible!"

Thank god. I was beginning to feel really uncomfortable with Hilly's brazen approach.

"Thanks," I said, the only word I seemed to have in my vocabulary lately, and then filled my mouth with a large bite of avocado toast so I couldn't say any more. My performance had a bittersweet taste now, after Jennson took my Worths away, and I didn't feel like talking about it.

"She's good at *everything*," Silliah interjected before tactfully turning the conversation to Unity. I thankfully managed to have next-to-no input in that conversation. They were all too happy to share their opinions, and I could get away with pretending to listen. Right up until…

"What is that?" Hilly pointed to the birthmark on my left wrist.

"A birthmark," I told her, pulling down my jacket sleeve to cover it.

"Is it? It's a bit *squiggly* for a birthmark, isn't it?" She leant over as if to get a better look.

Is this girl serious? "I don't know." I moved my hand away from her. "I don't have another one to compare it to."

"I've never seen one like that. It looks more like a tattoo."

She wasn't wrong; it did resemble a distorted number eight with an open, swirly underside. Around the bottom left half, eight small freckles curved with the bend.

"It's a birthmark," I repeated with a pursed-lip smile. *Go on, mention it again.* I stared fixedly at her, waiting for her to try me.

Silliah reached over the table and placed a hand on my forearm. "Well, it was lovely talking with you all." She smiled round at everyone. "We best be going now. See you in the Khakidemy."

※

The First-years took to their seats for an hour of history with Sir Iddle Praeter, a short man with a narrow face, a tidy grey beard, and watery eyes. His classroom had glossy black panels covering the walls, and the room was empty except for a circle of special black chairs called augreals. I jumped up onto one of the high-backed chairs next to Silliah. Unfortunately, I didn't manage to escape Hilly and her friends. They appeared unaffected by our sudden departure at breakfast this morning and took up the next four augreals next to me. We all sat quietly in the circle, swinging our legs, waiting for Sir Praeter to begin.

"If you haven't done so already," began Sir Praeter in a slow, fragile voice. He turned around and clambered unsteadily into his master augreal, joining the rest of us. His black uniform, not so different to the Navies', camouflaged well with the chair, rendering his body almost invisible. Back when I was a child, an unfortunately placed spotlight reflecting off his baldness became the cause for one of my run-ins with Jennson. The camouflaged uniform left Sir Praeter's head floating with his large round eyes glowing from the spotlight's reflection. The first time I saw it, I succumbed to fits of laughter before being exiled from the lesson. My fight for composure was lost when the spotlights flickered on and off, making him vanish. Each time the bodiless face reappeared, I fought back a laugh so hard it turned into a high-pitched squeal. In the end, I had the whole class of Mustards roaring with laughter. Needless to say, I spent the entire lesson nervously waiting outside Jennson's office.

"Put on your headsets," continued Sir Praeter, taking a flimsy headset off the dock attached to the side of his augreal and putting it on, adjusting the probes to touch the wrinkled, fleshy skin on the sides of his head. "And we will begin."

The clinking of headsets being removed from their docks subsided, and Sir Praeter took this as a cue to proceed. Our chairs reclined back, taking the weight of our legs, and my spine moulded into the squishy leather. I straightened the probes on my temples and waited for the spotlights to dim. Then my eyes closed.

A flash of white light replaced the darkness behind my eyelids. My new eyes blinked as they adjusted to the brightness, gradually an image emerged, and I could see. Becoming accustomed to my new hands, I turned them over, opening and closing my long, thin fingers. In our avatar state, we lost consciousness of our real bodies lying in the chairs in the classroom, and we became animated avatars in an augmented reality decided by our instructor.

The class and I were now on rigid, wooden benches in an old dingy courtroom. The light seeping in through small square windows created crawling sweeps of dust and obscured my view of the judge. He sat behind a bench as a frightened young woman stood in the dock.

"Aurora?" whispered an elderly lady sitting next to me.

"Yeeeah," I replied. "Silliah?"

"Yeah." She nudged me with her elbow. "What do we look like?"

"I don't think much of sixteenth century fashion." I tugged at the white V-shaped headscarf on Silliah's avatar.

"Shhhh," Sir Iddle Praeter requested our silence from across the room. He animated an avatar that looked like a thirty-year-old version of himself with a full head of curly brown hair.

We obeyed and watched a lengthy court hearing of a woman accused of witchcraft. The court found the lady guilty before gruesomely sentencing her to death by hanging seven days later. The trial finished, the courtroom faded into darkness, and I reopened my real eyes.

I was always a little dubious when I regained consciousness of my real body because a few years ago, Sir Praeter played a trick on us all. He made us believe he had revived us from our avatar state, waking up in the classroom. Turns out, it was a replica, and we were all still unknowingly animating our avatars in a virtual reality world. We thought we had regained consciousness, and when we tried to take off our headsets...none of us could move. We thought the headsets malfunctioned and kept us in a state of paralysis. We sat freaking out with locked-in syndrome, unable to move, our frantic eyes pleading for help. I think the only person to find it funny was Sir Praeter. I, for one, did not appreciate it, and my distrust towards people flourished that day.

"In 1542," Sir Praeter began. He paused and stared vacantly across the room. "Parliament passed the Witchcraft Act, defining witchcraft as a crime punishable by death." He paused again and I stifled a yawn. "Maleficium, the use of magic, is still illegal today, although no cases have been reported for many years. The last known use of maleficium came from an ancient civilisation whose descendants were eventually wiped out in 1684, but that's a lesson for another time."

"Sir," intervened Silliah, waiting for an invitation before continuing. "Isn't maleficium the use of magic *with the intention of causing harm*?"

"Yes, Silliah, but have you ever heard of witchcraft being used for good? Why do you suppose it was made illegal? It is dangerous and unsafe for humans to possess powers."

"So, all magic is maleficium? No magic can be used for good?"

"All magic is unsafe, dangerous, and threatens the human race. Magic changes a person; the power goes to their head and evil prevails. But you don't need to worry because the inhabitants of the aforementioned Puracordis civilisation were the last known users of maleficium, and it no longer exists. That's all for today, class. *Serve,*

Honour, Protect, and Defend," finished Sir Praeter with a closed fist over his heart.

"*Serve, Honour, Protect, and Defend,"* we aped.

"So much for Hogwarts," Silliah said to me, jumping down from her augreal.

"Hog-what?"

"Never mind."

We joined the queue of First-years bundling out of the classroom into the corridor. Outside, Pipila, Ryker, and about eight members of her gang waited for their history lesson. I managed to keep myself hidden amongst my classmates and avoided any further antagonising from Ryker.

"Hi, Pax," said Silliah suddenly. I was too busy concealing myself in the crowd to see him coming.

"Silliah," returned Pax, passing her with a single pat on the head.

Still embarrassed about the incident in the Food Hall, I kept myself from looking up at him, and instead watched a small cluster of Second-year girls ogling Silliah with open mouths. They clearly wished they knew him enough for a pat on the head.

"You know him?" I asked curiously.

"He showed me where the Unity assessments were being held on Monday," she said quickly, ruffling up her thick walnut-brown fringe. I watched her suspiciously, but before I could say anything, she continued, "Which reminds me, I kept meaning to tell you." She checked over her shoulder before speaking in a hushed voice, "I overheard Pipila talking at dinner on Monday. She said she had changed some of her Unity answers this year to try and match with Pax."

"Whoops, I'm not sure that's going to work."

"I know, that's what I thought," she said, returning back to her normal volume.

"That test had everything monitored, but if it works, good luck to her."

※

"Has everyone done their Unity assessments?" asked Shola at dinner that evening. Apparently, sitting with them once gave them an open invitation to sit with us whenever they liked. "It's our last chance tonight."

Silliah answered first, "I did mine on Monday."

"Yeah, me too," chorused Tyga and Hyas in unison.

"Me too," I said. Hilly nodded with me.

"I don't understand why this bit is three days," whined Hilly. "I've hated these last two days; I just want to know the results."

"I think it's too much for everyone to get done in a day," said Silliah reasonably. "Navies have duties to do, so it would be hard fitting it in. Could you imagine having twelve hours for—what? Over three hundred Navies to turn up at any time, in that one room? They would have to make a rota or something."

"Just think," began Shola with passionate dark-brown eyes. "This time tomorrow we could be sitting here with our betrothed."

Tiny pins prickled across my pale skin. I couldn't think of anything worse.

After retreating to my room later that evening, I struggled getting a good night's sleep. The thought of a husband being decided for me made my chest hurt. I tossed and turned in bed, getting frustrated with my active mind. I tried playing the soothing hum of white noise; I tried focusing on my breathing; and I tried imagining myself on a beach, all proving useless. The moment I fell asleep, I stirred five minutes later and needed to try just as hard to fall back to sleep again. It was the longest, loneliest night I'd had for years.

I woke before the alarm and sat down in the shower, allowing the hot water to pour down my face and bounce off my knees held into my chest. The weight of the stream forced my eyes closed. My mind faded into darkness.

Still. Empty. Peaceful.

A high-pitched beeping shook me out of my meditative state, placing me on high-alert until it registered in my brain as the alarm. I gingerly leant my bare skin up against the cold tiles, taking my head out from the water. The moist steam softened my aching face, and I felt my muscles relax to the mixture of musical tones made by the trickle. *Of course I can fall asleep now. Why wouldn't I?*

I woke with a jolt, shower still pouring, and confusion muddling my heavy head. *How long did I sleep for?*

"Soami, turn off the shower. What time is it?"

"Zero five forty-five hours," Soami replied. "You have—"

"Yeah, I know." I flung open the shower door. "One hour and fifteen minutes until breakfast ends. It's all good. Bye, Soami."

Silliah must be wondering where I am. I grabbed a towel and checked my Fellcorp Slate for any messages from her. My Slate was clear. Perhaps she wasn't thinking about me at all. Maybe she had eaten with the Fanciable Four and didn't even notice my absence.

Drying my body roughly, I wrapped myself in my dressing gown and left the ensuite. When I opened my wardrobe for a fresh Navy uniform, my gut twisted in a knot. The wardrobe was completely *empty. Where the hell is my uniform?* My 'AA' initialled pyjamas were still in my trunk from leaving Mustard, but I should have had six pairs of clean Navy uniform hanging in my wardrobe. It was always that way.

I scanned the bedroom rapidly, trying to remember if I had thrown my dirty one down the chute already. It was there on the floor at the end of the bed, and I thanked my lazy self for a moment. Holding the dirty one up in front of me, I examined it for imperfections. It had only been worn for an hour or so on Monday before I went to bed, and then on Tuesday, I wore my Mustard uniform, so it was only yesterday I had it on for a whole day. If only I'd hung it up last night, then it would be fine to wear today, but the night of guarding the floor by my bed had etched in a thousand untidy creases. I only needed to wear it until I found the whereabouts of my clean ones, but I didn't know who to ask. Nanny Kimly would have been my first thought when I was in Mustard. Disturbingly, the Navy receptionist kept oozing her way into my head now. I would rather throw myself down a never-ending staircase. *Maybe Silliah will know.*

After failing to brush out some creases, I left for the Food Hall. The Navy residential corridors were unusually quiet. I didn't see a single person, not even a team on Uniform Delivery. I quickly checked by the Navy reception to see if the night receptionist was still on duty. As I rounded the corner, I could smell the ogre's sickly perfume and knew it was a wasted trip before I even saw her. Weirdly though, today she seemed to have replaced her usual lemon-sucking expression, and I was sure I saw her smirking at me.

My Slate vibrated in my pocket, and a message from Silliah displayed onscreen. '*Where are you?!*'

I was almost at the Food Hall, so I popped my Slate back into my pocket and took a brisk walk down the corridor. Nearing the Food Hall entrance, I began to sense something wasn't right. My eyes met with fifty-odd Young Enforcers, but not a *single one* of them wore navy. Where were all the Navies?

"Aurora," yelled Silliah from the end of the corridor. "Come on!"

Her tone of voice concerned me. Without thinking, I ran towards her. "What?"

"What are you doing?"

I didn't like the distress I saw deep in her eyes. "I-I-I-dunno-I-fell-asleep-in-the-shower-and-I-didn't-have-a-clean-uniform," I rambled without taking a breath, all the words merged together in one big jumble. Silliah grabbed my arm and we ran.

"The Unity pre-meeting," she explained, leading me round to Khaki Quartz. "It was supposed to start ten minutes ago. We are all waiting for you."

"The what?"

"The Unity pre-meeting, before the results are announced this afternoon. Did you not read your welcome pack?"

"Oh." I pictured the untouched pile of paperwork sitting on the desk in my room. I was going to get around to reading that.

Silliah yanked the silver bar handle to the Auditorium, allowing me to walk in. I braced myself for what was on the other side. As I expected, every single Navy sat in a ground-swallow-me-up silence. They all watched as I entered the room through a door right by the stage. I kept myself from catching anyone's eyes, and prayed the low lighting was hiding the scruffiness of my uniform.

Seeing all the First-years in the first row, I spotted two empty seats on the far side. My chin tucked itself into my blotchy chest, and I began making my way towards them. I didn't remember the Auditorium being this long, and I felt sorry for Silliah, who, because of me, also had to endure the gruelling walk. Finally, we made it to our seats, glad for the attention to be averted on stage.

When I looked up from my creased navy combats—dismayed the creases hadn't magically disappeared—I was greeted by what could have only been death staring me in the face. It was my favourite person, Seioh Jennson. *Great.* I swallowed hard.

"How nice of you to grace us with your presence, Miss Aviary," Seioh Jennson's mono-tone voice filled the Auditorium. He stood in one of his timeless black suits, impatiently tugging at his buttoned cuffs. "Good morning, Navies. Whilst you are sat here this morning, the results of the Unity assessments are being analysed. For some of you, this will be the most important day of your lives. Those of you who are already matched, and those of you who will be matched today, are bestowed with an extra responsibility. You select few have been chosen to bequeath your upbringing on to your future offspring. Who better to raise a child than two former Enforcers, who, themselves, have had the soundest upbringing? You will leave here continuing to contribute to the growth of a peaceful population.

"This afternoon, Seioh Boulderfell will be paying a special visit to announce the results. Whilst he is onsite, you must all be the picture of perfection. Uniforms are to be freshly laundered. Your boots and badges are to be polished." His cavernous eyes lingered on my creased uniform for a moment. I pointlessly crossed my arms and legs in an attempt to hide it. "The Show of Force Display will begin at eleven hundred hours, so all morning duties and classes have been cancelled for rehearsals. However, the Food Hall will remain open all day to accommodate for the disrupted schedule.

"If you see Seioh Boulderfell at any time during his visit, ensure you stand to attention throughout any interaction unless he orders you at ease. You will all be back here at twelve hundred hours for the announcements to commence at twelve thirty hours. Miss Aviary, you will be here at eleven hundred hours. That will be all. *Serve, Honour, Protect, and Defend.*"

"*Serve, Honour, Protect, and Defend,*" the Auditorium repeated. I closed my fist, but it wasn't to place over my heart. I stayed tight-lipped as I computed that last sentence. I could not seem to cut a break this year.

"If I have to be here at eleven hundred hours, I can't take part in the Show of Force Display," I moaned to Silliah, storming for the exit and trying really hard to quash the anger bubbling up inside.

"Oh, Aurora," Silliah empathised, trotting after me.

"I have been in that display five times. Only two Musties are chosen every year to lead the march, and I have never done it with you. Now we are in Navy, we get to do it together for the first time, and Seioh Jennson has taken that away from me." I kicked the Auditorium door as I exited.

"MISS AVIARY," shouted a severely displeased Sir Hiroki, my martial arts instructor.

"Sorry, sir, I tripped," I said through gritted teeth.

"Calm down, Aurora," whispered Silliah. "Before you get yourself into any more trouble."

"I have had enough. First, he makes me wear my Mustard uniform during training, then he takes my Worths away, and now I don't get to participate in the Show of Force Display. I hate him." I barged past a group of Musties on my way out of the Khakidemy.

"He took your Worths away?"

"Yes! The ones Lady Maxhin gave to me yesterday."

"I'm sorry. I didn't know." Silliah held a hand to her cheek, searching for something to say. "It's okay, Aurora, we will get to do it loads of times now we are in Navy; it's held every week."

"No but this one is special." I stood still to face her. "This one walks Boulderfell into the institute. It has every single Navy doing it, and the two Musties leading in with the martial arts routine." I didn't do a great job masking the resentment building in my stomach when I said, "I don't care about that clart, anyway. It's only put on to intimidate the civilians into submission." Silliah's face lit up like I said something really naughty. "Well it is," I carried on. "Show how strong we are every week just to remind them we are here, so they might as well not try anything. Act like military, look like military, and they'll treat us like military."

※

To cool off, I sought refuge in my bedroom. With all the morning classes cancelled for the Show of Force Display, I had nothing to do with my time except find my clean uniform. I thought it best to remain in my room until I was certain I couldn't be easily provoked by the ogre. I settled down on my bed, staring into space, braiding my long white hair.

"Nanny Kimly!" I gasped, her arrival snapping me out of my daydream. Discarding my hair instantly, I threw my arms around her. She stood quietly, allowing me to hug her, as if she knew I needed it. I closed my eyes to stop the stinging. I'd felt so alone without her this week.

"Ahem," came Nanny Kimly's soft voice from the back of my head. "Now, you wouldn't want to crease up this uniform too, would you?"

I didn't realise I had sandwiched a fresh Navy uniform between us. "My uniform! How did you know?"

"Seioh Jennson paid me a visit. Surely you don't need a nanny as a Navy, do you, Aurora?"

"They weren't in my wardrobe," I said defensively.

"Evidently, but it's Thursday, Little Lady. I know you can organise yourself better than that." The shame kept me from looking at her. When I didn't speak she continued, "Somehow, you were left off the list when you transferred to Navy."

"But it's automated, isn't it?" I reacted, the weight of shame leaving me as quickly as it arrived.

"Yes, but it happens. Rarely, admittedly, but it does happen."

"Do receptionists have access to the system?"

"Of course they do, and you have always had a wild imagination, Little Lady."

My frown must have said it all. I would bet Worths on it that the ogre had something to do with my name magically disappearing off that list.

⚔

Later, when I walked into the deserted Auditorium, a glowing light shone on a chair at the start of an aisle, and I knew it was meant for me. On the back of the chair, a screen displayed my name. Calix Bane was assigned a chair next to me; Hyas and Tyga Cicero were after that. I searched the row for Silliah's name. Silliah Van de Waal, I found her at the opposite end, sitting as far away from me as possible. But this time it wasn't personal—we were to be sat in alphabetical order.

Contrary to the Unity pre-meeting, the First-years were to be in the back row, with Thirteenth-year sitting in the first row. This was their last chance to be matched before they were discharged from the institute next January.

As I sat alone for almost an hour in my immaculate Navy uniform, I knew the Show of Force Display would soon be over, and within minutes, groups of well-groomed Navies began to pile into the Auditorium. The girls hugged each other before parting and taking to their seats. It was nice to see that the alphabetical seating was not only meant for First-years.

Silliah came to give me a cuddle, wished me good luck, and disappeared to the end of the row. Pipila sat a few rows in front. She clearly knew her alphabetical neighbours and seemed to be chewing their ears off. I scanned her row and saw Brindan and Pax sitting next to each other leaning their heads towards one another in quiet conversation. Ryker, like me, sat on the end of an aisle. He was craning his neck, peering around the entire room. As he found my row of First-years, he stopped, and his dark eyes made their way down the row to me. I pretended to find something really interesting on my nails and fought with the urge to look up. I examined the white tip of my thumb nail, feeling him watching me, waiting for me to catch his gaze.

Silence spread around the Auditorium, and I felt safe to stop playing with my thumb nail. Seioh Jennson walked into the room and commanded with a hand gesture for everyone to stand. Then, a very tall, very skinny man entered the room. With an inflated chest, he pompously walked onto the stage. He straightened up the side split of his tailored suit, swept back his (probably fake) black hair, and stroked his (notably not fake) short grey beard.

"Goooood afternoon, my dear *children*. Please, at ease; relax, relax; take your seats," Seioh Boulderfell spoke in an annoyingly exaggerated voice. "It's an absolute pleasure to be in the City of Vencen today. It is my most treasured of cities, and it's no coincidence that you, my children, are raised in the very heart of it.

"Shall we get straight to it? Straight in with the good bit? The results! Thank you, Sir Jennson," said Seioh Boulderfell, taking a tablet from Seioh Jennson. Weirded me out the first time he called Seioh Jennson 'sir,' but apparently, you only call your superiors Seioh.

Boulderfell was Venair's ruler, and you can't get much more senior than that. I didn't suppose he called anyone Seioh.

"Oooh, interesting. Most interesting, I do say," Boulderfell continued, grinning sideways over the top of the tablet at us all. "First, the gentlemen! When I call your name, come and join me on stage. A big round of applause for Ninth-year, Thorn Jelani. Congratulations!"

The Auditorium burst into applause as the big guy I saw on the Ascendant II stood up. Thorn walked along the row, shaking the hands of everyone he passed. He met Boulderfell on stage, who then physically manoeuvred Thorn by the shoulders in position to stand.

The same happened for Second-year, Treese Harper; Seventh-year, Geosar Weaver; and Fourth-year, Sunworth Littlewood—all of whom I did not recognise.

"Now, could I please invite on stage Third-year, Ryker Boulderfell. Congratulations!"

Ryker leapt out of his chair and pointed at me. I couldn't help but curl my lip. Instead of taking the empty aisle to the stage, Ryker insisted on walking all the way down his row of Third-years, hugging his friends, and really making a big show of it.

"Boulderfell? As in…Boulderfell?" I asked Calix during the commotion. This talented blue-eyed boy was my Show of Force partner back when we were in Mustard.

"Yeah, one of Seioh Boulderfell's sons," he replied, combing his fingers through his bright-blond, straight, preppy hair. "He has all his children raised in the institute. That's how much he swears by our upbringing."

"OK, last but not least," continued Seioh Boulderfell. "Please can I welcome on stage Third-year, Paxton Fortis. Congratulations!"

Pipila shuffled to the edge of her seat. It looked as though changing her answers this year worked out. She certainly seemed to think so.

"Lovely! Wonderful! Take a look at these fine young men." He danced around the line-up of six. "OK. Let us meet your future wives, shall we? Thorn Jelani, I would like to introduce to you Ninth-year, Celeste Antares. Congratulations!"

Celeste jumped from her seat and skipped hurriedly on stage. The hall screamed with cheers and wolf whistles. She flung her arms around Thorn's thick neck and kissed him. I remembered her from the Khakidemy, the day I performed on the Flexon, the same day Seioh Jennson...

...I completely lost focus! Boulderfell announced the matching of three more Navies and I didn't even realise. I was dragged back to reality by the sound of one person's name.

"Ryker Boulderfell."

I checked the stage to find him glaring at me with a thin creepy grin much like his dad's.

"I would like to introduce to you..." Seioh Boulderfell paused for dramatic effect.

Please not my name; please not my name; please not my name.

"...Third-year, Pipila Darlington. Congratulations!"

Phew! I could breathe again.

Pipila didn't move.

"Pipila Darlington?" repeated Seioh Boulderfell.

Pushed by her alphabetical neighbours, Pipila slowly rose from her chair. She stood still as a plank, staring at the stage. Before things got too awkward, she headed to the front, taking the shortest route to the aisle and avoiding the congratulations from her year. She greeted Ryker with a painfully forced kiss on the cheek. Ryker looked as sick as she did.

"Are we saving the best till last, ladies?" asked Boulderfell. "Paxton Fortis, I would like to introduce to you..."

The audience sat up straight, several of the girls turning to hold their neighbour's hands.

"...First-year, Aurora Aviary. Congratulations!"

CHAPTER FOUR

AND I, YOU.

I stared, unseeing, words echoing in my brain. '...First-year, Aurora Aviary. Congratulations!' *But I'm only sixteen; I don't want to be engaged.*

Calix slapped my knee, snapping my attention out of my head. "Congratulations, Aurora," he yelled over the noise. "Go on."

"This must be a mistake," I muttered in a daze.

"It's not. Go."

He got to his feet and pulled me up into a hug. My eyes found the exit at the front of the room and I turned for it. Calix pivoted me back the other way towards Hyas, who wrapped his arms around me. Before Hyas had even let go, Tyga already pulled me in for a hug. A stranger participated in the congratulations, and I found myself being led down the aisle as if I were on a conveyor belt. My body was being hugged, my cheek kissed, and my arm passed onto the next person.

"Congratulations, Aurora," shouted Silliah. "Enjoy this."

I held on to her tightly, never wanting to let her go, but she turned me around, giving me a small nudge towards the stage. Pax watched with raised eyebrows and a soft smile. He seemed amused by something. Maybe he remembered my outburst in the Food Hall. My cheek muscles felt too hard-set to return the smile. Only my lip twitched as I tried to swallow the pressure building in my throat. I concentrated on the sparkly flecks in the black floor, the light catching on my polished black boots, others' footprints pressed in the red carpeted steps leading up to Pax, anything, before I had no choice but to lift my eyes off the floor.

Pax threw his arm over my shoulder, bringing me close, and whispered, "You."

"You," I said back. *What does that even mean?*

He kept his arm around my shoulder and guided me to face the audience. "Did you want to find a match?" he spoke out the side of his mouth.

"No." I wasn't going to lie. "Did you?"

"No."

Well, kudos for honesty.

I couldn't concentrate on a word Seioh Boulderfell was saying. I'm not sure anyone was paying attention at this point. Everyone wanted to discuss this year's matches. Luckily, Boulderfell kept it short, and after a *Serve, Honour, Protect, and Defend*, the next I knew, Pax led me off stage following behind Ryker and Pipila.

"I was trying to match with *her*." Ryker jerked his head backwards in my direction.

Pipila gave me a brief look from over her shoulder. She flicked her cocoa-brown ponytail, looking away, and then kept her back to me the whole way out of the Auditorium. Pax removed his arm from around my shoulders the moment we were out of view. It was just for show, and I was pleased he wasn't going to pretend we liked each other just because a stupid test said we should.

Seioh Jennson escorted the newly betrothed couples down the corridor, straight into a spacious, brightly coloured office. There was a boring white desk, as expected in an office somewhere as dull as the institute, but this room had a seating area in the far corner with a mismatched theme. The designer had clearly unleashed their creativity as if it were their own home. I assumed they spent a long time in here. The yellow sofas had patterned teal cushions facing a teal coffee table, and placed next to the sofa, by a large potted plant, a fuchsia-pink armchair adorned a single yellow cushion. My eye was forced down to the rug on the floor pulling the living space together with a blend of yellow, teal, and fuchsia.

But evidently this was not where we were going. In an area by the door, twelve white, S-shaped plastic chairs faced the desk. I sighed internally at one of the items laid out on the desk. In two neat lines, twelve identical Slates were placed on top of twelve large brown envelopes. *Great, another welcome pack to NOT read.*

Pax and I took seats in the back row next to Ryker and Pipila. Nobody looked as comfortable as Celeste and Thorn. They were in the front row by the door, holding each other's hands. Celeste gently pecked at Thorn's cheek as if they were alone, stopping only when an older instructor entered the room. The instructor stood at the front observing each of us in turn, her head tilted back slightly, her eyes slightly squinted. She stroked her pointy chin several times before speaking.

"Hello, Navies. Congratulations are in order. I am Lady Merla Liddicott, your new relationship coach. I am here for guidance and advice, helping you to achieve a harmonious relationship. This is where I'll be if you ever need to find me.

"It is of the utmost importance you pay close attention in this meeting. Its content must be taken seriously, for in the past, those who did not listen have suffered the consequences, as I'm sure some of you are already aware."

I had no idea what she was talking about, but from a few exchanged looks in the room, apparently some did. With a furrowed brow, I hung on to every word Lady Merla Liddicott spoke next.

"Now that you are all betrothed, you have adopted a new responsibility on top of your existing responsibilities as a Young Enforcer. Now, you not only *Serve, Honour, Protect, and Defend,* but additionally, you have been chosen to bequeath your upbringing on to your future offspring.

"However, *this* is not to be acted upon until you are discharged from the institute. You must finish your duty as an Enforcer first. It is for this reason that sexual intercourse is strictly forbidden. It is imperative that you exercise discipline and self-control whilst you remain enlisted here at the *Boulderfell Institute for Young Enforcers.*

"It is a frightfully serious offence for Young Enforcers to conceive a baby out of wedlock. It is illegal and carries a thirty-year prison sentence. Babies are not get-out-of-here-early cards. The mother will be obligated to see the pregnancy through, the parents will be issued a dishonourable discharge, and the child will be enrolled into Mustard whilst the parents complete their thirty-year imprisonment.

"Double beds are for *sleeping.* They are not for more you-know-what space. Under no circumstances are you to practice coitus interruptus to prevent insemination."

"Coitus interruptus?" I asked Pax quietly.

Pax held back a laugh and closed his eyes tightly. He gradually leant closer to me and whispered, "Pull out."

We both snorted together. I hid my face in my hands. *Why did I have to ask that?*

"Yes, yes. We are talking about sexual intercourse. Will you two grow up?" Lady Liddicott glared at us with hooded steel eyes.

We wiped the smiles from our faces and continued to listen to the rest of what Lady Liddicott had to say. To sum the meeting up in a few words, it would have to be serve, honour, protect, defend, and thirty-year-old virgins.

Once the new Slates and brown envelopes were distributed, Liddicott gave us permission to leave the room. An electrifying current met me in the corridor. Clearly the excitement had not yet passed, and for a moment, I felt like a celebrity. The noise coming from the eagerly awaiting Navies was deafening in such a tight space, and apparently, it had become acceptable to invade our personal space uninvited. If this was what a real celebrity endured by adoring fans, I felt sorry for them. Although, I was grateful for the crowd for one thing—I had completely lost sight of Pax. I navigated the mob single-mindedly, intent on seeking refuge in my room. But before I got away, I was dragged sideways through the crowd, straight into the embrace of Silliah.

"Can we get out of here?" I wasn't really asking; I felt extremely claustrophobic and needed space. Silliah took my hand to lead the way, but then someone took hold of my other hand. *Tut, not now, Hilly.* I just needed to be with my best friend alone.

"Congratulations, Aurora." Hilly's shrillness transcended the noise of the mob. "You are so lucky! The only First-year to be matched this year, and to Pax of all people."

That word 'congratulations' was really starting to annoy me. I didn't want this! Why was I being congratulated for it?

The crowd faded into the distance, and I could hear my own thoughts again. In a quiet spot by the Khaki reception desk, Silliah turned to talk to me, "How are you? Are you happy?"

I hesitated before answering, aware Hilly was there. She was that hair; that hair in your mouth when you have dirty hands and can't get it out: mildly irritating, you know it's there, but there's nothing you can do about it. Silliah must have known because she changed the subject. "Has your schedule been cleared now?"

"Yes, until Monday. Lady Merla Liddicott said it was because newly betrothed couples had a lot to digest, and it prevented absent-mindedness. What am I going to do now?"

"Get to know Pax," blurted Hilly, looking up at me with widened blue eyes.

"You'll have plenty to do with all the celebrations coming up," said Silliah. "The Promises Ceremonies are tomorrow, and then the dinner-dance on Saturday. *And* you could always read your welcome pack."

I actually felt a natural smile grow on my pale face, but then it fell quickly when I remembered what I put her through this morning. "I will, I promise. I'm sorry about earlier."

"Don't be silly. I'm going to really miss you—"

"It's okay, Silliah," interrupted Hilly. "You've got me."

"I've got to go check into my new room," I told Silliah, mainly needing to get away from Hilly, but partially just wanting to be alone.

"It'll be in that envelope." Silliah understood and obliged to my unspoken need.

I backed away, peeling open the brown envelope. She was right; inside was my new room number: 4-3-2. I decided to find the room to see if I could gain access without going to check in. A chance of not seeing the ogre was worth the risk of a wasted journey if it worked. I scanned my picoplant and prayed.

The door slid open.

Oh. I wasn't expecting the room to be so big. It was massive in comparison to my old one. The window display, currently playing a tropical fish tank, took up the whole length of the back wall. I managed one small step in the door before watching the colourful fish gliding through the crystal-clear water, crisscrossing each other as tiny bubbles escaped from their delicate, radiant bodies: striped ones, orange and white ones, bright-yellow ones, and shiny multicoloured ones. I closed my mouth and took a look around an archway in the back left-hand corner. A walkway turned right into an all-white tiled ensuite with a roomy corner shower and a wide floating sink.

I turned back into the bedroom, climbing up two small steps surrounding a huge king mattress. Crawling onto the navy-blue duvet, my urge to faceplant the bed became repressed when I noticed another door on the far side of the room. It was open, so I went to investigate.

It confused me to find another bedroom—an exact mirror-opposite to mine—but it didn't take me long to learn of the room's occupant. Slouched on the end of the bed, unaware of my company, was Pax. Although he still held on to his envelope and new Slate, he looked like he'd been sitting there for a while. The warmth in his eyes had gone and the blood drained from his usually radiant face. I fought with the need to back out the doorway.

"Are you alright?" I forced myself to say.

The sparkle returned to his eyes as they met with mine. "Sorry, Aurora, I didn't see you there. I'm fine. It's just a lot to take in, isn't it? You can sit down." He nodded to the white leather corner sofa on my left.

"You didn't want to match either, did you?" I replied, taking a seat lightly, not leaning up against the backrest. "I thought I would be the only one because everyone loves Unity."

"Not me. Unity ruined my life."

Wow. That was rude.

"No, not you. Not being matched with you." Pax back-pedalled, seeing the look on my face. "Sorry, that must have sounded really rude. No. Unity is the reason I'm here."

"Unity is the reason you are here?"

The troubled expression washed back over his face. It unsettled me somehow. He opened and closed his mouth as if to speak but then changed his mind. He exhaled, looking down at his knees. "My parents are still alive."

"What?"

"My parents were Young Enforcers matched in Unity and had me illegally. They were dishonourably discharged and are in Avalon of Second City, carrying out their sentence in Maximum Security."

"Whoa," I said breathily.

"I know, sorry, bit deep for our first conversation."

"No, it's fine, honestly. I just can't believe your parents are still alive."

"Yep. Sentenced to thirty years and their baby taken away to be raised in the institute. That's all I know about them since we're not really supposed to talk about our lives before the institute. If it wasn't for Nanny Kimly, I wouldn't have been told about them until I was discharged. My whole life I wouldn't have known they were alive. But that's why I hate Unity. It forces two people together who *could* develop strong feelings towards each other, but then they are told to have self-control. No. How about you don't force them together?"

Although Pax spoke out loud, I felt as though he really spoke to himself, as if he was the one who really needed to hear it. I remained quiet, allowing him to get it all off his chest.

"But then, on the flip side of that," Pax continued, returning back with a level head, "they broke the rules. Why couldn't they have waited until they were discharged?"

A silence crept over us. I didn't know what to say. *What do you say to that?* 'I'm sorry' didn't feel adequate, so I didn't say anything. I peeled my eyes off my knotted fingers to see a vacant look back on his face. He had returned to that place in his head. I sunk down into the sofa and quietly put my feet up on the coffee table. I kept checking over at him and saw when his expression changed.

"You get to leave with me, you know?" he said, his eyes sharpening on me. "The year I turn thirty and get discharged, they grant you early release."

This wasn't news to me, and I'd already done the math. "I'll be twenty-seven."

"See, I'm good for one thing at least: I'm your get-out-of-here-early card."

⁂

When I walked into my room after dinner that evening, I found the interconnecting door closed. I welcomed the privacy like a sweet scent, inhaling it slowly and savouring it. The mood lights around the ceiling were already set to a calming blue, so I slid into a pair of my charcoal pyjamas, preparing for an early night. I settled in bed with my welcome pack, certain it would put me to sleep. Before I drifted off, I discovered Pax and I were scheduled for our clothes fitting first thing, followed by our Promises Ceremony shortly after.

In the morning, Pax and I left our bedrooms separately, and we found each other upstairs in the Tailors. I had visited this room a few times growing up, whenever I grew out of my Mustard uniform.

"You made it," Pax said, turning as I entered the room. "I really wasn't sure if I should have checked on you."

"Checked on me?"

"Yeah, to avoid a repeat of—sorry." He turned back the other way, but I already saw his smile.

"No, a repeat of what?"

"Nothing. Sorry."

He meant the Unity pre-meeting. I forgot he would have been in the audience somewhere. "If you must know, I read my welcome pack."

"Never said you hadn't." He dismissed the conversation, looking busy and pressing buttons on a capsule. "Now, come on, get in the capsule. It will give you your dress for the Promises Ceremony. They have set the room up next door so we can get changed."

"I know," I responded petulantly, managing to hold his gaze for a few beats before becoming intently interested in the large institute logo embellishing the floor. It was safe to say I didn't know.

The wait for the ceremony was agonizing. I didn't feel like talking to *Paxton-Presumptuous*, so I was prisoner to my own thoughts. I toyed with the idea of running away from the institute and living in isolation somewhere, but I would probably be tracked down by my picoplant and brought straight back. I could always try cutting the picoplant out, but that thought disturbed me more than this stupid ceremony did.

The Promises Ceremony was being held in the rooftop garden on the first floor. I hadn't been up here too often, and it was probably the most exciting part of my day. This floor was home to the Banquet Hall currently being set up for tomorrow's dinner-dance, and Seioh Boulderfell's office, which I'd heard to be the only office with a real window and glass roof. A complete waste, in my opinion, since the room was empty most of the year.

I stepped out onto the rooftop garden and paused. A canopy of snow painted the already picturesque landscape a brilliant white. It was odd how it made the familiar city look so foreign. I watched the snowflakes drifting lazily on the breeze, coming to rest on its sparkly blanket. Evergreen branches in the far distance hung low under its weight.

The retractable glass roof protected my bare arms from the icy wind. I dreamily stroked my fingertips around my shoulder, staring at the angelic white bouquets crowding the rooftop. In amongst them, hundreds of flickering candles melted away the hardness in my chest.

"Paxton. Aurora. This way, please." Lady Merla Liddicott stood under a square arbour wrapped in dark-green vines and soft-white fairy lights. Her small face poked out of silky white curtains draping down from each corner.

As Pax stepped forward, an intrusion of buzzing cameras honed in on us like flies on clart. The cameras circled around our heads, flying high and low, catching all angles.

"We are not getting married, are we?" I asked Pax, riveted to the spot and not going anywhere.

"Yes, Aurora. Sorry to break it to you, but that's kind of the point of Unity."

"Har, har," I broke in before he could sass me anymore. "I mean *now*. Is Liddicott marrying us *now*?"

"No, relax. This is just a Promises Ceremony. It doesn't mean anything officially."

"OK, good. I was worried because you look like a groom dressed like that, and I look like a bride. It's all ridiculously over the top."

"You look beautiful, sweetheart. Now, shut up, and let's go get married," he joked, holding out his hand for me to take.

I gave him a look saying *not funny* and walked myself to the arbour, ignoring his hand. My long white dress trailed behind me, dragging the scattered white petals with me as I went. I hated dresses but at least this one was plain. Only the V-neckline had a small amount of detailing with a few crystals.

Pax met me at the arbour with that familiar amused smile he wore when I met him on stage. He stood opposite me in a classic suit, a bit like Seioh Jennson's, but this one was navy and had a long back and a silky navy-blue waistcoat.

Standing here, I noticed Pax's eyes for the first time. They were an artist's muse, perfect in shape, and the colour of melted honey. It was the most unusual shade I had ever seen.

"What?" Pax gave me a quizzical look.

"Nothing." I averted my eyes.

"Are you two ready? Please take these." Lady Liddicott gave us each a thick piece of paper with an embossed lacey pattern. "You are to read these to each other where instructed. You can begin when you are ready."

Pax regarded the words on the fancy parchment and gave a weak laugh. Lady Merla Liddicott and I caught each other's fleeting glances. We could tell Pax wasn't done by the way his shoulders still bounced. I quickly checked my paper to see what it was. My smile weakened Pax's self-control and he broke.

"This is a highly important ceremony, Paxton. Please take it seriously."

"Sorry, ma'am," Pax said with a cough, trying to pull himself together. He began to read, amusement coating every word. "I was made to love you."

If he wasn't grinning like that, I might have been able to hold it in, but I couldn't, and we burst out laughing together. I knew it wasn't meant in the way we were taking it; it was just the irony of the sentence. We were literally being *made* to love each other.

"This is being recorded for you to keep. It is also being televised for the whole of the institute to see." The wrinkles around Liddicott's mouth cut deeper as she grew irritated. "Now pull yourselves together."

"S-s-sorry. Sorry, ma'am." Pax wiped his eyes. "I was made to love you," he tried again in a voice several octaves higher than normal.

"And I, you," I replied, pursing my lips together hard.

Pax stared down at his parchment, taking a few moments to read through his next part. His eyes no longer squinted from his smile. They held still, blinking, before bouncing from the words to me. Then with a different, sensible tone, he continued to read, "I promise to be more than I am, better than I was, and above what I have been. I promise to be all that I am for you. I have never had more of a reason to. You give me courage, and now we are together, I am braver than ever."

"And I, you," I said, before reading my part with the same composure. "I promise to protect you, care for you, and never let anything come in between. I promise to put your life before mine, and learn to love you in time. You give me strength, and now we are together, I am stronger than ever."

When I finished, I looked up to see Pax watching me closely. "And I, you," he said without looking at his parchment. "I promise to love you more every day."

"And I, you. I promise to love you in every way. I was made to love you."

"And I...you," he finished.

I don't know how long we stood still for. His seriousness took me off guard, and I kept staring into his golden eyes.

"Absolutely wonderful, you two." Lady Liddicott broke our attention on each other. "That was beautiful. Incredibly touching—a rocky start, but the most heartfelt Promises I have had the pleasure of witnessing. All that's left to do now is exchange Promises rings. Take these. Aurora, if you could place this on the tip of Paxton's third finger of his left hand, and Paxton, if you could do the same with Aurora."

Lady Liddicott held open a white marble box displaying two platinum bands. I fumbled to get the ring out of the presentation cushion, and we waited with the (heavier than expected) plain bands hovering on each other's fingers.

"Please repeat together this wish:

"*I ask you to wear this ring as a symbol of my Promises to you. I ask you to wear it, and think of me, and remember all that I have promised you here today. It is a reminder of my faith in our strength together. I believe I was made for you.*

"And now, as a way of accepting each other's wishes, I would like you to push on your own rings."

CHAPTER FIVE
JUST PLAIN STUPID

"He *so* loves you already, Aurora," insisted Silliah, her rectangular glasses sitting diagonally across her little nose, barely hanging on by one ear. She had come running into my bedroom the day after the Promises Ceremony and flew onto my bed, landing on her belly. She brushed her ruffled walnut fringe out of her eyes, straightened her glasses, and shoved her Slate in front of my face. I had to lean away to allow my eyes to focus on the image she showed me. But something else caught my attention.

"Hang on a minute. What is this?" I referred to the device she held. It almost looked like the new Slate I had been issued the other day, but Silliah's was triple the size and noticeably thinner.

"Never mind that—watch." She scurried up next to me and played the recording of my Promises Ceremony, pausing it on Pax's face right after he had finished the last 'And I, you.' "Look at his face. See the way he is looking at you?"

"Don't be ridiculous. He hates Unity just as much as I do." I took off my Promises ring and dropped it on the bed.

"Trust me, he loves you. I can tell. You have never been very good at picking up on these things. I tried telling you years ago in Mustard that Hyas liked you, but you wouldn't listen, and now he has actually admitted he wanted to match. Take my word for it, Pax loves you."

65

"He doesn't love me. We don't even *like* each other. I'm sure he thinks I'm an idiot. He was the one who stopped me in the Food Hall, remember?"

"I do remember, but that doesn't mean he doesn't like you."

"He doesn't like rule breaking, and I always seem to get into trouble."

"HE. LIKES. YOU!" said Silliah, holding a short pause between each word.

"Er-hem," coughed Pax, standing at the interconnecting door with a secret smile. "Do you want me to close this?"

Silliah, who had her back towards the door, slapped her hand over her mouth, panic strewn all over her face. I quickly put my platinum ring back on.

"No, it's fine. Silliah was just *leaving*." I eyed Silliah strongly.

"*Sorry,*" Silliah mouthed silently to me, climbing off the bed backwards. She couldn't get out of the room quickly enough. At the same time, Pax disappeared from the doorway, and I was left alone wondering how much Pax had overheard. I tried to remember the whole conversation, working out if it was that bad. Either way, I was mortified.

Next thing I knew, I found myself at the open door between the two bedrooms. My legs carried me there without consulting with my brain first. I felt so awkward, and I needed to know if Pax was going to say anything about the conversation. I leant against the door frame and peered inside. Pax was lying on his back with his feet up on the display screen. He held on to the same device Silliah had earlier, and I spotted my opportunity.

"That tablet…where do you get one of those from?"

He tilted his head to see me at the door. "Come," he said, patting the bed next to him.

I tried to act naturally, but I was so conscious of how my body moved, it was as if I had forgotten how to walk. I made it to the bed and joined him, lying with my feet up on the display screen the same as him. As soon as I did, though, I regretted it; there was nothing normal about the way I was acting. It was too late now. If I sat up, he would definitely know I felt weird.

"Have you got your new Slate on you?" He put down his device and held out a flat hand.

"Yes. Why?"

"Get it out, and I'll show you."

I reached into my trouser pocket and pulled out my new Slate. As the screen came on, a message from Silliah showed on the display, '*Ahhh, I'm dying inside! Has he said anythi—*' I whacked the Slate down onto my stomach, preventing Pax from reading anymore.

"Tut, just give it here." He took the Slate, swiped the message from Silliah to clear it, and proceeded like nothing happened. "You just bring up your apps and press this one." He touched a blue and white icon resembling an open book. The Slate began to unfold itself in thirds, revealing a tablet exactly like Silliah's. The front lifted and folded right whilst the back folded itself out and to the left. The icon changed to a narrow rectangle. "And if you want your Slate back, just press it again." He pressed the narrow rectangle, and the device folded itself back in thirds again, returning back my Slate. I examined the glass screen for signs of stress—there were none.

"I like it," I said, turning the Slate over in my fingers.

"Yeah, it's cool. Basically like having a tablet on you all the time."

"Thanks for showing me," I finished, running out of things to say. It wasn't uncomfortable though; he made me feel oddly at ease given the situation. Even though we were both staring at the fish swimming around our feet, I was hyper-aware of his every movement. He was quite still, clearly unbothered by my presence. Only his broad chest floated up and down in a gentle rhythm.

"Not having a schedule makes time drag, doesn't it?" he said lazily, keeping his attention on the fish. His chest inflated fully, held there for a moment, and then sunk back down deep.

"Tell me about it. I actually enjoy training."

"You're pretty good, aren't you?"

"I'm alright." I shrugged. "I was chosen to lead Boulderfell's Show of Force Display quite a few times when I was in Mustard. You know the boy and girl who lead in the Navies doing a martial arts routine?"

"Yeah, I remember seeing you. Pee'd Pipila right off that year you got chosen over us." He gave a short breathy laugh.

"Over *us*?" I had to ask.

"Pipila and I were chosen a few years in a row, and then one year a younger, 'cuter' boy and girl were chosen instead of us," Pax said, making quotation marks with his fingers as he said the word 'cuter'.

"Oh." It was weird to think we were all in Mustard together; he seemed so much older than me.

"You've got nice little feet, haven't you?" He changed the subject, touching my white sock with his white sock.

Well, that got really strange, really quick.

⁂

"He said I had nice feet!" I explained to Silliah during the dinner-dance that evening.

"He said you had nice *feet*?" Silliah repeated over the loud music. "Explain to me in detail; what were you doing?"

"After you left, I had to find out if he was going to mention anything about our conversation. Don't ask me how I got there, but I found myself lying on his bed next to him, our feet were up against the display screen, and we were talking about the Show of Force Display. Then he randomly came out with, 'You've got nice little feet, haven't you?' It's not just me, is it? Isn't that *weird*?"

Silliah laughed. "He was flirting with you, Aurora."

"Flirting with me? How was *that* flirting with me? You're just still trying to convince me that he likes me." I searched the crowd, checking he was nowhere near me. I wasn't having a repeat of earlier; he would think I had nothing better to talk about than him.

"He does like you, and no, that is not what I'm doing. Did he touch you when he said it?"

He did, but how did she know that? "With his *foot*." I tried to play it down.

"Like I said, flirting with you." She created a heart with her two index fingers. "Do you want to go dance?"

"No," I replied, a little annoyed at her. "I think I've done my share of dancing tonight." I referred to the Near-touch dance Pax and I had to do earlier alongside all the other newly betrothed couples. The Near-touch dance was a simple routine taught to us in Mustard. All six of us girls lined up on one side in our matching white dresses, facing our handsome future husbands dressed in their identical tailored suits. The dance wasn't so bad because, as the name implies, we didn't have to touch each other at all. Maintaining eye contact was the only challenge. Then, after we completed the routine once through, we had to repeat it again, but this time, every single betrothed couple joined in. It was something quite special once the whole room was swirling with bodies. The dance symbolised intimacy in a relationship without the need for touching. Loosely translated to: '*you don't need to have sex to have an intimate relationship.*'

Silliah left me sitting alone on the top table with Boulderfell only a few chairs away. I watched glumly as she had fun on the dance floor with Hilly, Shola, Tyga, and Hyas. Multicoloured lasers whizzed chaotically around the room, occasionally reflecting off the crystal glasses and silver cutlery, splitting the beams of light on to my dress. The white cloth was the perfect backdrop, transforming me into a living lightshow.

Snow caked the glass ceiling, concealing the late-night sky. Unable to stargaze, I leant back in my chair, crossed my arms, and watched the slowed-down Promises Ceremonies playing around the walls. Ryker and Pipila's recording was funny to watch. Apparently neither of them had gotten used to the idea of being matched, and they both looked like they would rather be jumping off the Ascendant II unaided.

Not long after having finished our four-course meal, the round tables were being cleared by a horde of Juvies. They seemed happy to be out of their cells and able to witness such a rare celebration. Unity was the only time of year Young Enforcers had a big party. Even the Musties were allowed to enjoy this evening's dinner-dance. They currently ran around the room, really letting off steam. Some were even skidding across the dance floor on their knees, covering their Mustard uniform in nice dirty stains. Everyone wore their Mustard or Navy uniforms except the newly betrothed couples. We had to wear our Promises Ceremony attire. But whatever: it wasn't the first time this year I stood out like a sore thumb.

The music stopped, and Seioh Boulderfell cleared his throat. The walls changed to show Boulderfell's unnaturally smooth face and shiny jet-black eyes. The camera zoomed out, showing his head and torso. Under his neat grey beard, a golden small-link chain held closed a silly black cape covering his black evening suit.

Everyone stood to attention.

"At ease, my dear children," sang Seioh Boulderfell, flapping his hands. "Tonight's celebrations have been spectacular. Another Unity almost over, and what a wonderful start to the year it has been. The special send off for the discharged Thirteenth-years will commence tomorrow with the marriage of eight couples. I look forward to seeing you all there. Unfortunately, I am not as young as you are, my children, and I am quite ready for my rest. Please, do continue to have fun, my wonderful lot. *Serve, Honour, Protect, and Defend.*"

"*Serve, Honour, Protect, and Defend.*"

Seioh Boulderfell turned to leave, and at the same time, his team of Fell agents automatically emerged from the shadows and obediently followed after Boulderfell like a pack of dogs. Their EU was as black as the night's sky, and they were hard to make out in this dimly lit room. Why he needed to be escorted around inside the institute, I had no idea, but I supposed paranoia, once under the skin, grew like a parasite.

Unity was finally over. I hadn't gone to watch the many, many weddings yesterday. I had one last day of avoiding Pax before our duties started and we would practically be joined at the hip. He didn't go to the weddings either; I could hear faint movement coming from his room most of the day. This morning, as I sat lacing up my boots, I heard a light tapping on the interconnecting door.

"You can come in," I called out.

"Ready for your first day as an Enforcer?" asked Pax at the door. His fresh haircut from last week had grown out slightly, and I thought he looked better this way, with the sides a bit longer and the blondish top starting to curl again.

"I guess so." I wasn't sure if it was a good idea mentioning I felt nervous. In fear of making him think I was weak, I kept it to myself.

"Our schedules have been uploaded to our Slates. We are on a restricted schedule for a week to ease us in; not many Enforcer duties unfortunately, but this morning, we are Juvie chaperones at breakfast."

"I'm ready when you are," I said, attempting to sound nonchalant.

Only the ruffling from our uniforms could be heard as we walked side by side to Claret Quartz to pick up our Juvies. This quarter of the institute had dull-reddish panels on the floor, walls, and ceiling, making the corridors feel awfully narrow. I thought by having colour on the walls it would have livened the place up, but there was something I really didn't like about it in here. A dungeon crossed with an insane asylum came to mind, and it wasn't helped by that strange chemical smell singeing my nose.

"You get used to it." Pax responded to my scrunched-up face.

"What is that?"

"Laundry room down that corridor. It's the chemicals used to dry-clean the clothes."

In the detention centre, huge white numbers identified the cells. Pax stopped outside cell J-16 and turned to me. "OK," he began softly but still direct. "I'm allocated the Davoren Sisters. They are our 'resident' Juvies."

"Resident Juvies?" I parroted.

"It's a long story, but basically, they used to get caught on purpose, so now they don't even get discharged and are free to leave whenever they want."

"What? They *choose* to be here? Why would they do that?"

"Well, their mum is Band D—only one Worth per hour—so when their dad died, she couldn't afford to look after them. Normally, they would be taken into care, and adopted by the institute. They would become Young Enforcers like us, but they don't want that. So, they found a loophole, so to speak. Until there are signs of neglect, the authorities can't touch them, and they can't be enrolled here."

"But what about school? They will end up Band D too if they don't study."

"Take a look." Pax gestured for me to look through the observer window into the cell. Two fair-haired girls sat on bunk beds with their noses deep in books; opposite them—a white plastic bookcase. The books on the shelves weren't arranged like the ones in Seioh Jennson's office, where all the books were placed neatly in size order. No. The girls' bookcase was organised in colour, no matter the height of the book. The rainbow display was very aesthetically pleasing, and I felt fond of the girls without even having met them.

"Since Juvies aren't allowed to be seen with any electronics," explained Pax, "we have sourced as many books as we can find for them. They study at every opportunity. Maigen is fourteen and is almost ready to take the exams that assign the Worths Band—two years early. Bethoney is only ten. She'll be home with her mum in no time, thanks to her sister."

"Smart kids," I said, pulling at my lip, mulling it over. "I'm surprised Boulderfell allows that; isn't it seen as dishonourable to prevent children from being raised in the institute?"

"Well, what Seioh Boulderfell doesn't know can't hurt him. Seioh Jennson doesn't care—they provide training for us."

"But Ryker could tell him." I grimaced, aware I stated the obvious.

"Why do you think he hasn't been allocated them?" He winked. "Anyway, these two get allocated as a pair because they are pretty much free to leave if they wanted to. You have been given Tayo next door: J-14. He has his ankle trap on; you'll need to scan his picoplant to gain access to it. I'll get the girls and wait for you here."

Oh my god. Just like that and I'm about to chaperone my first Juvie. I pressed the shining blue access button so slowly it didn't make an audible click.

"Hi, erm…can I…I mean, I need to…tut, just hold out your wrist," I fumbled like an idiot, really struggling to find the balance between authority and politeness.

The Juvie blinked at me with round, piercing-blue eyes and a stupid smirk across his face which I wanted to slap. He flicked his jet-black hair out of his eyes, stared a little more, and then stood in front of me. I didn't know whether it was because he was quite a few inches taller than me, or because he had come into my personal space a bit more than comfortable, but either way, I took a small step back and scanned his wrist with my Slate.

"You're Band A? Four Worths an hour," I blurted after reading his personal information. "What are you doing *here?*" He was rich! He could earn a week's wages in two days. Plus, only the best jobs were given to Band As.

"Broke Curfew…ma'am." There was something about the manner with which he spoke that felt insincere, almost like he was pretending to be respectful. I should know; I'd used that tone many times pretending to be.

"Right. Well, this way, please." I decided to give him the benefit of the doubt.

Pax waited outside my cell with Bethoney and Maigen. *Why couldn't I have been allocated the Davoren Sisters? Look at them with their matching plaited pigtails and sweet, innocent faces.* Pax gave the Juvies a gesturing nod, and they walked ahead of us, leading the way to the Food Hall.

"How was that?" he asked. "Did you gain control of the ankle trap?"

"I scanned his picoplant. I control it with my Slate, don't I?"

"Yes. When you increase the slider, the trap will get heavier until they can't move their foot—means you don't have to watch them whilst you eat."

"Tayo Tessan? Is that you?" squealed Pipila, speeding past us and stopping Tayo dead in his tracks.

"Pipila Darlington," Tayo sang back fondly with a warm smile.

"What are you doing here?" probed Pipila.

"Curfew."

"Ah, that's a shame—"

"What are you doing talking to the Juvie scum?" butted in Ryker, coming level with Pax and me. "Paxton. Aurora." Ryker nodded at Pax then winked at me. "Come," he ordered for Pipila to follow him. "And it's *ma'am*," he said to Tayo, placing a hand on the back of Tayo's neck and swinging his fist deep into Tayo's stomach. It forced the air out of Tayo with a harsh *hoofing* sound. Tayo doubled over and fell to his knees, clinging on to his stomach, reaching for air. A small cry escaped from Bethoney as she knelt down to help him. Ryker continued on to the Food Hall like nothing happened. Pipila obeyed after eyeing Ryker scornfully, holding her chin up in the air, and walking off in a huff.

"*What do you think—*" I tried to shout at Ryker, but Pax turned me to face him.

"Don't," he whispered, shaking his head jerkily.

"*Why*?"

"You can't interfere with an Enforcer doing their job, Aurora. You'll be the one to get into trouble."

"Doing his job? How is punching a Juvie doing his job?" I wasn't looking for an answer and stormed off.

Pax helped Tayo to his feet. "You alright?"

"Yes." Tayo brushed down his overalls. "Sir." A punch didn't appear to have taken away that air of arrogance about him.

I stood under the Food Hall archway searching for Ryker and saw he made it to the meal dispenser already. *Come on, listen to Pax. Leave it. You'll only get in trouble.* I controlled my urge to confront Ryker and instead scanned the busy hall for a free table as far away from his crowd as possible. I wanted to take my usual seat in Claret Quartz, but I felt obligated to sit with Pax since we came to the hall together.

Before I made my choice, Tayo appeared by my side. I turned to tell him where to stand, but he pretended I wasn't there and went to stand where he wanted to, taking position at a vacant chute. I purposefully slid his ankle trap to the maximum weight, rendering his foot almost impossible to move. I saw when he realised because he gave me a confused look. I returned the look with one that said *you can ignore me all you want; I still have control.* My mood lifted an inch, and I dutifully joined Pax at a table in Navy Quartz.

"Have you booked yourself on to any lessons yet?" Pax asked me as I sat down. He read my expression and laughed. "I thought you said you read your welcome pack?"

"Some of it."

"Navies have duties with partners from different years, so lessons aren't done in year groups like they are in Mustard. You have to book yourself on to lessons when you have a lesson block on your schedule. Look." He showed me our schedule on his Slate. "We have the same schedule so we can do our duties together, but we don't have to take the same lessons. After all, I may have already done the subject you need. See here, the lesson block, touch that and it will bring up all the lessons available for that time. Then choose one to book yourself on to. Talk to Silliah and see if she has a lesson block at the same time as you. Maybe you can book on to the same lesson together?"

I was listening, but I didn't respond. My body remained completely frozen as my eyes followed him crossing the room. *No, it can't be. He isn't coming to sit here.*

He's only gone and done it.

"I'm sorry you had to see that earlier," said Ryker, sitting down at the table with his food tray. "I was thinking we should be friends again, Paxton."

"We were never friends, Ryker," Pax replied, his eyes returning back to the tabletop screen.

"Hmm, yes. I hear what you're saying." Ryker pretended to think. "Well, I think we should be friends now."

"Oh, right?"

"Yeah, it's not fair on poor old Brindan having to wait for you to leave the Food Hall before he comes to sit with us, when we could all sit together."

Ryker continued to prattle on. I absently scrolled through the breakfast items on my screen, but the words passed in a haze, one by one, failing to be computed by my distracted brain. I was busy thinking of my exit strategy. Pipila came and stood at the empty space opposite me, next to Ryker. If someone had told me that this week I would be sitting on the same table as Ryker and Pipila, I would have told them to put their straitjacket back on. Only, Pipila didn't sit down. Instead, she used the tabletop screen to program another table on the other side of Ryker and Pax. She placed herself down and a few of her cronies joined her.

Pax was deciding what to eat and only looked up from his screen to greet Brindan after he came and placed his tray on the empty space next to Pax. I was in utter disbelief of the unfolding situation, and to make things worse...Pax stood up to retrieve his breakfast from the meal dispenser. *No. Don't leave me here.*

"Since when did we start allowing the trash to sit at the table?" Pipila spoke to her bowl of porridge. *Is she really that spineless to not even address me?*

"Well, I took the Show of Force Display from you when we were younger, so I thought I'd take your seat at the table, too. You would rather be sitting in my spot, wouldn't you?" I retaliated, hinting at the fact I knew she wanted to match with Pax. The table fell completely still; it was as if they rehearsed a Mannequin Challenge. The long-nosed, sandy-haired girl next to Pipila even had her spoon in mid-air, inches away from her open mouth. Ryker moved first, leaning back in his chair, folding his arms, and switching to look between me and Pipila as if he were watching a tennis match. *You're actually enjoying this, aren't you? You vindictive little—*

"Get—the F—off—of my table," snarled Pipila, finding the courage to lock on to my eyes.

The F? Did you really just say the F? I know we're not allowed to swear but come on! I won't tell if you won't.

"Everything...OK here?" Pax returned.

When nobody spoke, his head turned from me to Pipila as he attempted to work out what he walked into.

"It's fine," responded Ryker. "The ladies were just sharing memories from the Mustard days. Ain't that right, girls?"

"Everything's fine," said Pipila, turning her emerald-green eyes back on to her porridge.

"See, like I said, fine," said Ryker, sneering. Then conversations began at the table again.

Pax sat down slowly. "Not eating anything?" he asked, turning to face me. I could tell he was still trying to gauge the situation.

"I'm not hungry." *Funny that.*

"You should eat."

"This was fun," said Ryker, getting up from the table. "We should do it again some time." He lifted his tray of half-eaten porridge and beelined towards Tayo.

Tayo straightened up, reaching for the tray. Before Tayo's fingers found the rim, Ryker let it go, spilling porridge down Tayo's overalls. There was a crash of smashing china and shards scattered around their feet. Then, a few moments of quiet as the room gawked at the stand-off commencing between the two boys.

"I prefer to *eat* my porridge—" The words barely left Tayo's mouth when Ryker pulled Tayo's face down into his rising knee, splitting Tayo's lip. Blood sprayed the white china splinters around them. Ryker didn't stop. He drove his knee into Tayo's abdomen again, again, and again, until Tayo collapsed in a heap on the floor. Ryker continued to pelt Tayo in the ribs with his weighty leather boots, every blow provoking an involuntary grunt from Tayo. He curled up into a ball, protecting his vital organs. Playing dead was his best option.

Horrified, I hurtled out of my chair towards them. *Is nobody going to stop him?* Too quick for Pax's attempt to stop me, I ducked under his arm, only to be captured by Brindan.

"You can't." Brindan hooked my arms behind my back in a double arm pin.

"Watch me." I stepped my foot between his legs and twisted my body downward, freeing myself from Brindan's lock.

"Ryker," called Pax in a firm, even tone. Ryker snapped out of his rage and held eyes on Pax. They stood motionless, eyes locked on. It was a tense few moments, but nothing else needed to be said. Ryker understood their unspoken conversation: enough was enough.

Ryker gone, I ran and kicked the china shards away from Tayo's lifeless body. Blood gushed from his busted nose, flowing freely into the open wounds on his lips. It was hard to recognise that lofty boy from earlier as he lay here on the floor, defenceless.

"Didn't feel like releasing the ankle trap?" *Oh, I was wrong; there he is.* Tayo spoke the words without opening his eyes. I felt for my Slate and immediately disabled the trap. Tayo struggled to sit, wincing as he held on to his side.

"You okay getting up?" Pax asked Tayo.

"Yes, sir," Tayo said weakly, pulling himself up to stand.

"You stopped Ryker," I let slip, getting myself up off the floor.

"Will you be alright taking Tayo back to his cell whilst I get the nurse?"

"Of course," I replied. *Although, I think the dude could use a psychiatrist. He's absolutely crazy.*

"Girls, come," Pax called for Maigen and Bethoney to follow him.

I aided a limping Tayo out of the Food Hall. A drone of gossip began from the stunned spectators behind us.

"Well, that was bloody stupid, even for my standards," I said, letting go of Tayo's arm and allowing the idiot to walk by himself.

"Yeah, well, I never have been very good at following the rules."

"You ought to start practicing. Unless you want to be beaten to a pulp again. You can start by addressing me properly."

"Undressing you properly? That's a little inappropriate, ma'am. We've only just met; I mean, give it a day."

"You really don't have any respect, do you? You deserve everything you get," I retaliated, a little flustered. "And that's not why it's inappropriate. It's inappropriate because it's inappropriate!"

"Profound." He burned me with a single word.

CHAPTER SIX
BEWARE THE WHAT?

"No, stop. Don't do that." I was being ignored by an undressing Tayo after reaching his cell. As soon as we stepped through the door, he began unzipping his blood and porridge covered overalls. "I'm warning you. I said don't do that."

Tayo still didn't stop but instead turned away, pulling the overalls off his shoulders. I averted my eyes quickly, staring out the window into the corridor. *Oh, Tayo, please put your clothes back on.*

"Will you relax? Why are you so uptight?" Tayo argued back. "It's only skin, Roar."

"It's *ma'am*," I said through gritted teeth. This boy was making my life miserable. All the other Enforcers managed to get Juvies to treat them with respect. Why was I so useless at this?

I gradually turned my head to face forward, trying to see him out the corner of my eye. I didn't want to see too much, and he was so unpredictable, I had no idea what I was letting myself in for. I knew one thing for sure, I did not want the first boy I saw in their underwear to be *this guy*. Thankfully, I saw claret-red shorts.

Tayo finally gave in and dropped the tough guy act. He sat down on the edge of the bed and, with his feet still on the floor, collapsed sideways into his pillow. He was clearly in pain and couldn't hide it anymore. From this angle, I couldn't tell he'd been beaten. One arm— heavily tattooed from shoulder to wrist— clung on to his lean, naked torso, and the other cast a shadow over his face. His long legs seemed

81

untouched. Actually, now I looked for it, I could make out a rather nasty purple bruise developing on his right shin.

"Can you stop staring?" Tayo said without moving. "It's creepy."

I snapped my eyes away. *Dammit.* The arm over his face clearly wasn't covering his eyes. I pursued my inspection of the corridor outside.

"Or you could join me?" he continued. "There's room for you here." He swung his white plimsoles onto the bed and slid back, making room in front of him.

"I'm serious, Tayo. You need to stop that."

"Stop what? I'm just saying, instead of staring at me, you could come join me. I don't mind. Just be gentle."

"I'll give you frickin' gentle—"

"Calm down, Roar. I'm only playing with you. God, you're easy to wind up."

"Well, don't! And it's *ma'am.*"

Tayo turned his blood-stained face into the pillow. I was in two minds about this boy. One minute, I felt sorry for him; the next, I hated his guts.

"I saw you coming to help me, you know?" Tayo mumbled into the pillow.

"I was…Ryker is—" I didn't know what to say. I shouldn't have tried to stop Ryker. Pax risked *himself* getting into trouble to stop *me* from getting into trouble. We'd only been betrothed for four days, and I was already pulling him down. Matching with me had to be the worst thing to ever happen to him.

I didn't need to finish my sentence anyway because a lady entered the cell. She was a nanny I recognised from Mustard, the one with dark-brown hair twisted in a tight bun, and the scary, hostile face which made me clench.

"Why aren't you applying pressure to the Juvie's wound, Miss Aviary?" asked Nanny June Damiano, attending to Tayo.

"Wound?" I repeated. *I can't exactly apply pressure to a split lip.*

"Yes, Miss Aviary. You have had your first aid training, am I correct?"

"Yes, ma'am."

"Then why aren't you applying pressure to the Juvie's wound?" She glanced over with close-set brown eyes.

I looked at Tayo dumbfounded, but then I gasped. Smeared blood soaked his body.

"Nature of the incident?" Nanny June moved on, taking a seat on the spare chair. Tayo flinched at the pain as he drew a breath to speak. "Quiet, Juvie," she ordered. Tayo bit the side of his bottom lip and exhaled noisily through his nostrils. "Speak only to answer my next question, Juvie. Do you have a problem with being told to be quiet?"

"No, ma'am," said Tayo, wide-eyed.

Wow, he's better at that fake respect stuff than I am. I would have believed him if I hadn't experienced firsthand what a jackass he was.

"Nature of incident?" repeated Nanny June, examining Tayo's ribs.

My shoulders and voice lifted higher and higher as I spoke, "Errr, being beaten to a pulp by an Enforcer?"

"Correctional protocol." She changed my answer.

A snorting noise forced its way out of my throat.

"Something amusing, Miss Aviary?" She cleaned up Tayo's bloody face with an alcohol wipe, turning his head from side to side by his chin.

"No, ma'am." I held my lips closed with my fingers. *Don't laugh!* My chest trembled at the pressure as I held it in. Tayo's chin had been released, and his acknowledging smile made my belly flutter. I smiled back...until I registered it was Tayo. *Yuck.*

"Nature of this injury?" Nanny June now wiped the blood from Tayo's body. As she cleaned the area, I saw the culprit for the mass of blood. I couldn't see it before. Nanny June uncovered an incision, about the size of my little finger, sliced under his ribcage.

"There was a smashed china bowl involved," I guessed.

Once the bleeding stopped, Nanny June used sterile strips to close the wound, applied some antibiotic ointment, padded it with a large cushioned plaster, and wrapped an extremely long bandage around Tayo's body.

Nanny June cleaned up after herself. "You will need to change the Juvie's bandages once a day, starting this evening."

"*Me?*" I choked.

"Of course, you. He is your allocated Juvie, is he not? Who else is going to do it?"

"You?"

"Pffft. I have more important things to do than to change bandages, Miss Aviary." Nanny June reached into her self-standing bag and pulled out a dozen bandages, plasters, and alcohol wipes. "Juvie, speak only to answer my next question. Are you at risk of using these bandages for anything other than their intended purpose?"

Tayo's face wrinkled at such an unusual question. "No, ma'am?" His tone rose at the end.

"Then these can stay in here." She plonked the first aid kit onto the empty surface opposite Tayo's bed, pushed the two stiff-leather sides of her bag closed, and left the cell with a, "Good day to you."

Tayo and I looked at each other with a thin smile. "Speak only for my next question," we said together, both having the same idea and moving our arms and bodies like robots.

I touched the metal institute logo on my hip after having a small swirl of guilt. I probably shouldn't have done that with Tayo, but I couldn't help myself.

"Looks like I'll be seeing you tonight, Roar."

"MA'AM! You have to go and ruin it, don't you?" Balance was restored. He was an absolute toolbox. "Can't you just change your own bandages?" I whined. I didn't want to go anywhere near him, let alone *touch* him.

"But then cutting myself would have been for nothing."

My face fell. "You cut yourself on purpose?"

"No, Roar. That's sick. It was a joke."

I walked out of that cell disturbed. My first day as an Enforcer couldn't be going any worse. I stepped into the corridor as Pax left Beth and Mai's cell. Seeing him felt weirdly comforting, and I almost missed the time we'd just spent bored in our rooms.

"How was that for timing," said Pax, meeting me with a small elbow nudge. "I wasn't sure if we were going to miss each other because I've got my lesson soon."

"Oh! My lesson block. I didn't book on to anything."

"Come with me to Advanced Mixed Martial Arts. You'll do alright in there, I reckon. You did private lessons for the Show of Force Display, right?"

"I did. But…"

"Honestly, come try it. I can stay partners with you if you would like, but you're going to be fine."

I thought about it for a minute. I didn't want to be alone after the morning I'd had, and if Pax did stay partners with me, it might not be so bad. "Alright."

It was settled. We set off together to Khaki Quartz.

"I thought, being betrothed, we wouldn't be with the Juvies on our own?" I broached the subject on our way out of Claret Quartz. The white panelled walls were as refreshing as the morning sunshine outside. I was glad to be out of those suffocating corridors.

"Sort of. We *never* go out there on our own," he motioned out in the city. "But most of the Juvies are kids, so inside it's fine."

But I didn't have a child. He may have had the maturity of one, but Tayo was most definitely an adult—a pig-headed, moronic adult.

"Is there any way of changing our allocated Juvies?"

"Why? You're not uncomfortable with Tayo, are you?" asked Pax, walking by my side, studying my face.

"No!" *Yes...* "I was just wondering," I lied to stop the burning in the side of my face.

"Unfortunately not." His honey eyes trained forward again. "Unless they do something wrong, and then you can get the adults sent to Maximum Security. But that never happens. Juvies always do as they're told."

I placed my hands into my pockets and tried to keep my voice casual. "How do you get them to do as they're told?"

"Just tell them. They will do it. If you wanted to be tough, you could threaten them, but make sure you can follow through with the threat. If you're talking about on the outside and you get a difficult detainee, then that's what our training is for. You know your pressure points, right?"

"Yes—collar bone, jaw zone, temples, shoulder blade." I listed a few.

"They help. Locks and holds come in handy too. I wouldn't necessarily recommend Ryker's approach."

My stomach tightened at the reminder of what I did. I pulled my hands together from inside my pockets, hugging myself. "No. Thank you for stopping him earlier."

"You didn't leave me with much of a choice now, did you?" he asked, holding open the murky-green doors to the Khakidemy.

"I was afraid you would say that." I knew he thought I was a dim-wit.

"I'll do what I can for you, Aurora, but *try* to rein it in? What were you going to do once you got there, anyway?" he asked, poised outside the male changing rooms.

"Rugby tackle?" I joked with a meek grin, backing away from him. He gave me a reassuring wink before disappearing through the door. *Okay, my belly really needs to stop doing that—that's twice today.*

I changed quickly into my gi—a bleached thick-cotton uniform—then met Pax in the corridor outside the dojo. We were a little late, and everyone had made it inside already. Eager waves from people I didn't know met us at the door, and the not-so-discreet whispers made me feel like we were hot gossip.

"Aurora," sang an enthusiastic Sir Hiroki. "I'm pleased to see you in an advanced class. Here, let me get you a different belt. I'll grade you later."

He scurried off to a cupboard towards the back of the dojo. I gave a small bow to the room before stepping onto the green mat. My special white socks had grips on the soles and prevented me from catching my toes. Looking around, I was the only First-year in the room, and the only person wearing a white belt. Grading, an exam used to award higher belts, was not available to Mustards.

Sir Hiroki returned, giving me an orange belt, *two* grades higher than white! I would only be one grade lower than Pax, who sported a green belt. I couldn't hide my elation, and Pax met my toothy smile with another wink. Today's events slowly drifted to the back of my mind; maybe this class wasn't such a bad idea.

"Perhaps you would prefer an Uke more your size, Aurora?" Sir Hiroki referred to Pax being my training partner. Pax was only marginally taller than me, but he was a share stockier compared to my tiny frame. Sir Hiroki, being more my build and height, was my suited partner, but I wasn't planning on being thrown around like a dog's toy by this Whippet.

"And will my opponent on the outside always be my size, sir?"

"Good point. As you were; don't go easy on her, Paxton." Sir Hiroki stuck his tongue out at me before turning away. I *knew* he wanted to put me through my paces.

As part of the warm up, we had to try and get each other on our backs. Pax didn't go easy on me. He was surprisingly quick for his solid build. But even though he easily swiped my feet from underneath me, he did always lower me down gently. It was a shame

I couldn't offer him the same courtesy. On the one time I got him down, I put my heel into his stomach, rolled onto my back, and threw him over my head. He counteracted the throw by leading straight into a rolling break-fall (a special roly-poly), but that didn't stop him from looking stunned when he turned around.

"You know that doesn't count, right?" He disputed my point.

"Yeah, I know. Still worth seeing that look on your face." I made an exaggerated shocked face.

He came at me. My futile attempt to get away was practically non-existent, and he threw me effortlessly with a hip throw, allowing me to hit the mat harder than usual. But then he held out his hand to help me back up. I took it, for him to swipe both legs out from underneath me, tripping me up onto my back once again. *Alright, I get it, you're clearly better than me.*

"OK, class. Can I borrow you, Aurora?" Sir Hiroki requested my assistance. He gave a demonstration of a technique used to break a double arm pin. The same technique I'd used on Brindan in the Food Hall trying to stop Ryker. "So, I want you to step, twist, and go for the double leg grab," explained Sir Hiroki, breaking my arm lock and taking my legs so I fell onto the mat. My face burned hot, but it had nothing to do with the impact of falling.

"I think you're already a pro at this one," Pax said upon my return.

I fidgeted on the spot.

"I'm kidding, come here." He grabbed hold of my arms.

My toes scrunched at the strange sensation squirming through my body as he held me.

"Number yourselves *one* and *two*," instructed Sir Hiroki. "I want *ones* to stay put, and *twos* to switch partners. Perform the technique on each other once, and then *twos* move on clockwise."

I stayed put and for the first time cared who was in the room. What if Ryker and Pipila were in here? One swift glance around confirmed they weren't. *Phew.* But I did see a familiar face. Thorn

Jelani, Celeste's betrothed, made his way round to me wearing a brown belt, one grade lower than black.

"Hi, Aurora," said Thorn in a deep, silky-smooth voice. I knew that voice! It was *The Tank* from the Khaki reception that day I got my uniform taken off me and performed on the Flexon.

"The Tank! Sorry. I mean, hi, Thorn," I said, warmth rising to my cheeks. I circled behind him, reaching to hold on to his massive arms.

"Looking forward to the Parkour Games on Saturday?" he asked, bulldozing me to the ground.

"Shi-ugar." A four-letter word almost escaped my lips. The Parkour Games! I had completely forgotten. I wasn't ready for that. I could just about cope with my new duties as an Enforcer.

"You'll be fine. It's Celeste's and my first game, too. Don't worry, it'll be fun." He threw himself onto the mat after I struggled to lift his giant leg.

❧

After a session in the Colosseum that afternoon, I made sure I went to dinner with Silliah, safeguarding myself from Ryker. I was happy we got our usual seats in Claret Quartz, and I didn't even mind when the Fanciable Four pulled up a seat.

"Who's the hotty?" asked Hilly, craning her neck to look towards the back of the Food Hall.

"*Tayo*?" I nearly had my casserole squirt out my nose. "No. He is disgusting."

"He's your Juvie? I'm so jealous. I've got Crazy-Tattoo-Head, over there." She used her head to point.

I looked up expecting to see an adult, but what I saw was a child, possibly about eight years old, just at the age to be a Juvie. The even stranger part was he had the whole side of his face and a portion of his forehead tattooed with an intricate pattern.

"He is about as strange as they come," Hilly added.

She could say that again. He was looking over at our table with the most intense, fixated stare. It was freaking me out.

"What's with the tattoos?" Tyga took the words right out of my mouth.

Hilly started laughing before taking an imperious tone and saying, "'It is the insignia of my people used to show we are Taheke. It is believed that one who is touched by magic cannot bear such a mark.'" She changed back to her normal voice. "I'm not even kidding. That's what he said. It gets funnier. Apparently, it's why they shave their head like that, too, because your hair will grow back if you have magic in your blood."

"Oh no, we're all screwed," ridiculed Tyga, his black quiff holding perfectly in place as he shook his head.

"Do they not realise their hair grows back every day?" said Hyas. *Whoa, he speaks!* "Why do they think they have to *keep* shaving it?"

"What's '*Taheke*,' anyway?" intercepted Shola.

"He said no magical blood, or something. And what's more, he said his people, the Kalmayans, are *Puracordis hunters*." Hilly found this hysterical and tears began to well in her glistening blue eyes. "Doesn't he realise they no longer exist? Their hunting sessions must be as eventful as tracking down unicorns. Oooh, ooh, I got one. Oh no, wait…it's just another horse."

"Wow, just when you think you've heard it all," said Shola, giving him one last look from over her shoulder.

"What about your Juvie, Silliah?" I asked.

"I've got Natashly, that lady over there." Silliah pointed to a teary-eyed, blonde woman, not much older than Tayo. "It's a bit sad really: the night after the Unity results, I had my first Curfew Duty with Roman. Natashly was stuck outside her apartment block, banging desperately on the door for someone to let her in. She finished work and needed to pick up her food shopping before she got home. Well, just as we reached her, so did a ground floor tenant who heard her banging. The tenant opened the door to let her in, but Roman wouldn't let her go, saying she's broken Curfew. The sad part is she had a four-month-old with her. Suddenly, Natashly shoves the baby in the arms of the gentleman who answered the door, and says, 'He is the father. *Please,* I'll be back in *six months…*six months.'" Silliah lowered her voice, "I'm not convinced he was the father. Her baby would have been taken away from her if she didn't have anyone to look after it whilst she was in here. Imagine, a six-month sentence and she wouldn't see her baby for thirty years."

"She should get a food delivery subscription," Hilly said matter-of-factly.

Tyga and I caught each other's eyes briefly at her comment, but after a long blink, we continued listening to Silliah. "She said she copes with the cost of child care, her rent, and other subscriptions like energy, but she can't afford delivery on her Banding."

"Definitely sounds like a single mum then." Shola pursed her wide berry-red lips.

"Oh no," I said, my attention catching on someone else. I didn't even know he was in the hall.

"What is it?" Silliah turned to see what I was looking at.

"Ryker," I answered, watching him target Tayo with his food tray.

"What about him?" asked Hilly.

The crash of china answered her question. Every muscle in my body tensed. *Not again.* Tayo's face didn't show much for punishment, but I didn't think his body could take any more damage. Tayo and Ryker were at yet another stand-off after Ryker dropped his tray before Tayo had a hold on it once again. I wasn't even sure of the right action for Tayo to take; it was a game of roulette. If Tayo didn't speak, Ryker could beat him for not saying thank you, but if Tayo did speak, then Ryker could beat him for being sarcastic. The room was thick. I jumped at the stroking sensation on my shoulders. It was only Pax. He'd come and rested his chin on my head, wrapping his arms around me. To everyone else, it was an innocent hug, but I knew it was a precautionary measure.

"Thank you, sir." Tayo had chosen.

"You're a clumsy git, aren't you? Get this cleaned up immediately." Ryker ended the stand-off, leaving the hall.

"What was everyone worried about?" asked a confused Hilly, twirling her sun-kissed-blonde hair around her finger.

Pax stood up straight, running his hands up my arms, massaging my neck and shoulders. The tension melted away with every squeeze. Hilly elbowed Silliah in the side and they both smiled dotingly.

"I best take Tayo back to get cleaned up." I sobered up at their stupid faces. "Coming, Pax?"

"Yep. Girls," he called to Maigen and Bethoney.

"Do you guys wanna go back, too?" Hilly addressed the table.

Small nods and empty plates meant they did.

Tayo and the Davoren Sisters led the way, with Pax and me following close behind. Suddenly, Hilly's Juvie grabbed my wrist. "Beware the angel with the devil's mark!" he spat at me, pulling up my jacket sleeve and recoiling at the sight of my birthmark. The kid tripped over himself and fell onto the floor. His brown eyes twitched in terror. Staring up at me, he scuttled back against the wall.

I know I wanted Juvies to treat me with respect, but putting the fear of god in them was a bit much. *Why do I always attract the weirdos?*

"Hey! Don't you *dare* touch an Enforcer," shouted Hilly, kicking the boy in the thigh. "Go. Move on up front."

The kid ran, looking round at me as if I were about to give chase. I could tell everyone held it back for my sake; they knew it was inappropriate to laugh in earshot of the crazy kid. Even Tayo showed restraint. A tiny squeak came from Silliah. The whole way, nobody could speak a word in fear of bursting. To them it was the funniest thing to happen all day.

"I have to change Tayo's bandages tonight," I told Pax on our way into Claret Quartz.

"I'll meet you back at our room?"

"Sure."

Back in Tayo's cell, it didn't take long for the taunting to start.

"'Beware the angel with the devil's mark!'" Tayo imitated the boy in a malevolent voice.

"Don't." I rubbed my aching face.

"What the hell was that?" he said, laughing.

"I have no idea. Why me? There were eleven of us in that corridor."

"Freaky, *freaky* child." Tayo shuddered.

"Right, can we hurry up and get this over with?"

"Hmm, if you say so." Tayo slowly unzipped his claret overalls and walked towards me.

"Go sit on the bed, Tayo," I said firmly as he swaggered closer until my back was pressed up against the wall. Unsurprisingly, he didn't listen to me. He lowered his face closer to mine. I thought about what Pax said earlier about pressure points, and I thought about how Hilly booted that kid in the leg to get him to move on. Then, I dug my thumb into Tayo's bandage. "I said *go* and *sit* on the bed," I repeated, applying a little more pressure to his wound. I could tell by the gaunt look on his face that he was trying to fight it. The muscles around his mouth twisted. I stepped forward, pressing harder.

Tayo retreated. *I did it!*

"Alright, Roar. Play nice."

I gave up trying to get him to call me ma'am. He only called me Roar when we were on our own, so I knew he did it intentionally to goad me.

I pushed him backwards to sit on the bed, and Tayo sat quietly as I unwrapped the bandage from around his body. As much as I wanted to hurt him, I resisted the temptation and peeled back the padded plaster carefully. A dribble of blood fell down his waist. The force from my dig had caused it to start bleeding again.

"I'm not wrapping that big bandage around your waist," I told him bluntly. "You can do that."

"Ohh, why not? I was looking forward to you putting your arms around me."

"That's exactly the reason I'm not doing it."

I held pressure to his wound, waiting for the bleeding to stop, and I finally asked the question that nagged at me all day: "How do you know Pipila?"

"You two looked like best friends at breakfast this morning. Especially the way she came to sit opposite you, but then used the screen to pull up another table just so she didn't have to."

"I don't know what her problem is. Are you going to tell me, or not?"

"I'll tell you anything you want, my little Roar."

"How do you know Pipila?" I repeated, ignoring his pathetic attempt to get a reaction.

"How about you spend the night in here, and I'll tell you all about it?"

I latched on to his hair and yanked his head backwards. "I think you are REPULSIVE."

"Ow! You are feisty, aren't you? I quite like it rough."

"You disgust me, Tayo." I let go of his hair, disappointed he got a reaction from me.

"You are funny," he said, rubbing the back of his head.

"You are an idiot."

I was done—with both Tayo and the bandage. I couldn't be bothered with the hassle of trying to have an adult conversation with him. Who cared how he knew Pipila, anyway.

Back in my room, Pax left the interconnecting door open.

"Can I come sit with you?" I asked, holding on to the door frame for moral support. Tayo had wound me up once again, and I really needed distracting.

"What are you asking for, silly? Come on." Pax gave a subtle head tilt.

I crawled onto the bed next to him. "What a day," I said with a sigh, facing up at the ceiling.

Pax snorted. "I can't stop laughing at that crazy kid from earlier."

"Oh, don't remind me. I *do not* know what the *hell* that was." I twisted onto my front and smooshed my face into the pillow.

"That was so funny. Of everyone in the corridor he could have chosen and he chose you. If he is like that at the age of eight, can you imagine what *his people* are like?"

"Absolute nut-jobs," I grumbled into the pillow.

…I froze at the fingers tenderly stroking up and down my spine. Goosebumps covered my immobilised body.

CHAPTER SEVEN

I'LL TAKE THAT

M y eyes had barely adapted to the bright lights after a long night's sleep. I slept quite well considering, and I still had the sleep wrinkles on my cheek to prove it.

"A straight, horizontal beam about knee height?" a fully-dressed Pax fired at me from the doorway.

"You don't have to do that every day."

"If I'd have known you didn't watch the Parkour Games in Mustard, I woulda been doing it every waking minute. Knowing the Bounty can be the difference between life and death."

"Death?" I repeated, pulling a face. "That's a bit strong, don't you think?"

"Well, if you see it as death, it might help you survive."

"I think the debilitating electric shock is enough for me to try and survive."

"A straight, horizontal beam about knee height?" he fired at me again, coming to rest his foot on the platform steps surrounding my bed. He stood there emanating a spirited energy.

"If anything comes at me, I'll just run, okay?"

"A straight, horizontal beam about knee height?"

"Get out," I moaned, throwing my pillow at him.

"Now, now, that's no way to talk to your betrothed, is it?" he said, dodging my attempt to shush him. "Come on, I'm excited! Meet you at breakfast." He scooped up the pillow, walloped it over my head, gave it a few jabs, and then fled from the room. With the pillow's dull *thud* still ringing in my ears, I uncovered my face to an empty room.

"I'll get you back," I shouted after him. "You wait!" I lingered for a moment, checking he had actually gone. Then, I slithered out of bed and down the platform steps until I was lying rigid on the hard white floor, my fists closed tightly by my sides in protest. It was the morning of the Parkour Games.

Finishing my tantrum, I pulled myself up, got myself ready, and left for breakfast. Overnight, posters had appeared on the walls throughout the institute. From what I could tell, they were fanmade posters supporting their favourite teams. Two couples in particular were hugely popular with their posters repeating over and over. A black and red poster played a video loop of a boy and girl flexing their muscles. The chubby-cheeked girl had tiny square teeth and big pink gums. The boy was lanky and had oddly familiar shiny black eyes. Underneath the video loop were the words *'Unholy Reign'* written in what could only be described as blood. Not real blood, obviously. The designer just did a good job making it look like it was.

The second (extremely popular) poster was the polar opposite of the first. This white and gold poster had an exceptionally photogenic couple standing stiffly side by side, arms crossed in front of them. It was difficult to tell it was even a video loop because the only movement I detected was their blinking royal-blue eyes. Both of them had slicked-back, dead-straight, blond hair, not a single strand out of place. The girl's hair was longer than mine, and his was around chin length, but he combed it back, tucking neatly behind his ears. I wondered how much hair product they went through maintaining that level of perfection. Underneath them, the words *'Sovereign Skill'* glistened in beautiful golden calligraphy.

When I entered the Food Hall, everyone was already there to greet me. Pax had organised a table in Claret Quartz with Silliah and the Fanciable Four. He patted the empty seat next to him and pulled a tray towards me.

"I know what you're like when you're unsettled," said Pax, handing me a fork. "You don't eat. So, I ordered your breakfast for you." He tapped a platter of chopped fruit, the same platter I'd left on the table on my first day in Navy. He must have remembered—which was both sweet and embarrassing. If he remembered the food on the table, he had to remember the whole incident.

"*The Red Queen*," I said, sitting down heavily. "A straight, horizontal beam about knee height…it's *The Red Queen*." I answered his question from earlier about Bounty.

"Good. And how do you get Bounty?" He continued to quiz me.

"By eliminating another player. When you touch them, they get electrocuted and pass out. Then a Bounty ring appears on our arm."

"Yes, one for each of us, regardless of who eliminated the player because both players in the other team will pass out. But we can only use our Bounty once we touch each other and activate it. The ring on our arm will change from red to gold."

"Oh god, my brain hurts."

"You'll be fine. Once we find each other in there, I will be able to walk you through it."

"Of course." I dropped my fork and facepalmed. "We enter the arena separated from our partners."

"Aurora. It's a game. As in, *fun*. Try and enjoy it," said Pax, pulling me sideways in a half headlock, half cuddle.

Silliah left her empty food tray and stood behind me. She took the hairband out from my loose ponytail and began securing my wavy white hair into a tight French plait. "And what is Bounty?" she asked, cottoning on to our conversation.

"I'm not entirely sure to be honest," I replied. "They are rewards for actually playing the game and not hiding, but they have ridiculous names, and you don't know what they do until you use them."

"Unless you *watch* the games and *learn*," interjected Pax.

"I'm sorry I've put you at such a disadvantage, Pax," I snapped, pain from getting my new hairstyle bolstering my reaction. "But I didn't ever intend on matching and taking part in these stupid games."

"Hey." Pax spoke direct but soft. He pivoted me around using my knees until I was looking into his warm honey eyes. Silliah still hadn't finished with my hair and she rotated with me. The Fanciable Four kept their bodies animated, pretending not to listen, but the chatter had stopped. Hilly, the least tactful of them, kept glancing at us intermittently.

"Hey," he said again. "I wouldn't want to be playing the games with anyone else, Aurora. I mean that, okay?"

His hands holding on to my knees tickled, distracting me from being annoyed, so I just said, "OK."

"OK," he repeated after me, letting go of my legs. "It'll be fun, I promise."

Twisting back around in my chair, I saw Brindan enter the hall. He spotted Pax in Claret, and a mischievous grin spread across his freckled face.

"Good morning," he welcomed everyone. "So, look what I came across on my way round here." He opened his cupped hands to reveal a silver badge with a smouldering double-edged battle axe on it. Under the battle axe were the words '*Smokin' Axe*' written in hazy, wispy writing. I seemed to be missing the point. What did we care about someone's TPG fan badge?

"Right?" Pax also seemed to be missing the point.

Silliah clapped her hands over her mouth. Behind her glasses, her big green eyes glinted with excitement. "*Smokin' Axe*," she said with a chuckle. "Aurora...Pax...Axe." She broke it down for us.

"No way," said Hilly. "You have a fanbase already?"

"That's pretty cool," agreed Tyga, lifting off his seat to see the badge over Hilly's shoulder.

"Umm," mumbled Hyas, trying to quickly finish his mouthful of food. "You've not even played *one* TPG yet and people are already rooting for you."

"Wow." Shola stared at the badge with glossy dark-brown eyes. "Pretty sure that's unheard of."

"You're right," agreed Brindan, throwing the badge in the air and snatching it back one-handed. "You have to come close to winning before this type of thing crops up."

"*Smokin' Axe*?" I interrupted, frowning at the badge now being held up between Brindan's thumb and index finger. "What kind of team name is that?"

"Axe is a portmanteau of your names," explained Silliah. "And smokin'...because you're both..." Silliah's cheeks grew rosy red.

"Hot!" finished Hilly.

"What?" I said in disbelief. "No. That's just embarrassing. Get rid of that."

"Get rid of it?" Brindan asked with a small laugh. "So, will you guys not be wanting these?" He pulled out from his pockets a dozen of the horrid things. Everyone reached for one and began fastening them to their Navy uniforms.

"I hate you all," I said, dropping my head into my hands and hiding my face.

"It's alright," reasoned Pax. "At least our video loop isn't on it."

"Not yet, anyway," said Brindan. "After today they will have it, and then you'll probably have your own smokin' hot posters."

※

After breakfast, Pax and I split up from the others to prepare for the games. In the Khakidemy, Pax held open a plain white door I'd never noticed before. I stepped into a long, narrow corridor lit up by dingy porthole spotlights. Turning left at the end of the corridor, I began to hear the low hum of conversation. And after descending a noisy metal staircase, we entered a room longer than it was wide, with glass booths lined up in two long rows. Leading down the centre, between the booths, smooth circular pillars had black sofas built-in around the bottoms.

"This is where we get changed into our picosuits," explained Pax, although somewhat unnecessarily; I already watched a couple leaving a booth in their skin-tight uniforms. "This booth is free. You ready?"

I took a deep breath, exhaling as steadily as I could. "Yeah."

"We need to place our hands on the door together to open it."

As we did, the red edges of the booth turned to gold and the double-doors parted. Pax allowed me to walk in first, and once we were both inside, the doors closed behind us, turning the clear glass walls an opaque black.

"Welcome, Paxton and Aurora," greeted Soami in her relaxed voice. "When you are ready, please take your positions on a plinth and disrobe, leaving on only undergarments and socks."

"In front of each other?" I asked suddenly, not wanting to believe my ears.

"I won't look," reassured Pax, stepping up onto the right-hand plinth and removing his jacket. "I'll face this way the entire time."

I dithered. This was not right, not to mention unfair! But what choice did I have? I stepped up onto the left-hand plinth and slowly unzipped my jacket. To my overwhelming relief, my step onto the plinth triggered a partition wall between us. Before it concealed our view of each other, Pax gave me an attentive smile.

"Oi!" I yelped. "You said you wouldn't look."

"Oh, behave. You were undressing like a snail. I could have looked over in half an hour and still seen nothing."

I undressed quicker, hanging my Navy uniform on the hooks provided.

"Please place your feet on the markings," instructed Soami. "Then elevate your arms above your head."

The podium to my front showed a rotating turquoise diagram of the position I was required to take. A contraption lowered from the ceiling and plastered an elasticated black material around me, enveloping my entire body in a skin-tight jumpsuit with a high-neck. The picosuit was so lightweight and stretchy I may as well have been naked. Inspecting the suit closer, I saw a mesh of tiny golden thread running through it, creating odd patterns and geometric shapes. If they wanted it to look like a computer spewed-up on me, they succeeded.

"Please hold your arms out to the sides," instructed Soami with a new rotating diagram displayed on my podium.

I copied for a new device to lower from the ceiling, placing a lightly armoured chestplate around my torso. Slightly better, I thought. At least it was now harder to tell my gender. The same happened around my waist and thighs. *Phew.*

Before I put my arms down, cuffs were secured to my forearms. Each one had an identical screen. Then, two cold metal probes attached to the chestplate were placed on the back of my neck. The podium screen switched off and revolved backwards, revealing a pair of picosuit gloves. On each fingertip was a special diamond of golden wire with an even smaller diamond in the centre of it. It was fair to say, I was impressed, and I actually really liked my new outfit.

The partition wall gone, Pax tried to hide his feelings regarding my new look. "What? I'm allowed to look now, aren't I?"

"No. You're making me self-conscious."

"Don't be so silly," he said, passing me my black running trainers. "Only this booth can take the suit off, anyway."

My mouth fell open.

"I'm joking, I'm joking. Sorry, I'm joking," Pax spluttered.

"Yeah, you look sorry with that stupid grin on your face."

"No, I am. I'm sorry," Pax coughed out, forcing the smile from it. "I'm sorry."

"Hmmm," I hummed with a frown. I wasn't letting him off the hook that easily.

"Come, we need to do this video loop." He reached to put his arm around my shoulders. "Come on, pretend we like each other for a minute? Or we'll look silly in this thing."

"Fine, for a minute."

He pulled me in front of the camera between the two podiums. I awkwardly placed my arm around his waist. *Hashtag hover hands.*

"Recording will commence in three, two, one," counted Soami.

When we left the booth, the room outside had gotten a lot busier. The sudden realisation of the fast-approaching games sent nerves stirring in the pit of my stomach. Not helping the feeling was the sound of pounding drums and the penetrating shrill of violins being used to gear us all up for war.

"We need to wait here to be called through," said an unrecognisable Pax. He looked strong and confident. His short blond-brown curls and honey-coloured eyes were dashing against the pitch-black picosuit. "When we get in the arena, all you need to worry about is finding me. I will show as a white dot on your radar." He touched the computer on my cuff. "This is a team game intended to strengthen our bond, so alone, we are sitting ducks. We can only begin to eliminate other teams once our hands unite.

"The middle of the arena is the quickest route to me, but it is a war zone, so stay at the edge. I know it will take longer for us to reach each other, but we will have more chance of uniting. Go up. You're skilled and can navigate the upper tiers better than most of them."

The dramatic music cut out and Lady Joanne Maxhin's voice cut in, "How are we all doing? Are you ready, Youngens?"

People responded with a weak whoop.

"I said ARE YOU READY?"

This was met by a deafening roar of cheers and whistles. My hair stood on end.

"Alright, good! Now, once you are inside the arena, you are no longer friends. The only person who matters to you is your betrothed. Hunt, target, pursue, and annihilate. This is survival of the fittest, okay? Let's go!"

"We're going to be separated in a minute, Aurora." Pax took hold of my hand so he didn't lose me in the crowd. The music started again, but this time only louder. He leant into the side of my face until I felt his lips brush the top of my ear. "Find me."

Lady Maxhin led us into the next room, where everyone lined up in their pairs. "Put your hands into the bag together," she instructed. "Take a token, then enter the corresponding cage."

One by one, couples reached into the bag, pulling out either a purple or yellow token. Up front, I saw Ryker pull out the purple, and Pipila, the yellow. On our turn, we placed our hands into the velvety black pouch together. Pax placed a token in the centre of my hand, and I closed it in a fist. I stared down at my knuckles. This was it. *When I open my hand, I will be on my own.* Such a simple action of opening my fingers, and it was taking every ounce of strength I had.

A purple token branded with the words, 'The Parkour Games, January, 2119.'

Pax stroked my chin before turning away, and I walked down the illuminated purple runway into my cage. I had the tiny-teethed girl from *Unholy Reign* with me. She slid her finger across her throat to the boy from *Sovereign Skill.* He returned it with a middle finger. The cage door slammed shut behind us. Now we were all divided.

The lights went out. With one of my senses lost, the darkness intensified a vibration pulsing through my whole body. Lengthy deep notes boomed behind an ear-splitting air raid siren. Through strobe lighting, I saw Ryker climb up onto the bars and shake them violently like a wild animal. Smoke billowed out two archways at the front of the cages. One had a purple arrow pointing left, the other, a yellow arrow pointing right. Everyone began shouting and stomping their feet.

The cage doors opened and we were released. I coughed through the smoke as I entered the archway. It veered off sharply to the left. Guided only by purple spotlights, everyone broke out into a jog whilst navigating the blackened tunnel. Around me, the purple team burst into a repetitive chant:

Unity united us,

You and I, unite us.

We will fight and we will fall,

Together we can do it all!

I will fight and I will fall,

I WILL FIGHT,

I WILL FALL,

And for you, I'll do it all!

I couldn't help but wonder if Pax ran and chanted in the same fashion. The thought perked me up. 'Aurora. It's a game. As in, fun. Try and enjoy it.' His words from earlier brought about a new mind-set. Maybe I did need to lighten up.

Ryker entered a capsule on the right-hand side of the tunnel. Confused, I tried to work out what I was supposed to do. Then I saw above his pod, in bold purple letters, the words '*Ryker Boulderfell.*' I ran faster, passing capsule after capsule. The tunnel began clearing out as everyone found their names. I still ran down this once lively passageway, but now the noise faded as they readied themselves in their closed-off pods. I reached the end and had to double-back, this time in a sprint.

Finally, after keeping everyone waiting, I found my name at the very start where I'd first entered. I missed it through the commotion. The capsule door locked me in the dark, and I felt the ground move from under my feet. We were being taken underground, deep down beneath the institute.

I jolted to a stop and steadied myself.

"Five, four, three…two…*one*," a male voice came from nowhere.

With a *shoooze* noise the capsule opened. I walked out rubbing my eyes, desperately needing my vision to be restored. I appeared to be in a dead-end, boxed in by four black walls. A low buzzing from behind me sent shockwaves down my spine. It was only a camera following me out. The screen on my forearm showed a blueprint of the arena. On the opposite end from where I stood, a tiny white dot made its way anti-clockwise. *Right, go up.*

The two walls either side of me were double my height. There wasn't enough room for me to take a running jump, so I reached out to see if I could scale both walls at the same time. They were too far apart. Suddenly, the echo of hollow footsteps resonated above, getting closer and closer. A boy leapt from one wall to the other, front-flipping directly above my head. He didn't see me. *But how has he gotten up there already?*

Taking a look at the end of my enclosure, I discovered I was not trapped in. There was an exit at the end. I peered around the corner. A six-legged robot crawled in my direction. Whether it was friendly or not, I wasn't going to hang around to find out. I ran back towards my pod, wall-running around the right-side wall and kicking off the back one until I was high enough to grip onto the ledge on my left.

I had a better view from up here, and I could see video loops playing around the edge of the arena. Just then, a five-note victory tune played, and *Sovereign Skill's* video loop turned from black and white to colour. I assumed that meant they had united. Seconds later, another tune—*Unholy Reign* found each other, and I instantly began to feel like prey. Not too long passed when a deep electronic drone sounded. The video loop of Treese Harper and his partner immediately turned red—the first elimination of the game.

Pax had covered some distance and was half-way to me. I jumped from my platform over to a rail, launching myself up onto higher ground. Glimpses of bodies leapt in and out of view all around the arena. I found myself on a nice flat surface. As I took a step, a bell rang from under my feet. My muscles stiffened. Some runners in the distance looked in my direction. I took another step only for another bell to ring. The *'nice flat surface'* was booby-trapped, and I was giving away my location. Above my head was a long pole. I jumped, hooking my leg over, and I stood up cautiously. It was no wider than the rail in my wardrobe. Slowly placing one foot in front of the other, I crossed with meticulous care and precision, toe after toe.

A rapid chain of victory tunes led to an even faster succession of elimination drones. The war zone in the centre hit full scale, and Bounty lasers missed their targets and zipped across the arena. Just then, as I neared the end of the long bar, a fury of short yellow lasers skimmed past my ear. Still keeping my balance, I checked behind me. Ryker and Pipila had united and they hurtled my way! Pipila clearly tried to hit me with Bounty but missed. Ryker still had his golden Bounty ring on his arm. He could send out another attack.

Off the bar, I raced over springy ground which aided me in propelling my body up towards an overhang. Dangling from it with straight arms, I managed to hook my ankle over, heaving myself up. Ryker and Pipila had been slowed down by the long bar, so I would be able to get a head start. Watching them wobbling across it, I took a few strides before I ran full pelt into a padded wall. I would have almost knocked myself flying if it wasn't for two arms catching me, enclosing my body in a tight hold. The padded wall wasn't a wall at all, it was a person.

"Whoa there, I gotcha," said a voice, soothing me to my soul. "As lovely as that was, sweetheart, we only need to touch hands to unite."

I didn't move straight away, savouring the security of the embrace for a moment. That familiar smell I was becoming accustomed to; that expanding broad chest; those solid arms which, more often than not, confined me in a headlock. I had run straight into Pax.

"Why did you fire your Bounty so early?" We could hear Ryker moaning. "She didn't know we were after her, and we would have got her already."

"I thought I could get her," argued Pipila. "Why didn't you fire your Bounty at all?"

"Because I've got *When We Set Out to Deceive*. She was on that bar, and the web would have helped her keep her grip."

"What about when she was on this springboard, then?"

With a pressed finger over his lips, Pax knelt down, encouraging me to do so with him. "Shh." He held out his hand for me to unite. My hand was small and childlike in the palm of his. A five-note victory tune played, and the picosuit sent a blaze of glowing light swirling around our interlaced fingers. Our greyed-out video loop returned to its full glory.

"Ryker, wait!" yelled Pipila.

But Ryker didn't wait. His fingers gripped on to the platform by our feet, shortly followed by his shoe, then the top of his head. The last thing we saw was his traumatised beetle-black eyes. The last thing he saw was our smug faces side by side before Pax touched the back of Ryker's glove, imparting a paralysing electric shock. Ryker gurgled at the pain through a clenched jaw. His body fell to the floor. Perhaps next time he wouldn't be so conceited and would listen to Pipila. I stood up to see what had become of her. She, too, was lying on the ground unconscious.

From the touch that eliminated Ryker, a red ring burst forth, encircling Pax's wrist, travelling up his arm, and coming to rest around his bicep. A matching ring appeared on my arm. Pax held up a high five. I swung for it, and our rings turned into shining golden halos. Our first Bounty.

"What did you get?" Pax's face radiated delight.

The screen on my left arm turned on showing a menu. I only had one item in my inventory. "*Back to Square One*," I answered. "What does that do?"

"*Back to Square One* breaks the connection between a couple, meaning they lose all their Bounty and need to join hands to unite again. It's a good one actually, and how *Unholy Reign* won last year's game against *Sovereign Skill*. It fires as a small black square, tripling in size as it approaches the target, making it a difficult one to evade."

Impressed with my weapon, my eyebrows lifted. "How do I use it?"

"Have it selected on your screen, and then extend a flat palm." Pax threw his arm out like he ordered someone to halt. "The picosuit will do the rest."

"What did you get?"

"*Peek a Boo, I See You*. It turns our radar on for sixty seconds. Wanna go kick some butt?"

"Let's do it!"

My radar suddenly had a dozen white dots crawling around us. We headed towards one. Pax front-flipped over a gap.

"Was that really necessary?" I laughed.

"It's the Parkour Games, Aurora. Got to give 'em something in the form of entertainment." He referred to the audience watching us through the tailing cameras.

We waited with our backs up against a wall as a pair of dots made their way down a narrow pathway. Our radars switched off, but the couple still didn't stand a chance. They walked straight into Pax's outstretched hand as they rounded the corner. The drone sounded, and their bodies writhed from the searing pain. Again, two helpless players dropped to the floor.

"Good night." Pax slapped my low five. "I got *Don't Count Your Chickens*. It kills off an opponent's Bounty ring."

"That's cool," I replied, checking my inventory. "I got *Mere Trifle*."

"I have no idea what that does. They come up with new ones all the time."

"I saw a robot before when I first entered the arena. What does that do?"

"Er…what did it look like?"

"Like a huge spider, but with six legs."

"That's either Ly or Ty. They are so fast, but their strengths lie in the upper levels. Their limbs extend so they can navigate the obstacles as if it were solid ground. All the robots basically try to eliminate you but in different ways. If you can get close enough to them without detection, you can program them to work for you. Then, if they kill, it effectively becomes yours with a Bounty reward. They are good to get—if you're brave enough to try."

"How do you program them to work for you?" I asked slowly, checking over my shoulder, thinking I saw movement in the shadows.

"They will have a handprint on them somewhere. It's red when it hasn't been programmed, and gold when it—"

"—Run!"

"What?"

"I saw someone," I said, pulling Pax by the arm.

"Why are we running away?" Pax laughed at me.

"Oh. I dunno." I felt the heat leaving my cheeks. "I panicked."

"Look, there's no one there," Pax said gently, slowing me down to a walk.

"I could have sworn I saw..." I stopped talking out of embarrassment. *I can't believe I ran. What an idiot.*

The arena was eerily quiet. With all teams united, no more victory tunes played, and an elimination drone hadn't sounded in a while. The competition had thinned significantly, but I was glad to see Celeste and Thorn's video loop still shone in full colour.

"You realise if we survive two more kills, we make it into round two," said Pax.

"Wait," I said, stopping Pax by the arm. I definitely saw Tiny-teeth that time; I was sure of it. Something wasn't right. She made eye contact with me but didn't even attempt to pursue us. "I think we're being herded, Pax."

"Why? What is it?"

"*Unholy Reign.* The girl, I think she's herding us. I'm sure I saw her earlier, and I just saw her again back there."

"Let's change direction, then."

We turned a corner, running down a short alley. The lanky boy from *Unholy Reign* slid in, blocking the exit. We turned back the way we came. Tiny-teeth blocked the way we came in. She fired a Bounty laser towards us.

"Teeny blue bubbles," whispered Pax. "It's only *Crocodile Tears*."

As the bubble lights hit us, our eyes began to water, turning our predators into blurry outlines.

"Awww," ridiculed Tiny-teeth, stalking forward. "It's okay, ickle babies, don't cwy. It will only hurt for a minute."

Then I heard Tiny-teeth's voice in my head: *Come on, Beignley, use The Red Queen already.*

"He has *The Red Queen*," I warned Pax.

Just in time for a red horizontal beam to come at our knees. We both managed to jump over it. The red beam rose up, tearing back towards us at chest height. We ducked under it. Then the beam spread into a huge grid swarming the entire alleyway. I grabbed Pax's arm and ran towards Tiny-teeth. She reached out her hand to release another Bounty attack, but I got there first and fired *Back to Square One*. The black square spiralled at Tiny-teeth, and her golden Bounty rings pinged off her arms. She was at our mercy.

We chased her to higher ground. As she was in mid-air between two platforms, Pax suddenly yanked me back. An elimination drone filled the air. A hand had reached up and grabbed Tiny-teeth's ankle. Then the *Sovereign Skill* duo sprang into view with a swift curvet. Just like that, we were prey again.

A black spear immediately struck Pax in the heart.

"*Blind Leading the Blind* takes both our sight." Pax hauled me into his chest, tucking my head under his chin. "You did amazing today."

Oh, no. Ow. His voice faded far in the distance as I disappeared into a deep pocket in my mind. *The pain.* It felt as though my body was being savagely stabbed by a hot needle, splitting my skin and piercing my veins. Hot, sharp, and unrelenting, my body rigidified uncomfortably. *Stop. Stop. Please stop.*

But even as our bodies convulsed aggressively, and despite the excruciating pain, Pax never let me go.

CHAPTER EIGHT

NA-NUTTA

Before meeting everyone in the Food Hall, I visited Tayo's cell first. "I've only come to change your bandages. You can sit back down."

"But I haven't been out of my cell all day," he argued, continuing to stand in front of me, picoplant arm stretched out.

"Yeah, I do know. My schedule was cleared today."

"Let me come do some work. I'm going stir-crazy in here." He stepped forward, bringing his picoplant closer for me to scan.

"Pfft. No. Unzip your overalls, please."

"Come on, Roar. Take me to dinner."

"I said, no. I'm not taking you to dinner. Now, unzip your overalls so I can get going."

"No. You want them off. Unzip them yourself."

"Tayo!" I stamped my foot. "You incessant moron. Unzip your overalls. Otherwise, I will leave your bandages tonight."

Tayo didn't move, so I did—towards the door. "Fine, sod your bandages."

"Aurora." There was a long pause before he said, "Please," in an airy voice, his outstretched wrist emitting desperation.

I made a strained murmur, battling with the inner conflict. Why I felt sorry for this idiot, I had no idea. "I don't want to," I told the honest truth. Every day since the tray incident, Ryker had been dropping his food in front of Tayo tirelessly, and I could really use an evening without the anxiety.

"Please." The helpless look in his eyes gave me an unexplainable ache in my chest.

"Aah. Alright!" I caved in. "Give me your wrist." I scanned his picoplant and engaged the ankle trap. "You really do annoy me, Tayo."

"I wouldn't have it any other way," he replied, flashing a smile and showing a set of beautiful, straight teeth.

My entrance into the Food Hall coincided with the arrival of *Sovereign Skill*, and the room was very lively. The victors crowned, they were met with a standing ovation. A large congregation of their fans swarmed them, chanting lustily, "*Sovereign Skill! Sovereign Skill! Sovereign Skill!*"

Pax and the others were in the back of Navy Quartz, close to the archway. Having a long line of tables joined together was becoming a regular occurrence now, and the bombardment of conversation was hard to keep up with. Pax always saved me a seat next to him, and today, I sat between him and Silliah. Once our account of the games had been told, and praises given, conversations turned on to the victors.

"They remind me of elves, those two," Silliah commented on the alluring duo.

"Christmas elves?" I said, watching as the girl's wide hips swayed from side to side, not resembling an elf in any way.

"*No*, Elves, like High Elves or Woodland Elves from the old 2D movies." Silliah kept trying but gave up. "No?"

"No. You like all that old stuff, don't you?"

"Why not? It's as good as today's stuff." She gave a mellow shrug. "I'd say those two are more like High Elves with the amount of Worths they've won in the games. Ten thousand Worths each for every game they've won. That's more than a whole year's salary if they win both the new year game and the mid-year rematch."

"What year are they in?" I sat up tall, trying to see the number on their arms but failing due to the crowd swarming them.

"Saulwyn and Theodred are Tenth-years. They united in Second-year and won every game for three years until *Unholy Reign* united. Then they lost their crown to Beignley and Romilly in the 2114 mid-year rematch; they've been competing ever since. No one else has won except from one of those two teams."

"Beignley and Romilly are the guys from *Unholy Reign*?"

"Yeah, Beignley is an Eighth-year, and Romilly a Sixth-year. They united five years ago," Silliah explained before Brindan butted in.

"Eleventh place! Nice going, you two," he called out from behind us.

"She did good," said Pax, hooking an arm around my neck and pinching my cheek.

"Good game today, *Smokin' Axe*," congratulated Celeste, passing our table with Thorn and their friends.

"That team name isn't catching on already, is it?" said Pax, letting go of my head.

"I saw a poster in the corridor with you both on it," answered Thorn. "So, I'd say so. Did you enjoy it, Aurora?"

"It was fun," I admitted, patting down my hair after it had been messed up by Pax. "Better than I thought it was going to be."

"After she eventually found her capsule," roasted Hilly from across the table. She combed her fingers through the front of her blonde hair.

"Yeah, alright, cheers, Hilly." I flashed her a sideways glance. "How did you two end up doing?" I focused back on Celeste.

"Tenth place," she replied. "We were the first to be eliminated in round two. You two came in just behind us. I can't wait to see you both in action when I watch the games back." She gave me a little affectionate nod as she turned away.

"How on earth did you know Beignley had *The Red Queen*?" Brindan asked me, gesturing for Hyas to move so he could sit opposite Pax. The whole table stopped to listen to my answer.

"The picosuit told me."

My reply was met with a flat silence before Tyga finally laughed.

"Good one, Aurora," he said, evoking the same reaction from everyone else.

"Yeah, good one," agreed Brindan. "It would be good if the suit could do that. Seriously though, how did you know?"

Now I was confused. The suit did tell me. How else did I hear Tiny-teeth's voice in my head? "I just...figured it out," I lied. "Why else did they lure us down that alley?"

"That's true," said Brindan.

"Order ready for Mr. Fortis," called Soami from the meal dispenser. "Order ready for Mr. Haywards."

Pax and Brindan left the table. I concentrated on diffusing the burning in my cheeks after having to lie to everyone. Minding my own business, an arm came from behind me, strangling my throat. I immediately dropped my chin to my chest to block the choke.

"My brother's gunning for you," came a slimy, tormenting voice in my left ear.

"If you don't remove your arm from my throat, Ryker, I'll break it."

He squeezed tighter. I reacted without warning, using a wrist lock to straighten his arm, ducking my head to the right, and pivoting his elbow against the side of my neck, bending it back the wrong way. He followed the pain and face-planted into the table. I had him standing beside my chair with his face flattened against the tabletop and his whole arm in a lock.

"You bitch. Alrigh'—alrigh'," he cried. I released his arm to a crowd of aghast faces all telling me I wasn't getting away with that.

Ryker took a seat in Pax's empty chair. "Damn, girl—you're hot on your training." He rubbed his sore elbow.

"I warned you."

"Yeah well, I'm warning you. My brother is coming for you."

"*Uggh*, I don't even know who your brother is, Ryker."

"Beignley Boulderfell," he said as if it were self-explanatory. "He says you cheated in TPG."

"How?" I scoffed, disinterested, resting my cheek in my hand.

"He doesn't know. He just knows you cheated. How else did you know he had *The Red Queen*?"

"It was obvious." Pax came to my defence after arriving back at the table. "Get out of my seat, Ryker."

Ryker obeyed without question and sat opposite me by pushing Hilly out onto the next chair. To Hilly's delight, Pipila and the motley crew joined the table with her. Sitting with Third-years was clearly her idea of climbing the social ladder.

"I suppose so," agreed Ryker. "Well, you aren't going to be so lucky next time. *Unholy Reign* are coming for you."

"Let them," said Pax, unbothered.

I zoned out of the chatter. I wasn't used to the room being so busy, and I couldn't keep up with the conversations flying everywhere. Plus, my hair was still in a French plait, building pressure on my scalp. In my own little bubble, I contemplated spending the evening soaking in the shower with the lights off and ambient sounds washing away my day.

I ate quickly, attempting to get Tayo out of the Food Hall before Ryker had a chance to get to him, but I gave myself indigestion for nothing. Ryker got up before me. Yapping on about the games to Brindan, he approached Tayo with his tray. I think everyone was getting used to the regular crash of crockery at meal times. It really was getting boring; even Seioh Jennson stopped paying it attention.

Tonight though, Ryker was distracted, and he held out his tray to give to Tayo *without* dropping it. But this was Tayo we were talking about. Instead of taking it, like any sane person, the deranged, foolish berk slapped it out of Ryker's hand, sending it to the floor forcefully. I didn't want to watch the next episode of *KO Tayo*, so I laid my head in my arms.

"I have to give it to ya," said Ryker in shock. "That is something I would have done, but there's one difference between you and me: you're Juvie scum, and I'm an Enforcer. I'm extending your sentence. Cross me again, Juvie, and I'll drop your Banding."

"Can he do that?" I asked Pax, who was also alerted by Ryker's words.

"Extend his sentence? Yes. Drop his Banding? No, not normally, but being who he is, Boulderfell's son, I reckon he could. I don't believe Ryker would give an empty threat."

"I extended Crazy Kalmayan Kid's sentence," piped in Hilly. "For grabbing on to you before. I doubled it. He has a year now."

Well, I wasn't going to say thanks to that. I would rather not have to put up with him trembling at the sheer sight of me for a whole year.

"But what did Tayo do to get his sentence extended?" Pax cut back in.

I shrugged. "Got fed up with a tray being dropped at his feet?"

"Hmm. Ryker has had crosshairs on him from the moment he spoke to Pipila," he said quietly, ensuring Pipila's attention was elsewhere.

Tayo hunched his shoulders, opened up his arms, and looked down at his gravy splattered overalls with a mild grimace. I nodded, acknowledging his unspoken request—he wanted to go back.

"Well, yet again, I best take my Juvie back to get cleaned up. See you all."

Tayo followed me out of the Food Hall with dirty overalls for what had to be the fifteenth time this week.

"Thanks," he said, catching up with me.

"Are you *insane*?" I rounded on him. "I saw what you did back there."

"I was friends with guys like him in school. They act like they can do anything just because of the family they were born into. I had to do something to get him to stop. I was just waiting for the right time."

"You're crazy. This isn't a school kid you're messing with. Do you realise he can get you thrown into Max?"

"No, I didn't, actually."

"It's not funny, Tayo."

"Look, I'm still here, aren't I? You act like you can't stand me, but I know you'll miss me when I'm gone."

"Oh yeah? When is that now? In a year? Two years?"

Tayo stopped talking, hopefully using his bloody brain for once.

In his cell, Tayo unzipped his overalls without me needing to ask. Perhaps his way of thanking me for taking him to dinner, or perhaps just knowing I wasn't in the mood for him.

"It's healing quite well," I said, reacting to the clean plaster.

His body, however, was black and blue. The bruising covering his ribcage had matured into a swollen camo-print of all purply shades. He was lucky to have escaped without any broken bones.

Tayo sat still whilst I slathered the wound with ointment. I carefully placed on a fresh adhesive dressing, stroking the edges firmly to his skin. After securing the dressing with a long elasticated bandage, knowing my visit was coming to an end, Tayo said the one sentence he knew would prolong my stay, "I went to school with Pipila. That's how I know her."

"How could you have? She was in Mustard when I was."

"She was eight when she was adopted here. I say adopted— she was given to the institute by her father. He's a family friend of the Boulderfells—absolutely obsessed with the institute and Young Enforcers."

"He gave her away. That's so messed up. Where was her mum?"

"Pipila's mother passed away when she was five. With her mother gone, her father grew infatuated with this place—regards it as the highest honour. He trained Pipila himself to get her ready. She used to come to school with cuts and bruises, and these ankle traps on, set so heavy they would imbed into her ankles."

I never thought I'd hear myself say this regarding Pipila but—"That's really sad."

"She was in the year below me at school. I noticed she was always on her own. When the other children were playing, she would be sitting on the side watching. Then one day, I saw she was wearing ankle traps. The sores around her ankles were so deep and angry, but the teachers would turn a blind eye because of who her father was. So, I went home and taught myself how to reprogram them. Her father didn't know it, but I would make them lighter during the day and set them back before home time. That's how we became friends."

I found Tayo to be almost human this evening. He answered my questions without being his normal difficult self, and I completely lost all sense of time. Creeping back into my bedroom later that night, I caught sight of Pax through the adjoining door. Luckily, he'd already passed out on the sofa. Hopefully he hadn't been waiting for my return.

※

In the weeks that passed, I changed Tayo's bandages for the last time, witnessed the end of Ryker's unrelenting tray dropping, had come to grips with a number of Enforcer duties, and kept myself out of trouble. The routine, everyday life of being a Young Enforcer was turning out to be far better than I ever thought it would be. The days were broken up with more choice, more freedom, and most of all, more time spent outside.

Tonight, on Curfew Duty, the low sun meant the city still held on to a fleeting glimmer of natural light. We were forbidden from dropping our visors, so I couldn't allow the sunrays to brush my face, but it was still better than being indoors.

Pax and I wandered the streets in a careless daydream. I was so thankful Pax enjoyed soaking up the atmosphere, too. We would often stroll along together in silence. The city, Vencen, was built of mostly glass and steel, each building an architectural masterpiece. I could spend all day admiring the impressive works of art. Once content with the breath-taking, man-made structures, we would find ourselves in the woods encircling the city outskirts. Being immersed in natural beauty was such a rare feast.

The sunlight blinked through the myriad of fluttering leaves, making a spectacle of the brilliant-green ferns below. A few moments later, shadows crept in. The sun was setting, so we re-entered the city, seeking the remainder of light. Walking in the middle of a deserted road, Pax began to speak. "I couldn't imagine what it must have been like for Bricks-'n-Mortar Men. They didn't have intelligent, pico-processing roadways."

"I know. I've walked on them in history. It was like a big flat stone."

"They called it tarmac," explained Pax. "It was broken stones mixed with tar."

"With painted-on lines!" I giggled. "That must have been so *weird.*"

"Not to them. It was normal, and they didn't know any different. They had a lot of issues with it, but they didn't have the technology to change it."

"It's only glass and lights."

Pax tipped his head towards me. Behind his visor, I imagined he probably raised his eyebrows at my major understatement. "Their roads were ridiculous." He peeled his eyes off me and carried on searching down the side streets. "In the winter, the snow would settle on them, and because the roads weren't heated, the snow would build up causing accidents and all sorts. Not to mention cover up the lines they'd painted on them. Bricks-'n-Mortar Men would either have to spread salt, which eroded the cars they drove, or keep sweeping it every day."

"Oh, of course, they drove their own cars. Jeez, so much effort and it's something we don't even need to think about nowadays. Have you seen those big pylons they used to have spoiling the green space? God knows how they put up with those."

"It was like they didn't think to put the wires undergro—"

"Pax, wait!" My body flooded with an icy wave. Between the apartment blocks, I saw a tall silhouette. Someone was breaking Curfew!

"What is it?"

"I s-s-saw someone."

"Let's go take a look." He broke into a brisk jog.

The sun was even lower now, and the street lights began turning on in its place. Pax used the computer on his arm to bring up a picoplant tracker. If there was a person in the street right now, we would be able to track them with it.

"Are you sure you saw someone?" asked Pax, head down, inspecting the tracker.

"Yes, there, look." I pointed down the street at the shadowy figure.

"Where? All I can see is a dog…"

"What?" I couldn't see a dog anywhere. "A dog? What are you talking about?" The person ducked out of view, hiding in the flowerbed. They knew we were onto them. "Quickly!"

The raised flowerbeds were a few yards away, and we were hot on their trail. The EU amplified the sound of rustling from the lawbreaker hiding in the tulips. I jumped onto the grey marble wall. "Aha!"

The black dog fled from the bushes with its tail between its legs. Pax laughed so hard he couldn't talk. "I tol…you…it…wa-a-daaaaaawwwwg," he howled, doubled-over, grasping onto his stomach.

"It's not that funny," I sulked, the embarrassment only made worse by Pax's lack of control.

"You're such a donut." He tried to pull me into a hug.

"Go away."

My reaction only made him worse, and he walked around in a drunken circle patting his chest. I stormed off—I didn't have to put up with this.

"Aha!" Pax imitated me jumping onto the flowerbed, before losing his voice to hard laughter.

"I'm going back," I shouted over my shoulder.

"Wait-wait-wait-wait-wait." He apparently sobered up at the thought of me walking alone.

Back in the institute, we entered the EU Changing Facility in Claret Quartz. This room was unlike most others in the institute, and I think the most recent to have been renovated. The spacious room had low lighting despite the many lines of bright-blue lights—of all different widths and angles—jutting through the dark-grey surfaces.

Pax and I stood on plinths to remove our suits.

"Finished?" I growled at him. But this just made him snort. He covered his mouth to hide his smile. His golden eyes were guilt-ridden, yet shining with a childish innocence.

In my room, I made a point of shutting the interconnecting door. It was always open lately, and I knew this would hurt. He messaged me before bed, '*Are you still annoyed with me?*'

I ignored it and fell asleep until morning.

A remorseful Pax woke me up the next day with a khaki-green takeaway drink cup.

"I don't drink coffee," I told him grumpily, resting up against the display screen with the duvet pulled up to my chin.

"It's not coffee," he replied.

"I don't like tea either."

"It's not tea."

"What is it, then?" I said, fed up with the game.

"Just try it."

I burrowed one hand out from under the duvet and took a sip of the warm liquid. It was creamy and chocolatey and—I took another sip—minty.

"It's nice, isn't it? It's a peppermint hot chocolate."

It had become my new favourite drink, but I wasn't about to let him know that. "It's alright."

"Mm-hmm," he hummed, seeing right through my falseness. "I'm—" A smile began to grow, and he held up his index finger. "I am going to say this with a straight face," he continued, struggling to relax his facial muscles. "I'm sorry for laughing at you last night."

"Please don't tell anybody."

"I won't tell a soul, sweetheart. I promise."

Before he turned to leave, he pulled a white tulip out from behind his back. It took me a second to realise it came from the flowerbed last night.

"Is this a joke?" I said, throwing the tulip at him as he ran back into his room. "You're not funny!"

Later on, I picked the flower up and stroked the silky petals between my thumb and forefinger. The long stem had broken in half when I threw it, but it was still tall enough to stand in my paper cup. So, I rinsed out the hot chocolate, filled it with water, and placed it on my floating bedside table. Although the memory of the dog was embarrassing, the flower reminded me more of Pax's laughter. I smiled at the image I saw when I closed my eyes.

The start of my day was pretty standard. That was until I took Tayo back to his cell after breakfast. A glimmer on Tayo's wrist caught my attention. He wore a bracelet made from a thin piece of woven golden rope.

"Hey! That's mine," I said sharply.

"Huh?" Tayo turned on the spot to face me.

"That bracelet—it's mine."

"No, it's not. It's mine," he said casually.

"Since when is your name Aurora?"

Around the golden rope were six small spherical charms made from a shiny black stone called Hematite. Engraved on the front of each one was a golden letter...spelling my name! It was a very distinctive bracelet, and I would recognise it anywhere.

"I've had this since I was a child. When did you lose it?" asked Tayo, standing by his bed, leaning up against the doorframe to his ensuite.

"Stop lying, and give it back to me. You've obviously found it cleaning my old room."

"If you can prove it's yours, I'll give it back to you."

I could prove it belonged to me. I had a photo in my trunk of when I was a baby. In it, my mum held me on her hip as my dad pointed at the camera. He must have been trying to get me to look down the lens, but both my mum and I were laughing at him, ignoring the camera. I was no older than three years of age, and encompassing my tiny wrist half a dozen times was that bracelet. The photo—posted to me one day in Mustard—had a hand-written note on the back which read, 'I knew your parents well. I hope this brings comfort in times of need.' I used to carry it with me every day until I became numb to the feeling of sorrow. I always wondered who'd sent it but there was no name.

"Tayo. Listen to me very carefully. Give me my bracelet, or I swear to god, I will leave you to rot in this cell for a week." And I meant it. Just because I could prove it was mine, didn't mean I was going to.

"Look at you getting all *enforcery* on me." He waggled his fingers as he said '*enforcery*.' "If you wanted to wear my bracelet, Roar, all you had to do was ask."

Tayo removed the bracelet and held it open to put it on me. I grabbed for the middle but he snatched it away. We had a short battle of wills before I relinquished my right wrist. But that wasn't enough for Tayo. After sensing the weakness, he pointed to my left wrist.

"You just can't help yourself, can you?" I swapped hands to end the nonsense.

He looped the bracelet around twice then closed the golden clasp.

"I'll think about whether I'm coming to collect you at lunch or not." I attempted to gain back some control. After all, I was the one who was *supposed* to have it.

"You will."

"Will what? Stop stepping into me, Tayo." I held my hand out to keep him at arm's length. "Will what?"

"Be coming to get me at lunch."

"Keep it up, Tayo, and watch."

"Ohh, you aren't going to do anything to me, my little Roar." He walked into my outstretched hand until it laid flat against his solar plexus. As a warning, I jabbed my knuckles into the sensitive area— not too hard, but enough to wind him slightly. It was just like Tayo to not let the pain show, and I wished I had punched him harder.

"You're such a patronising jackass," I said, pressing the access button to leave.

"See you at lunch, ma'am." The polite exchange was for the benefit of a Navy passing out in the corridor.

Annoyingly, I did intend on collecting Tayo at lunch, but only after I swapped the bracelet onto the other wrist, and placed it on top of my sleeve so he would see. I also intended to make him sweat a little first. So, that afternoon, I convinced everyone to go for Mando-sleep before going to lunch.

Mando-sleep was a two-hour slot allocated for a mandatory afternoon nap. It was discovered by observing the natural sleep habits of babies, and applying it to teenagers that our consciousness fluctuated throughout the day. The old habit of an extended sleep period followed by an extended wake period did not take advantage of these waves in consciousness. The peaks and troughs were being ignored, and Bricks-'n-Mortar Men were keeping their consciousness working flat-out all day. The high efficiency of the peaks was barely noticed and hugely unutilized, and during the low troughs, accidents were rife. So, we no longer pushed ourselves through the tired periods, or forced ourselves to sleep during the alert ones, and thus Mando-sleep was born!

Outside my bedroom, I was having trouble getting inside my room. Nothing happened when I pushed the access button. I had ignored Pax most of the day and hardly spoke two words to him, but now I was looking at his closed bedroom door, needing his help, and wondering whether to knock. I settled for tapping lightly enough to not wake him if he had fallen to sleep, but hard enough for him to hear if he was still awake. I stood with my ear to the door and listened to the muffled noise of movement…coming from everyone else's room but Pax's. *Reception it is.*

"Good afternoon, ma'am." I wasn't making that mistake again. "I am having trouble gaining access to my room."

The ogre straightened up to see me over the large counter. Her excessive makeup startled me, and I desperately tried to prevent any alarm from showing on my face. But when you're not expecting *that* to make an appearance, I seriously doubted I'd managed it. Thick blue eye-shadow congealed in the creases of her eyelids, and a black lump of goopy mascara collected in the corner of her eyes.

Behind her mask of thick foundation, I caught a brief flash of malice cross her face, sending a surge of adrenaline through me. It was so weird, and I felt as though I needed to protect myself.

Don't be so stupid. What was she going to do, jump over the desk and maul me? *Get a grip.* I pushed the thought to the back of my mind. Anyway, I must have been mistaken because the ogre smiled and held the phone up to her ear.

"Good afternoon, Seioh. It's Nunetta." The ogre spoke in a way that was quite alien to me. For the first time, I realised she was female. "I have Miss Aviary with me here at reception. She's being rather rude and—"

"You what?" I burped, the adrenaline quickly turning to anger.

"Yes, and abusive. Could you please come and retrieve her?"

"ARE YOU MAD?"

"Please calm down, Miss Aviary. I am not at fault for you being unable to gain access to your room," she spoke intentionally down the phone.

"I never said you were!"

"Thank you, Seioh. Come quickly." She hung up the phone and stared at me with dangerous eyes.

"You're insane! Nunetta, is it? More like Na-*Nutta*! What is wrong with you?"

"*Aurora Aviary*, get to my office this instant," Seioh Jennson's stentorian voice tore down the corridor.

"Seioh Jennson, she's lying," I said with tightness in my throat, forgetting to stand to attention and moving toward him.

"NOW."

I had never heard Seioh Jennson shout, and I froze. The sound rang right through me, causing my guts to shrink. I hesitated for a second before I acted. *Okay, maybe now isn't the time to explain.*

"You are insane," I hissed at the ogre before leaving reception.

In the distance, I heard the ogre talking to Jennson, "She's agitated she couldn't get into her room, Seioh. She is such a troublesome little girl."

"I know, Nunetta. Thank you; I will take care of it."

CHAPTER NINE

NOTHING HAPPENED

Pacing backwards and forwards in Seioh Jennson's office, the anger morphed into crippling fear. *What if he doesn't believe me?*

No, he will. Why would I lie? But why would she lie? Why did *she lie?* My temper flared once more, and I blindly hammered my fist on top of Jennson's wooden desk. The noise echoed louder than I expected, and I waved the desk down to be quiet. "Shhh!"

The display screen turned itself on, telling me Seioh Jennson was close by. I spun to watch the door. *Oh, for goodness' sake, Aurora. Will you pull yourself together? You're not eight anymore. What's the worst he can do? Take some Worths away. Big deal.* But then I took a sudden gasp at the thought of claret overalls. That was why he was taking so long. He must have gone to get Juvie overalls.

The door slid open. Seioh Jennson aided his overly dramatic arrival by standing still on the other side for a moment before entering. He held a closed fist up to his mouth as he stepped inside. I couldn't work out if it was rage or utter disappointment.

"Seioh Jennson, I swear, I didn't do anything," I burst out, remembering to stand to attention this time and placing my hands behind my back.

"Put these on." He threw a pair of ankle traps at my feet. They hit the ground, crashing together like a pair of dumbbells.

"But, Seioh—"

"If I hear anything other than 'yes, Seioh' come out of your mouth, I will get you some Juvie overalls to match."

I clamped my teeth together, conflicted by the injustice but scared to utter another word. I watched his face reflecting the raging fire roaring down in the pit of my stomach. Unable to defend myself, unable to explain, I knelt down silently, pulling up my combat trouser legs to place on the traps.

"No, Miss Aviary, put them on top of your trousers," he ordered. "And you can take that bracelet off as well."

I removed the golden rope—which was still over my jacket sleeve, ready for Tayo to see—and tucked it into my pocket. The bulky, brushed-metal ankle traps locked shut with a *click*, and I felt them constrict around my lower legs. Seioh Jennson held out his Slate to scan my picoplant and he gained control of them.

"Now walk." He used his head to gesture at the office door.

"I can't, Seioh. They are really heavy," I explained, showing him I couldn't lift my foot.

Seioh Jennson attended to his Slate and adjusted the slider. "Walk."

"You made them heavier."

Did the idiot not know how to use ankle traps?

Once again, Jennson held up his Slate to alter the weight. "Walk," he repeated for the third time.

I tried to walk, only to realise they were even heavier. The increase had been intentional. They were so heavy my body quivered taking a step. Lifting my leg wasn't going to work, so I tried dragging my foot instead; slightly easier but not by much.

"Which way is it to your room?" Seioh Jennson asked once I'd finally met him outside.

I couldn't believe what was happening. I didn't do anything! That stupid ogre set me up. And now, I was being punished in public for all to see; it was so unfair. Not trusting myself to speak, I pointed, and

Jennson began to lead the way. There was not a chance in hell I could keep up with him at that pace. Maybe he intended to meet me there.

A Sixth-year girl crossed Jennson up ahead. She gave my arm a light squeeze of encouragement as she passed me. She didn't hang around though, and I continued hauling my legs, one after the other. My leather boots could barely leave the ground, and the smooth white panels aided my endeavour. Pushing one foot forward, I dragged the other on its side to meet it. I pushed the other foot forward this time, bringing the next up to meet it—not that it made any difference; both were just as hard.

A few Navies standing up ahead stopped talking to gawp at me. Once level with them, they turned on the spot to watch me pass. I felt like a subservient Juvie, not even worthy to look them in the eye.

Almost there.

A bead of sweat dripped off my eyebrow, splashing onto the floor. Pushing one foot forward and dragging the next, I made it to my room at last. Seconds later, Seioh Jennson found me.

"This is your room?" he asked, eyeing up the silver door number.

"Yes, Seioh." *Obviously. I'm not randomly waiting outside someone else's room, am I?*

"Room 4-3-2 is your room?"

"Yes…Seioh." What was he not getting?

"Well, scan your picoplant, then."

The door *whooshed* open. I couldn't believe my eyes. *If that frickin' receptionist did this on purpose, I'm going to go mad.* First my uniform was missing from my wardrobe and now this!

"Tell me," began Jennson, straightening up his suit jacket. "Are you going to learn to control your temper, Miss Aviary?"

"I didn't do anything." A swirling darkness consumed my head. "That woman is a liar."

"Walk." He stepped to my side and pushed me between the shoulder blades.

"Where?" I barked back.

"Seeing as you like being the centre of attention, to the Food Hall."

No! I threw both hands over my mouth at my worst nightmare being realised. Not only was it lunchtime, it was also the time I'd arranged to meet everyone in there.

Jennson set off again, but I stood defiantly, staring into the back of his head, deciding if I was brave enough to disobey him. I wouldn't expect he'd know what to do in that circumstance. As I stood there deliberating, Jennson spun on his heel and came back my way. It was as if he knew what I was thinking. Was I that predictable? In a panic, I slid my foot forward and shook my head for forgiveness.

"I mean it, Aurora, this is your last chance," he said, pausing, eyes trained on mine, still, intolerant, and reprimanding. Then he turned back on his heel again.

Talk about almost signing my own death warrant.

I dragged my foot to meet the other. Sharp pains streaked through my shins. They were inflamed and rubbing up against the metal traps. Each step became harder than the last. More gormless bystanders watched me limp past as a demented mess. My knees gave way, and I collapsed on the floor. Panting there on all fours, I knew I was almost defeated. I wiped the sweat trickling down my cheek, and I forced myself back up.

At the Food Hall, Seioh Jennson was already waiting. "I want you at a chute, Miss Aviary."

The sentence made my blood burn under my prickly hot skin. "No," I said almost soundlessly. He wouldn't be so cruel. "Seioh, please."

"A chute—now."

A single audible breath escaped from my fallen jaw. I couldn't move, but it had nothing to do with the weight or pain.

"Seioh, *please.*" I tried again out of sheer desperation.

"A chute, Miss Aviary, *now*."

I choked on the pressure building in my throat. Even if I could talk, I didn't dare mutter another word. I blinked my misty eyes to lessen the sting. Limping my way to the nearest vacant chute, I managed to only take the attention of a nearby Juvie.

But I wore navy.

In an outbreak of murmurs, the news spread like a virus. Mortified, I kept my gaze downwards in an unfocused trance. Becoming aware of the room's change in mood, Pax turned to see what all the fuss was about. He stopped eating and lowered his fork at the sight of me. Silliah did the same. Soon enough, the Fanciable Four were setting down their cutlery too. I couldn't stand the look on their faces. They wanted to end my suffering but were helpless. Pax stood up slowly. I could tell he was compelled to do it even though he hadn't figured out what he was going to do. Crossing the Food Hall, he came to me. I reached out to take his tray, but he leant over me, putting his own plate in the vacant chute.

"Stay strong, sweetheart," he whispered in my ear as he reached past. "You're going to be okay."

Too much for him to handle, he collected Bethoney and Maigen and left the hall. The Davoren Sisters passed me with the same troubled, forlorn stare. Clearly nobody wanted to be in my shoes, and the word spread quickly. Musties popped their heads around the corner to see me, then stood back to let their friends look. A Navy being punished to such degree was unheard of.

A scream of despair wedged in my throat when I caught Nanny Kimly's eye. How disappointed she must be of me. But then, remembering I didn't do anything, the dark cloud returned.

The whole time I stood there, no one dared approach me to clear their plates, but it looked as though Ryker attempted to. I wasn't sure. Pipila held on to his arm, and they were arguing yet again. He aggressively wrenched his arm free and came my way. But then so did Pipila, so perhaps I wasn't what they had argued about.

"What did you do?" asked Ryker somewhat sympathetically, eyebrows raised and mouth crooked.

I shook my head and gave a small eye roll as if to say, "You wouldn't believe me if I told you."

"Well, make yourself useful. Here you go."

What I wanted to do was take the tray and smash it around his head, but Seioh Jennson was watching, so I took it begrudgingly.

"Thank you, *sir...*" Ryker urged me to respond, taking full advantage of my vulnerability.

"Back off, Ryker," I suggested, not caring if I got into any more trouble.

"I'm joking. We're friends now, remember?" he said, walking off and giving a hearty cackle. Pipila gave me her plate without a trace of emotion. I could have been a Juvie and it would have made no difference.

Seioh Jennson approached me with his tray. I accepted it painfully. He reciprocated with arched eyebrows as if waiting for me to say something. His blue eyes were barren; he really didn't have a soul.

"Thank you, Seioh," I complied, the anger churning over in my stomach.

"Are you going to learn to control your temper, Miss Aviary?"

"I didn't do anything," I said, turning my face away from him.

When he shoved me, I realised my ankle traps were released. He was probably about to let me go, but now he led me down the corridor towards the outer passageways. Outside, the city bustled with the usual weekly activity, and a lady in a patterned poncho caught my eye. She pulled up her oversized hood and passed with her head down.

"Go to your room." Seioh Jennson engaged the ankle traps.

I screwed up my face for two reasons: one, how old did he think I was? *I'm sixteen, not eight*; and two, we were right by Navy Quartz and my room was literally a minute away. With my tongue in my cheek, I turned towards the corridor, but Seioh Jennson rotated me by the shoulders to face the other way.

"That way," he instructed.

My first thought was, *I think I know where my bedroom is,* but then it hit me like a bucket of ice cold water—he wanted me to do a full lap around the institute! I thought being humiliated in the Food Hall was as bad as it could get. How wrong could I be? I could hardly move my legs, so for me this was going to take forever. Wishing I could turn back time, I began the arduous trek.

At first my body screamed. The short rest in the hall awoke the shooting pains through my knees. I strenuously pushed my foot forward, and the traps rubbed against my already-shredded shins. Grabbing around my calf, I helped move the other one to meet it. Doing that may have assisted my joints, but now my back started to hurt.

An hour later, when I reached Mustard Quartz, I lost my balance. I fell on my knee hard, cracking it against the solid floor panel. I held my breath to cope with the pain. By the time I got to my feet, a fleshy lump had already surfaced on the tender area.

"You can do it, Aurora," someone said whilst I nursed my sore joint.

By now, the corridor was ridiculously busy. This, I was sure, was not a coincidence. People could be so nosey, and I kept seeing the same faces again and again.

Pain was no longer my main concern—exhaustion was. I couldn't remember the last time I'd pushed my body this far, and I normally trained hard. The compulsion to rest was so strong I kept imagining my bed. But then, as I neared the Khaki reception, my vision turned into a sheet of white, I heard a whistling in my ear, and a splitting pain through my temple brought my suffering to an end.

"Aurora?" called a familiar voice in the distance. "Aurora, can you hear me?" said the same voice, only closer. I slowly opened my eyes to see Nanny June Damiano leaning over my face. She wiped my clammy head with an icy-cold flannel. In confusion, I tried to sit up, but Nanny June held me back down.

"Stay down, Miss Aviary," she said, pushing on my shoulders. "You've had a nasty fall and banged your head." She looked down at the ankle traps and asked, "Is this…Seioh Jennson?"

I nodded weakly.

Nanny June pulled out her Slate. "Hello, Seioh. Miss Aviary has fainted in the Khaki reception and sustained an injury to her head." She paused to listen. I couldn't hear what Seioh Jennson said, but I think I got a clear idea of his response. "No, Seioh, it is not serious, but what about the risk of concussion? Okay. Yes, Seioh. Thank you. Goodbye." Nanny June ended the phone call. "I'm sorry, Miss Aviary. I have been instructed to administer first aid and then be on my way."

Subdued, I closed my eyes and allowed Nanny June to fix up my head with a few sterile strips and a plaster. She mopped up the pool of my blood from the floor and helped me to my feet. She didn't say anything before leaving; she just bowed her head with a sorry expression on her face.

My accident in the corridor attracted more spectators, and I didn't appreciate being this afternoon's form of entertainment. "Do you not have somewhere to be?" I barked at a crowd of loitering Musties. They turned in all directions, bumping into each other before making themselves scarce.

I managed two more strides before I fell to the floor again. *This is hopeless.* I was too weak and depleted of energy to continue. Sliding myself backwards, I sat up against a wall, pulled my legs up into my chest, and rested my sore head on my knees—I had finally given up. I couldn't do it. Maybe I could sleep here and try again in the morning.

It wasn't too long after that the corridor full of people finally got to me. The noise of footsteps continuously passing by made it impossible to sleep and soon drove me into giving the task another go. Using the wall to help me, I hauled myself up.

Agonizing joints, shooting pains, and stinging shins eventually led to numbness. *Come on, Aurora. You can do this. Do not let that bastard break you. You're nearly in Navy Quartz. You are almost there.*

Vencen suddenly cleared out. It amazed me how quickly Curfew emptied the city. It must have been about twenty hundred hours, and I couldn't help thinking about Pax. We would have been out on our Curfew Duty, where we planned to wait until dark to see the full moon. It was the end of March, and we had been watching it getting fuller and brighter each day. But it would be at its fullest tomorrow, so at least there was that.

In the Navy Quartz residential corridors, I fell onto my hands and knees once more. The sight of my bedroom door allowed me to draw the power, getting myself on my feet again. Seioh Jennson must have done a lap to see where I'd gotten to, because he overtook me from behind. He stood outside my bedroom and watched me struggle to reach him.

But finally, I made it. My attempted stand to attention was limp and pathetic. The muscles in my body struggled with my own weight. I stood there fighting the urge to wipe the droplets of sweat running down my flushed cheeks.

"Are you going to learn to control your temper, Miss Aviary?" said Seioh Jennson.

"Yes, Seioh." I accepted defeat.

"I'm taking four thousand and eighty Worths from your account and wiping it clean. That's everything you've earned so far as a Navy, gone due to your insolent behaviour. Children do not earn Worths, Aurora, and you will not be receiving any further Worths until you prove yourself *worthy* of receiving them. Do you understand?"

"Yes, Seioh," I whispered so my voice wouldn't break.

"Now get out of my sight."

With that, Seioh Jennson opened my bedroom door, allowing me to walk in. He closed it behind me, and the ankle traps fell to the floor—that was the end of it. Demoralised, exhausted, and broken, I dropped down on my bed as thick tears gushed from my eyes.

The interconnecting door opened, and I frantically dried my face.

"Hey, hey, hey, it's okay. It's okay to be upset," said Pax, sitting on the bed behind me. He shuffled closer and tried to turn me to face him. I resisted, but he was unyielding, so I gave in to him. He guided my head onto his chest and held me with both arms. I curled up, resting my throbbing legs on his thighs, and with his lips resting on my hair, I cried myself to sleep.

When the alarm rang in the morning, we were still together. Pax had stayed with me all night. He still sat up against the display screen, my head still on his chest, and his arms still cloaked around me.

"I'm going to go and take a shower, sweetheart," Pax spoke softly.

I sat up automatically, allowing Pax to get off the bed. I didn't know if I was embarrassed I'd fallen asleep on him, or if it was just residue from the day before, but either way, I was thankful he was leaving the room. As he stood, he stretched his arms backwards, cracking his spine. He must have been so uncomfortable leaning up against that hard wall all night. I wondered how much sleep he'd actually gotten.

When I heard the shower running in the next room, I kicked off my boots and crawled back into bed. There was no way I could face the world today, no way I could walk into the Food Hall, no way I could be a Navy. How could I, after being publicly humiliated? I couldn't and I wasn't going to.

After his shower, Pax came back into my room and crouched on the platform steps by the side of my bed. He gently lifted the covers off my face. The fresh fragrance of soap and deodorant wafted under. With his eyes level with mine, he pressed his top lip on his slightly curled-in bottom one. "Come on, sweetheart. I know it's hard, but it'll only get harder the longer you leave it."

"I can't, Pax. I can't go out there."

"Why don't you get out of those dirty clothes, have a shower, and see how you feel?"

I didn't say anything and turned my head to face the other way. Pax stood up, keeping hold of the duvet. *Please don't try and force me, Pax. It won't end well for you.*

"OK. I'll come and see you at lunch," he said, setting down the duvet. I felt his hesitation before he left the room.

I must have fallen asleep because the next I heard was Nanny Kimly. "How did I know you would still be in bed, Little Lady?" she said, folding back the duvet to sit by my side.

I pushed my face into her leg. "I didn't do anything, Nanny Kimly."

"Shh-shh-shh." She wiped my wet cheeks. "Come on, shh now. You're okay." She peeled back the plaster on my forehead, reached into her first aid bag, and applied some ointment to my wound.

"Nanny Kimly, I didn't do anything," I repeated after calming down and getting a handle on my emotions.

"Little Lady," Nanny Kimly said sensitively. "Seioh Jennson said he saw you. He said he saw you get angry at Nunetta and was asking you to control your temper."

I blinked as I thought about what Nanny Kimly said. She was right. Seioh Jennson didn't mention anything about being rude or aggressive to *Na-Nutta*. He only asked if I was going to control my temper, which I didn't manage to do all day—I was so caught up on getting punished for no reason.

"Now come on: get up, have a shower, and take yourself to breakfast." She patted me on the leg.

"My body hurts too much to train," I moaned. I wasn't lying. Every inch of my body ached. My head was sore, my knees and ankles swollen, and my shins red raw.

"I said breakfast. Now, come on, Aurora—up." She removed the duvet from the bed.

I kept still, ignoring her, hoping she would leave me alone.

"Aurora."

I didn't move.

Nanny Kimly gave up, covered me back over, and left the room with a sigh.

"You have five minutes to take a shower," said Seioh Jennson, storming in, going into my wardrobe, and pulling out a clean uniform. "Take these, and start behaving like a Navy."

"Yes, Seioh." I dragged myself out of bed.

During the night, my trousers had stuck to the dry blood on my legs, and removing them reopened the sores. I had a nasty shock stepping into the shower when the water hit the open flesh; the sudden sting was unanticipated. The red stream of fresh blood trickled down my ankles and swirled down the plughole with the water. Knowing I didn't have time to dry my hair if it got wet, I secured it up high, switched the jets to below head height, and rubbed soap into my achy shoulders.

Whilst brushing my teeth, I stared at my sunken, pale face in the mirror and had a word with my reflection before leaving the room. I couldn't risk allowing my true feelings towards Jennson to surface, provoking further punishment from him.

"Come on, Miss Aviary. Time's up—out," Seioh Jennson ordered from the other side of the partition wall.

"Yes, Seioh," I responded, exiting the archway, walking straight past Jennson without acknowledgement, leaving the room, and turning towards Claret Quartz to collect Tayo. That was the best I could do at being reticent—even the sideways glance made my blood boil.

"You have got to be kidding me!" Tayo jumped down my throat as soon as I entered his cell. "I gave you that stupid bracelet back, didn't I? Why didn't you com—what's the matter with you?" He changed his tune at the sight of my weary face.

"Nothing. I'm fine."

"You look like you've been crying."

"I haven't. I'm fine. Give me your wrist."

"What did you do to your head? Is that why you've been crying?" Tayo wasn't taking 'nothing' for an answer.

"I haven't been crying," I snapped. "Now let me scan your picoplant."

Tayo seemed distracted by his own thoughts. He looked between my empty hand hanging by my side, and the other holding out my Slate. Then he came and yanked up my jacket sleeve.

"Get off." I snatched away my arm. "What do you think you're doing?"

"Where's your bracelet?"

"Tut, you didn't even put it on this wrist. You put it on this one."

"I *know*. Where is it?"

"*Here*." I put away my Slate and reached into my jacket pocket. "*Why*?"

"Aurora, tell me you didn't swap it over onto the other wrist?" Tayo watched my face closely for a reaction.

"How did you even know that? Yes, I did but…what has…why did…" I couldn't get my words out. I was so confused and my head was still muddled from yesterday.

"Oh, my little Roar, why would you go and do that?" Tayo spun slowly on the spot, fingers pulling at his cheeks, chin up in the air.

"What has that got to do with anything?"

"*This*." He flipped my open hand up to face the ceiling. Usually, I would have been intolerant to his touch, but something in my head told me to allow it. Still holding on to the back of my hand, he coiled the bracelet in my palm like a snake settling to sleep. He closed my fingers around it and pushed my knuckles against the access button to open the cell door.

Nothing…happened. The door wouldn't open.

Tayo let go. My brain went into overdrive trying to figure out what it all meant. I opened my fingers to see the bracelet. The spherical charms around the golden rope all gathered at one end, and on them, I read the word, 'ROAR.'

I clung on to the frame around the observer's window whilst flashbacks forced themselves through my mind's eye, clear as though they were happening right now. That young boy with those piercing-blue eyes and jet-black hair; us running hand in hand; being separated by the grown-ups; the old wand-like pico-reader being waved over and over; then finally, Tayo Tessan, aged six, parents Mr. Jarl Tessan and Mrs. Tora Tessan.

"It was you…" I said quietly, still trying to process the information.

Tayo walked backwards until he was propped up against the empty surface opposite his bed. "What was me?"

"You know who I am, don't you?" I asked, already knowing the answer.

He looked at the floor. His mouth stretched into a slanted smile. Then his eyes flicked up to meet mine. "So, you do remember," he said, holding my eyes intently. "You were so young, I wasn't sure you would."

Well, I didn't remember, as such. I wasn't certain if the dream was a memory because it never played from my perspective. Perhaps it was too painful, so my subconscious protected itself and filled in the gaps. I had so many questions I didn't know where to start. "You were trying to jog my memory yesterday when you asked when I lost my bracelet."

"See, I wasn't lying. I did have it since I was a child."

"I couldn't remember when I lost it," I said, spinning a smooth Hematite stone between my fingers. "There are two charms missing, the 'A' and the 'U.'"

"They must have slipped off when the bracelet broke. When I got home, only the four charms were loose in the bottom of my pocket.

I fixed the bracelet and put them on, spelling the only word I could with them."

"Roar…" I pre-empted, with a single breathy laugh at the realisation. "That's why you call me Roar."

"My little Roar," he said, staring down at his plimsoles. "I'm sorry I couldn't save you, Aurora."

"Tayo. You were six. It's fine. And anyway, putting yesterday aside, this place isn't so bad—better now I'm in Navy."

"I know, it's just," he huffed, rubbing his sole against the other, "you're a *Youngen*." Tayo said the word like it was dirt. Only Lady Maxhin ever called us that but always as a term of endearment.

"I *knew* you didn't like us very much, from the moment I walked in this cell."

"Oh, you mean the 'Hi, erm…can I…I mean, I need to…tut, just hold out your wrist' moment?"

"Hey! It was my first day, and you made my life miserable."

"Good."

"Why are you so horrible to me?"

"Oh shh, I'm joking. Why have you been crying?" He jumped up onto the surface so that his feet dangled.

"I told you, I haven't."

"Why are you lying to me? I can see you have." Tayo waited for me to respond, but I continued to look at the floor. "Listen. So, that night when your bracelet broke, the guy who couldn't scan my picoplant didn't appreciate being made to look stupid in front of that Nanny. He walked me back home and tasered me in the back repeatedly. Look." Still sitting on the counter, Tayo undid his overalls and showed me his back. At first, I expected to see some kind of tattoo or something, but I didn't see anything. Then as I moved closer, I saw pale electrical scars zig-zagging across his skin like tiny bolts of lightning. Unthinkingly, my fingers traced over the jagged forks, but Tayo, ever so slightly, flinched at my touch.

"Sorry," I apologised for my unsought behaviour, snatching away my hand.

"It's okay. You can touch me all you want, my little Roar—*anyway*—" He quickly broke in before I could retaliate, "I shared with you, now you share with me. Why have you been crying? Here, I'll start you off: I thought I was being clever by defying Tayo, and switching my bracelet over to my picoplant wrist, but now I realise it was foolish; your turn."

"I hate you."

Tayo didn't laugh often, but when he did, it felt very genuine. It was as warming as the sparkle behind his eyes when he smiled. "I couldn't help myself," he said with a cough, settling down and rubbing his eyes deeply with both palms. "No, seriously—tell me."

"I don't want to tell you," I said hotly.

"What did you do, lock yourself in a toilet, or something?"

"No! *Urgh*. I was punished, okay? I had to lap the institute wearing ankle traps, made to stand at a chute during lunch, and had all my Worths taken off me. And I didn't do anything! The stupid receptionist lied about me. I have no idea why, and I just want to forget about it, so can we please change the subject?"

Tayo blinked at me as he thought it through. Then his expression hardened. He sighed heavily, blowing his bottom lip out, directing the airflow to ruffle his long, straight fringe. He appeared to be respecting my request of dropping the subject and internalised his feelings.

"Alright, fine," he agreed. "Now, what I would like to know is what a three-year-old was doing with a bracelet that blocked her picoplant."

CHAPTER TEN

GLOWING

Tayo was on the counter, leaning back on his hands, one foot resting on the shelf underneath the surface, the other hanging down freely. He had gotten himself comfortable after he asked me a question I really couldn't answer. Why *was* a three-year-old in possession of a bracelet that blocked their picoplant?

"Maybe my parents didn't realise it blocked my picoplant." I finally came up with an answer. Tayo raised his naturally perfect eyebrows. He clearly didn't believe that to be the case. "Well, what was a six-year-old doing out at night breaking Curfew?"

Tayo's eyebrows arched even higher. He swooped his head backwards as if my words physically hit him. "Really? Best form of defence is attack, huh, Roar?" He leant forward, resting both feet up on the empty shelf, interlaced his fingers, and brought his elbows up to lean on his knees. "Your dear little bracelet has been helping me break Curfew my whole life."

"Tayo!" I gasped, covering my ears. "You can't tell me *that*. I'm an Enforcer. It's my duty to catch Curfew breakers."

"The day you report me for breaking Curfew is the day I become a Kalmayan and start Puracordis hunting."

"What is that supposed to mean?" I crossed my arms.

"It means, my little Roar, that it's never going to happen."

"Just please don't put me in a position where I have to act on it. I don't want to know if you break the law." I frowned at him, and he gave me an indifferent shrug of the shoulders. My thoughts turned back on to my dream. "Tayo, can I ask you something?"

Tayo nodded earnestly.

"Do you know *how* my parents died?"

"You don't know?"

"No. We are not really supposed to talk about our lives before the institute. If my drea—I mean *memory* serves me correctly, my dad was alive that night in the woods."

Tayo dipped his head, giving a slow blink confirming my belief. "Pass me your Slate. Let me show you something."

"My Slate? Why?" I held my Slate in my pocket, protecting it, as if just asking meant he could obtain it.

"So I can show you something," he repeated, holding out his hand.

"But, Juvies aren't allowe—"

"Trust me," he said convincingly. "Do you really still only see me as a Juvie, Roar?"

"Uh..."

"Come, sit up here, and you'll be able to see everything I'm doing. I swear, Roar, I'm just going to show you something."

I handed Tayo my Slate without speaking. It was as if I thought by not saying the word 'OK,' it meant my actions were less reprehensible. My Slate left my fingers, and suddenly, I became hyper-aware of the observer's window. All I could think about was getting it back from him. What if he deactivated his ankle trap and escaped?

Tayo searched through some kind of database and was nowhere near my apps, so I started to relax a little. Without warning, I snatched my Slate back from him and jumped off the counter—Pax stood in the doorway. He tilted his head backwards and beckoned for me to join him in the corridor. *Clart*. I was in so much trouble—there was no coming back from this.

When I met him outside, he cradled my body in his arms and held me with vigour. I devoured his touch, and for the first time, I returned the embrace by wrapping my arms around him. His muscles engulfed my fragile frame, and I burrowed my head into his bicep.

"You're up," he said, leaning back to look at my face. His fingers brushed around my jawline, finding my chin and tipping my head back until my eyes found his. "Come on, you've got fifteen minutes until breakfast ends. Grab Tayo, and I'll come with you." He let go of my chin, but as I turned away, he took hold of my hand impulsively. "Aurora, I trust you know what you are doing…with the Slate?"

Oh no. He saw. My nod was sluggish and uncertain at first, but then I realised I needed to be more convincing, and it switched to a jerky, twitchy nod. That ought to have done it…if Pax was a moron. Who was I trying to kid? I backed away into the cell before I did any more damage.

"Come on, Tayo. You ready?"

"Yes, ma'am."

On our walk round to the Food Hall, I really wished I had that lady's bright-purple poncho so I could pull the oversized hood over my face. Navies and Musties alike ogled me as if I had grown a second head. I felt like a circus act, and this stupid plaster on my forehead didn't help matters. Although Pax and I had only known each other for a few months, he already knew me too well, and his arm swooped me into his side, preventing me from retreating to my bedroom.

There wasn't anybody inside the Food Hall when we arrived except for the Juvie cleaning team and their chaperones.

"Give the cleaning team a hand, will you, Tayo?" said Pax.

Tayo glanced over at the group. I saw the disdain swamp his face even if Pax didn't, but regardless, he dutifully obeyed, dragging his feet lazily. The tables cleaned themselves once they retracted under the floor, so only the meal dispenser and chutes needed wiping; the floor panels would be polished after we vacated the hall.

Pax came and stood over my screen, giving it a double-tap. "Avocado toast?" he commandeered.

"Sure."

A three-minute counter appeared, and Pax left to retrieve my food. I fell forward onto the table. How could Seioh Jennson disgrace me in front of the entire Food Hall like that? The sight of the chute I stood at yesterday brought the memories flooding back. The luminance of my soul was smothered by the shame, and a single tear rolled out of the corner of my eye.

"Sweetheart—here you go." Pax returned, setting the tray down gently. His head tilted to the side at the sight of my tear. "Do you want to talk about it?"

"I didn't do anything, Pax," my voice cracked. "I swear to you."

"I believe you." He wiped my face clumsily, as though the sight of my tears caused him pain and he wanted them gone.

"I've tried really hard to keep out of trouble. I didn't want you to be ashamed of me; I didn't want you to regret *matching* with me."

"I am not ashamed of you, Aurora." He sat next to me and took hold of both my hands. "And I will never regret matching with you. I didn't want to match in Unity until I matched with *you*."

My heart skipped, but then it tripped over into the pit of my stomach. I wanted to believe him, but what if he just said that because I was upset. "It's just I know you don't like rule breaking. I'm so sorry."

"What are you sorry for? You didn't do anything." He squeezed my hands. "Now, come on, eat. Before the cleaning team retracts the tables from underneath us, and you find yourself eating your breakfast on the floor." Then a thought swept in and he pulled a face. "Or mangled up in a table beneath the floor."

I gave a small smile, and lifted my toast. At the first taste of creamy, mashed avocado, an insatiable hunger consumed my body. A low grumble in my belly made me realise I hadn't eaten since yesterday morning. Pax watched the cleaning team, so I granted myself permission to take larger bites than normal. My taste buds rejoiced at the zesty lemon and light seasoning of salt and pepper. I didn't even notice Pax chose crusty sourdough bread until I picked up my second piece. It was a nice change to my usual wholemeal thin slice.

"I heard she was pregnant. Can you believe it?" came a girl's voice from the corridor to my right.

"No, it can't be that," said a voice even whinier than Hilly's. "Both of them would have been taken to Max. I heard she cheated on Pax. I bet you it was with Brindan. So, apparently, Pax took his plate to her whilst she was at the chute, and then he stormed out of the hall."

I didn't see Pax leave the table. He was already at the corridor when I looked up from my plate.

"Well, I heard she—" a third voice broke off.

What I heard next was the offended tones of Pax's coarse voice. I couldn't make out any discernible words, nor could I see them down the corridor from where I was, but Tayo could. He stopped cleaning the sparkling white door of a chute and watched through narrow eyes. He didn't stop eyeing them even after the three Musties entered the hall. The girls, all probably old enough to be in Navy come January, glanced at me sideways as they hurried across the room. They all had faces full of makeup and matching yellow ribbons in their hair. The tall one with her blonde locks tied up in a high ponytail, boldly turned back to look at me before she exited through the archway towards Mustard Quartz. I wasn't sure about that one—she gave me weird Pipila vibes.

Pax returned, shaking his head. I had never seen that side of Pax before. I wondered whether his reaction was because he was really protective of me, or whether the mention of an illegal pregnancy stirred up harboured emotion. Or perhaps it was both.

"That was Crystal, one of Ryker's sisters," Pax explained.

"The tall blonde one?"

"No, the short blonde one."

"Oh."

"It won't be like this for long, sweetheart." He stroked a loose strand of white hair behind my ear. "It will be old news soon, and they will find something else to gossip about." He checked on Tayo's progress, and then turned back to me. "If you're finished, we are scheduled for Uniform Delivery."

My plate was empty (despite my sudden loss in appetite), so Tayo came and took it from me, and we made our way to the laundry room.

Once you got used to the pungent chemical odour, the laundry room wasn't too bad. It was a very busy one—not with people, but with moving machines, revolving conveyor belts, and mechanical arms. The clean clothes swung along on their hangers until being sorted onto trolleys. These trolleys were organised by room number and made delivery very simple.

"Aurora," called Silliah. Her bright-green eyes peered around the corner of the laundry room's double doors.

"Silliah," I returned in the same tone. We met halfway and threw our arms around each other.

"So," she began, letting go of me but taking hold of my hand. "Pax spoke to Roman and arranged for us to do our round together today."

"You didn't say anything about this." I turned to confront Pax.

"I know. I thought you two could use some time…just the two of you," he replied. "If you want to take the seven hundreds, Roman and I will take the eight hundreds?"

"Thank you, Pax," I said, amazed by his thoughtfulness. "Thanks, Roman."

"No problem." Roman tilted his square head forward, partially concealing his eyes beneath bushy brown eyebrows. He stood with the Davoren Sisters and his Juvie, a chunky teenage boy with an unruly tuft of ginger hair.

Overhearing our room allocation, Tayo and Natashly opened up the lockers beneath the conveyor belts to pull out our pre-sorted trolleys. The electric trolleys didn't require much effort and maneuvered easily. I assumed that was due to it being Enforcers who usually handled them. We were the ones who maneuvered the trolleys outside bedroom doors so the Juvies could take the garments and stock the wardrobes.

Once we were in the Mustard residential corridors, Pax and Roman walked up ahead, conversing quietly. I stopped outside the first room and opened the metal shutters to my trolley so Tayo could begin delivery. Silliah stopped at the room directly opposite, pressing the round access button, allowing Natashly to do the same.

"And you didn't do anything?" Silliah replied after I told her what happened yesterday.

"Nothing but tell her I couldn't get into my room. I swear she's got it in for me."

"Stay away from her, then. If you need anything, message me first. I'll go to reception with you, or *for you* if I can."

We continued moving forward habitually, stopping outside each room. Tayo was listening to our conversation, I could tell. So, as much as I wanted to divulge everything about the bracelet and whom I'd found out Tayo to be, I knew it wasn't the time or the place.

"We were all worried about you," said Silliah. "It was sickening seeing you standing at that chute. Personally, I think it was a little excessive. You're an *Enforcer*. I wonder if Seioh Boulderfell would have stood for that."

"I don't know," I said, sighing, wishing yesterday never happened. "Come back to my room later during lunch; I've got something I need to tell you."

Tayo smiled as he took hold of another uniform. I don't know why it made me want to slap him around the head. Luckily, Silliah missed his tactless indiscretion; she was busy attending to her Slate.

"Ooh, okay," she replied, before looking back down at whatever preoccupied her mind. "Natashly, is this the foundation you use on your clients?" She turned her Slate to Natashly, who was halfway through a doorway. Tayo rolled his eyes, shook his head, and disappeared into a room.

"Yes, that's the one," said Natashly. "It's the best on the market. It blends well, has light-reflective technology, and gives a real natural complexion, as well as being hydrating."

"You can tell you've said that before." Silliah smirked cheekily.

"I don't know why we have to say it. It's not like they are ever going to buy it. They pay a monthly subscription for us to apply their makeup."

"Well, you've sold one bottle," said Silliah. "I'm going to order it now."

Natashly smiled and continued on through the door.

Silliah finished her purchase and faced me. "How nice is it having Worths now we're in Navy?"

Tayo, who just arrived back to the trolley, bared his clenched teeth and moved swiftly on to the next room.

"Yeeeah." I rubbed my left temple. "Seioh Jennson took all of mine away. He cleared my account."

"*What*? Oh my god, I'm so sorry, Aurora."

"It's fine."

"Aurora, you need anything—and I mean *anything*—you tell me, okay? I'll get it for you, whatever it is. Do you want some foundation?"

I laughed at the worry clouding her judgment. "Silliah, when have you known me to wear makeup?"

"I know. Okay, not foundation. But anything else you want, I will get it, okay?"

※

After our morning duties, Pax and Silliah stayed glued to my side. They both booked on to a law lesson with me, even though I was pretty sure it was far too basic for Pax. Perhaps he was attempting to crush the cheating rumours and show we were still united. But nonetheless, it was nice having them both with me and not facing anyone on my own.

Once they ensured I ate food at lunch, they both escorted me to my bedroom for Mando-sleep. I sat for a while with Silliah and told her everything about Tayo. She said that she had always liked him and now she knew why. If only she knew how much of an ass he really was.

Because Pax and Silliah watched me all day, I hadn't been able to find out what Tayo was about to show me earlier. But before settling down to sleep, I stumbled across it. He had found what he was looking for before I snatched the Slate from his hands. Left open on my internet browser was a news article dated Monday, the tenth of August, 2105—not long after my third birthday. *This must be it: the night my parents died.*

Abandoned Nuclear Research Lab Discovered After Death of Family

Last night, an abandoned nuclear research lab was discovered buried beneath the City of Vencen.

The discovery was made after the bodies of a male and female were found dead in their home late Friday evening. A post-mortem of the bodies revealed the cause of death to be radiation poisoning. This led to the abandoned facility being uncovered by none other than Seioh Borgon Boulderfell himself.

Seioh Boulderfell investigated the family home after the bodies were identified as well-respected, retired Enforcers: Mr. Orin Aviary, 34, and Mrs. Averlynn Aviary, 26. The couple—who were both adopted and raised at the Boulderfell Institute for Young Enforcers—died tragically after only five short years of being honourably discharged from the institute.

In a statement following the incident, Seioh Boulderfell said, "The city has lost two of its own in this terrible incident. These young

157

people dedicated their lives to the City of Vencen, and it was the unknown depths of the city that took their lives. It is tragic, and they will be sorely missed."

Going forward, the site of the nuclear bunker—which is located in the woodland outskirts—has been quarantined, the underground facility destroyed, and the surrounding areas cordoned off indefinitely. These drastic measures are a consequence of the type of harmful radiation at the site being able to last for thousands of years.

This shocking and unexpected event will see the introduction of new radiation detectors being installed in all residential and business properties throughout Venair.

When I finished reading the article, my arm hair was bristling. For the first time in my life, I had an insight into who my parents were. They were raised in the institute just like me. They must have matched in Unity and had me like they were intended to. My mum and dad had walked down the same corridors as me and eaten in the same Food Hall. *I wonder if they made it onto the scoreboards in the Colosseum. I wonder if they were any good at TPG!* My mind was frantic, mulling it all over. Mando-sleep was out of the question for me this afternoon.

It was just as well nobody expected me to be 'with it' today. During my four-hour session in the Colosseum, I couldn't do much physical exercise due to my body being so sore, and I was left to my own devices, wandering around on the suspended observer platform. I was able to maintain that dreamy state for the rest of the day. Nobody felt the need to keep asking me if I was okay, or trying to engage in conversation with me. Yesterday's events were the perfect guise, and allowances were being made for me.

Later that evening, Pax once again escorted me to my room, and I *still* hadn't spoken to Tayo. I was relaxing on my bed in my pyjamas, mood lighting around the edge set to purple, re-reading the news article again and again, when Pax poked his head through the adjoining door.

"Aurora," he whispered, staring me dead in the eyes.

I kept my sideways glance on him as I replied in the same hushed voice, "What?"

"I'm bored," he whispered again, to which I smiled. I knew what that meant, so I shut off my Slate, and swung my legs off the bed. Pax grinned and disappeared back through the doorway.

When I entered his room, Pax was on his bed holding two takeaway drink cups.

"Peppermint hot chocolate?" He held out a cup.

He had propped up the duvet and pillows to face the display screen showing a stunning night-time landscape. Pouring from the centre of a deep velvety sky, the full moon bathed the rolling hills in soft ivory rays, illuminating the cheerfully swaying grass. Piercing the veil of blackness, not even the moon's mystical aura could extinguish the brilliant sparkle of celestial glitter.

I slowly took the hot chocolate from him as I spoke, "I didn't hear you leave the room."

"What kind of an Enforcer would I be if I couldn't be stealthy?" He shuffled into the duvet pile with his hot chocolate. "I thought it might help you sleep."

"Thank you," I said, getting comfy next to him. "Not just for this, but for everything."

"I promised to protect you, care for you, and never let anything come in between, remember?" He reached over and held up my hand, showing me my Promises ring.

"And I...you." My stomach swirled, realising for the first time I not only accepted my Promises to Pax, but I also meant them. I felt a strong desire to be closer to him, and I turned to read his expression. We held each other's eyes as we both tried to decipher each other's intentions. Testing the water, his hand came to my face. I pushed my cheek into his palm. His gentle touch was a new kind of contact. It wasn't a playful headlock; it wasn't a friendly hug—it was intentional affection. When his gaze lowered to my lips, I felt a warm rush in my cheeks. He leant forward.

"Ahem. Aurora," came Nanny Kimly's polite tone. "May I borrow you for a minute?"

"Sure!" I said, probably a little too overzealously, and I dashed to my room without so much as a backwards glance.

"I just want to check on your head," she explained, walking to my bed with her black first aid bag in hand.

"Oh, right."

"Unity not looking so bad now, huh?" she teased once I joined her.

"Shhh." I pointed at Pax through the wall, learning my lesson from that time Silliah spoke about Pax when he was next door. "How's it looking?" I changed the subject. I hadn't yet seen the injury underneath the plaster.

"The swelling has gone down. It's slightly purple, but the sterile strips are keeping the split closed. I'll be seeing you in the evenings for a few days."

"How long have you worked here for, Nanny Kimly?" I wasn't making sure she knew what she was doing—I had something else on my mind.

"Ooow, over thirty years now. I passed my Worths exam when I was sixteen and began working here the following year. I was about the age you are now, I'd say."

"I was wondering…if you remember my parents?" I blurted, unable to contain it anymore.

"Little Lady, you know it's disrespectful to bring up life before the institute."

"But, Nanny Kimly, is it though? Do you really think that?"

"That's enough, Aurora. It doesn't matter what I think. You have been lucky enough to be adopted by Seioh Boulderfell. Where would you be without him? He has seen to it that his children want for nothing. Now show some respect."

"Nanny, I'm not being disrespectful by talking about my birth parents."

"Aurora, this is the type of behaviour I expected from you when you were a child."

I knew when Nanny Kimly didn't mean what she said, and I could tell when her training was coming into play. When she spoke, her words and her face didn't seem to agree with each other.

"Please, Nanny Kimly?" I pushed.

Nanny Kimly looked off to the side and gave a subtle sigh. "I didn't look after Orin, but I was Averlynn's caregiver. Satisfied?"

"Yes. One day, I'm going to be discharged from this place, and then I'm going to come looking for you so you can tell me all about them."

"Are you now?" Her face softened. She leant over into my ear. "Will you be arm in arm with Paxton when you arrive?"

"Stop. You're so embarrassing!"

"Go on, go. Someone is waiting for you." Nanny Kimly stood up. "Hm, hold on." She touched the top of my head, seemingly trying to pick something out of my hair.

"What is it?" I asked as she came closer to inspect my head.

"A black hair."

She held it out for me to see. I crossed the room to get a better look in the wardrobe mirror. Nanny Kimly was right. I had a single black hair attached to my scalp, but the strange part was it was black from root to tip, as if it had been growing with the rest of my hair all this time.

"Maybe, because my hair is already white, I will go black instead of grey?"

"How strange." She touched her own greying fringe. "No, don't pull it ou—"

Too late. I had already plucked it from my head. I rubbed the stinging spot where the hair once grew and allowed the strand to float into the bin.

"I'm almost seventeen, Nanny Kimly. I'm not having grey—I mean *black* hair already."

When I returned to Pax's room, he had changed into his charcoal pyjamas, and he was lying feet crossed, staring at the nightscape.

"You do like to push your luck, don't you?" he said lightly. "I could hear you in there testing Nanny Kimly."

"Only when I know I can. She is the one person I've always been able to be myself around."

"I can tell you two are close. It's nice."

"I was asking her about my parents. I just found out about them from Tayo. Here, read this." I showed Pax the article on my Slate.

"Ahh. So this is what he was doing with your Slate earlier."

As he read, I watched the top of his head and concentrated on diffusing my guilty, blushing cheeks.

"Whoa, ex-Enforcers." He passed back my Slate. "It's no wonder you're such a natural. How are you feeling about it?"

"Yeah, I'm fine. Obviously, I wish they were still here, but it's nice knowing a bit about them."

"How did Tayo know about them?"

"He was there that night and tried to save me."

"*Tried*, yeah?"

I tripped up on Pax's weird response. "Err. Um. I guess he did save me, actually," I rambled. "I suppose I could have died that night, but I think he got me away just in—wait a minute…'*tried*, yeah?' What did that even mean?"

"Nothing."

I blinked at him as what I thought just happened sunk in. "Paxton Fortis, was that *jealousy*?" I nudged him with my elbow.

"No."

I sat up and thumped the pillow over his head, jabbing it a few times just like he had done to me the morning of TPG. "Good!" I called out in between jabs. "It better not have been."

Pax's reaction was fast, and before I knew what was happening, in one fell swoop, he pinned me with his body weight, trapping both my hands down with his knees. Straddling over me, he now hammered the pillow over my head.

"You really think so, do ya?" Pax only removed the pillow to speak. It came ploughing in the side of my face again after. A few punches later, he lifted it for his next sentence. "I thought you would have learnt by now," he shouted over my uncontrollable giggling. "You can't win."

I was a complete mess, hair sprawled across my face, stuck to the tears rolling down my cheeks. My attempt to lighten the mood had worked, but I couldn't believe I had allowed myself to get caught in such a compromising position. My only option was to propel his body over the top of my head, but that would mean hurting him, and he knew I wasn't going to do that.

"Wait! Is my plaster coming off?" I tried to ruse him.

"It ain't." He didn't fall for it.

"I'm sorry!" I tried something else.

"I know."

"I give up! I won't do it again." I kept trying.

Pax stopped biffing up the pillow and gave my neck a playful warning bite to end the fight. The instant I felt the pressure of his teeth on my neck, electricity flew around my body. My laughing ceased, and the instinct of filling my lungs with air was replaced by another.

Pax felt it, too. When I turned my head and swept away my messy hair, he checked my eyes, and then his lips came down to mine. Pax's mouth touched my mouth. For a brief moment I felt unvirtuous, but soon my fingertips longed for his warm skin. They travelled up under his cotton shirt and stroked the contours of his shoulder blades. I had never touched him in this way before, and in that moment, I realised how hard this was going to be.

Controlling my hips from pushing up against him, I pulled back and bit my bottom lip, our eyes still closed and our foreheads touching. We breathed deeply, both trying to extinguish the flames burning inside us. I opened my eyes first; his face mirrored my same pained expression.

When he opened his eyes, panic suffocated them and his face mutated with horror. "Erh!" He threw himself off me, pushing up against the display screen. "Your skin, it's...*glowing*."

I looked down to see my arms shining with the whitest of lights—and not in a radiant first-kiss kind of way. Then, just like that, my skin had a power cut and the lights went out.

"Yur-yur-you're *Puracordis*?" He backed away from me.

"What? NO! No, I'm not," I insisted, wounded by the hurtful allegation. "It has to be the radiation poisoning."

"You really expect me to believe that? This is real life, Aurora, not one of those old comic book things. Look, I'm not going to tell anybody, just stay away from me, okay?"

I could hear the fear behind his words.

"No, Pax, wait," I yelled as he backed away towards the door. "Pax!"

"Get out." His hand hovered over the access button, ready if he needed to exit.

"Pax, *please*." My throat strained to find my voice.

"Maleficium is dangerous, Aurora, not to mention illegal. It is punishable by death, with harsh penalties for anyone found encouraging it. I want nothing to do with it. I am not having a family reunion in Maximum Security. How dare you jeopardise my life like that."

"But, Pax," I said helplessly, not knowing what to say to make it right.

"No. I'm seeing Lady Merla Liddicott in the morning to see how I can end the betrothal. I will keep your secret, Aurora. Just stay the hell away from me."

CHAPTER ELEVEN

I AM

Knowing my presence only aggravated matters, I retreated into my room. As soon as I passed over the threshold, Pax pounded the access button, concealing me behind the interconnecting door as if I were a flea-ridden animal.

I slid down the door as my agonising cry broke into wheezy inhales and silent exhales. My mouth contorted in a gape as it tried to release the storm cloud building in my strangled airways. The raw pain from my shattered heart stabbed me in the chest with every pulse. My eyes were open, yet I could not see. I struggled to rationalise with the war raging in my mind. The one person I wanted to hold me right now was the same person who had done this to me.

The forceful tears came periodically throughout the night. I finally came away from the adjoining door and crawled into bed. The smell of Pax on my sheets crushed my throat, and the pillow stifled my broken wail. Last night he had selflessly lain with me, and tonight I had lost him.

When I woke, for a brief second, I had forgotten: a cruel trick played on me by my unconscious self. Pax was in the shower but my lights were still off; the alarm was yet to ring. Was his night as sleepless as mine? I lay unmoving on my front, head to the side, holding on to my pillow, staring through the darkness towards Pax's room, listening, until I heard him leave—to find Lady Liddicott, no doubt.

Before I opened Tayo's cell door, I thought I was going to be fine, but as soon as I entered, I lost all inhibition. The tears fell, and I stopped trying to hold them in. I had waited all day yesterday to speak to Tayo, and I wanted this conversation to go differently.

"I've ruined everything. He's never going to speak to me again. He thinks I'm Puracordis but—"

"Hey, Roar, slow down."

In my hysteria, I couldn't hear him, and I continued pacing blindly, flailing my arms. "—I'm not, I swear it. But he thinks I am. It must be the radiation poisoning. It's the—"

"Roar."

"—only explanation. Sir Praeter said it no longer exists. But if he won't believe me, then who will? I'm going to be sentenced to death if anyone ever—"

"Aurora, *calm down*." Tayo tried to break through my sobbing.

"—finds out. Maleficium is illegal. It's dangerous—"

Tayo yanked me into the ensuite and held me into his chest. If he was going for shock tactics, it worked.

"There." Tayo was relieved by my calmness. "OK."

The reason I pulled away wasn't because Tayo was a Juvie. It was the guilt I felt from finding solace in his arms.

Tayo checked the coast was clear and reached out to guide me through the doorway. He led me between the shoulder blades to the empty surface. "Sit." He used his sleeve to dry my face, took a deep breath preparing himself, and lowered down onto the spare chair. "Now, start again. What happened?"

"I've ruined everything, Tayo. He thinks I'm Puracordis, and if he doesn't believe me, then nobody will."

"Who thinks you're Puracordis—Pax?"

"Yes. But I'm not! I can't be. I don't have any magic."

"Why would he think you're Puracordis?"

"Last night, my skin"—my stomach turned over at the memory—"it…"

"It what?"

"It was *disgusting*. It…it…" Why couldn't I say the word?

"It?" Tayo pressed.

"Glowed!"

"Aaaaay, alright. I don't want to know what you get up to in your spare time."

"Oh, I don't know why I bother with you."

"Alright, no, I'm sorry. What do you mean it '*glowed*'?"

"It was like I had a thousand volts of electricity running through me," I explained. Tayo's mouth twitched as he suppressed a smile. "Get your mind out of the gutters, Tayo. It's not an innuendo; I'm being serious."

But his shoulders didn't stop shaking. "If I had known we were having a sex ed class, I would have brought my banana." And there was that stupid laugh of his. "Actually, come to think of it, I know a better way. I don't need the banana."

"I'm done."

"No-no-no, don't leave me in here, Roar. Roar? Ma'am!"

On my way to the Food Hall, I hoped Pax was still with Lady Merla Liddicott so I could be in and out without running into him. The last thing I wanted was to see him with everyone around before I'd had the chance to try and fix things. I wasn't too worried about the meeting because, as far as I was aware, ending the betrothal was impossible. If it weren't, Unity would be a complete waste of time. Also, I'm pretty sure, if it were possible, Ryker and Pipila would no longer be united.

At first glance, Pax and the others were nowhere in sight. Claret Quartz was empty, and Navy Quartz, although busy, did not have a familiar face in it. But as I stepped through the archway, my guts fell through to the floor. Pax and the others were sitting by the meal dispenser in Khaki Quartz. I attempted a U-turn before anybody saw me.

"Aurora," called Hilly. "We're over here."

Oh, it would be YOU, wouldn't it? I rotated back around to check the seating from a distance. Silliah and Pax were opposite each other, and Hilly was next to Silliah. To the left of Pax was Pipila and the gang, to the right…my empty chair and the remainder of the Fanciable Four. I felt sick to my stomach.

"Pax decided he wanted to sit here today," explained Hilly.

Yeah, I said to myself. *He was probably trying to get away from me.*

As I slowly lowered myself down in the chair—that may as well have been covered with broken glass—Pax shuffled away to the outer rim of his seat and didn't look up from the tabletop screen.

"Trying something new?" asked Hilly.

"Hmm?" I hummed, uncertain if she was speaking to me. Did she mean breakfast? She probably still felt sorry for me being punished and was trying to undertake a motherly role.

"With your hair. Are you trying something new?" Hilly asked again.

What are you talking about? I looked to Silliah to see if she could help me out. She stared back with an expectant smile, waiting for my reply.

"The black streak," enlightened Hilly, stroking the front of my hair.

I tipped my head forward to see a small section of black hair fall into my face. *What the hell!* Even Pax peeled his eyes away from the screen to have a look.

"Oh, yeah. Just seeing if I like it," I lied.

"I like it," said Silliah. "You should definitely make the streak bigger."

"Come with us to the salon when we go," squealed Hilly. "Silliah, Tyga, and I are going next week."

"I'll see if I like it first." I double-tapped my tabletop screen, pretending to be busy and hoping she'd get the hint.

"What the hell are we doing in Khaki Quartz?" Brindan curled his lip as if we were sitting in clart. He stood behind Silliah and beckoned for her to move so he could take his usual spot opposite Pax.

"Pax wanted to sit here today," answered Hilly.

Actually, he was trying to avoid me.

"Mind, Silliah," Brindan ordered with a hint of irritation when she didn't respond to his previous tap on the shoulder.

"No," Silliah said with a nose laugh. She looked at me with an expression that I knew all too well. It meant *get a load of this guy.*

"Get up," he reiterated in disbelief.

"Here, Brindan, you can have my seat." Hilly moved to sit on the far side of Hyas.

"If I wanted to sit there," began Brindan. He slouched over Silliah and picked her up by her legs. "I would have done," he finished, carrying Silliah in a seated position and shifting her over onto Hilly's empty chair.

Silliah's eyes flared with astonishment. She stared at the side of Brindan's head as he took his trophy seat opposite Pax.

"Sort your friend out, Aurora." Brindan jerked his head towards Silliah.

"Pax, can you sort *your* friend out?" Silliah retaliated.

"What the hell are we doing in Khaki Quartz?" asked Ryker, looking around at the tables in the same way Brindan did.

HE WAS TRYING TO AVOID ME.

Ryker placed a hand on Silliah and Brindan's shoulders. "Loving the hair, Aurora."

I returned a wry smile.

"What's wrong with you two?" His eyes regarded Pax and me. How could he tell something was up? Nobody else had said anything. "You both look like you've been up all night."

Well, I know I had, and evidently Pax had too. I really wanted to speak to him. It didn't need to be like this.

"I'm not feeling great," Pax replied, getting to his feet. "I'll see you lot later."

My body seized as I tried to quash the agony. Staring down at nothing, I attempted to appear natural whilst I coped with the wrath of Pax's coldness. But I knew I failed miserably to anybody paying attention. I checked around swiftly, catching only Ryker's eye. He flashed an eyebrow lift before I urgently broke his gaze.

After breakfast, most of us were scheduled for the weekly Show of Force Display. This morning it was for the benefit of the working class arriving to work at the earliest time possible in order to earn the maximum amount of Worths. Those on a higher Banding could afford the extra hour in bed.

In the EU Changing Facility, Navies were busy being dressed into their Enforcer Uniforms. The EU allowed us to hear each other digitally, but this clever technology imitated the way our ears worked by considering things like distance and volume. We could mute ourselves so nobody could hear us, and we could mute certain people whom we didn't want to hear. It was also possible to specifically select those whom you wanted to converse with, a bit like a group phone call.

I searched the room, scanning between both exits and all the plinths in between, looking for Pax. Assuming he managed to elude me already, I stepped up onto a plinth to be dressed—once in a uniform I would be able to see him on my picoplant tracker. The plinth under my feet lit up an ice blue, and a device lowered from the ceiling, suiting me up. I switched on my computer.

No Pax on my tracker. He must have made it outside already. We were to be marching alongside each other during the show, so he couldn't avoid me for long. I grabbed my taser gun off the rack ejected out of the wall and held the chunky white weapon across my chest. Out in the city, I took my position next to Pax in a row of four and initiated a private chat.

"Pax?" I waited apprehensively.

The silence, the absence of his voice, spoke volumes. *Have you really muted me?*

Then I heard a cold sigh. "What is it, Aurora?" His tone was hard and dispirited, empty, like his soul had been sucked out of him.

"Pax, you have to believe me. I'm not Puracordis, I swear."

"Look, Aurora, I believe you didn't try to keep it from me, but how do you know you're not?"

"Er…I…uh…" I croaked, unable to answer. "I'm just not!"

The stationary marching began but I wasn't moving. The squad turned right, and Pax bumped into my body. He grabbed my shoulders and turned me round, pushing me forward with the side of his gun in my back. I joined the march, stomping my feet in a steady rhythm.

"Has it not occurred to you," said Pax, "that Seioh Boulderfell could have spared your parents' reputation, and released a cover story on your parents' death?"

"What are you saying?"

"I'm saying, how do you *know* you're not Puracordis?"

"I…don't," I slowly admitted. I knew nothing about my parents, nothing about where I came from.

"Exactly."

"But, Pax—"

"I'm going now, Aurora."

"No, wait. Please don't mute me. I can't not talk to you."

The marching swallowed my plea.

"Pax?"

Still nothing.

"No, Pax, please. Can you hear me?" I asked the silence, realising how serious Pax was on not wanting anything to do with me.

"I don't want to mute you, Aurora. Don't make me have to."

My chest cramped. He was unfaltering with his decision, heart-obliterating, soul-crushingly unfaltering, and I was going to have to leave him alone.

⚙

After an incredibly slow morning, I decided to give Tayo another chance at lunch.

"You know I hate it when you leave me in here," he sulked, sitting up on his elbow when I entered his cell.

"Well stop being such a jackass, then."

Tayo huffed, threw himself backwards into the mattress, and stared up at the ceiling.

"Tayo, I fou—"

"I'm not talking to you," he cut me off.

"You're such a child," I said with a laugh, moving to lean back on the counter.

Tayo couldn't help but smile. "What?" He feigned enmity, turning his head to look at me.

"I found the article about my parents."

"You did," he responded rhetorically.

"Yeah, I did. Tayo, I was wondering…" I stopped, thinking carefully about whether I wanted to ask the question.

"Yes?"

"Do you think it was radiation poisoning that killed my parents?" I forced myself out with the question.

Looking at the ceiling, Tayo scrunched up his face and took a deep inhale through his nose. He leaned up on his elbow with a grimace.

Oh no. He doesn't. Pax was right on it being a cover up. "What?" I began to panic.

Tayo sucked air in through his teeth. "If you want, I can show you something."

Without question, I reached into my pocket for my Slate. I needed to know what he knew.

"No," he said. "Not on that."

"What do you mean?" I asked, fingers poised around my Slate.

He swung his legs off the bed and leant on his knees, fingers knitted. "I mean *actually* show you something—outside."

"Outside? In the institute?"

Tayo shook his head. "Outside in the woodlands."

"*What?* How on earth are we supposed to do that?"

"Do you have Curfew Duty tonight?"

"No."

"Good, because now *we* do." He tightened his linked fingers, stretched his arms out, and cracked his knuckles backwards.

"*Pfft.* No way, Tayo! Are you mad? If we get caught doing that…" I quite literally shuddered at the thought.

"We won't get caught. All I need is your bracelet."

"What is it you're even going to show me?"

"So I am going to show you it, then?"

"I didn't say that."

"The night your parents died, your father came up through a trapdoor."

"Hm."

"A few days later, I went looking for it. What I found—well, let's just say, with the exception of that night when I was six, I don't get caught breaking Curfew unless I *want* to be caught breaking Curfew."

"What does that even mean? You're a Juvie, Tayo. You got caught breaking Curfew."

"Exactly my point."

"Tut, can you stop talking in riddles, and just tell me?" I said, crossing my arms.

"From the moment I found that trapdoor, I planned the day I would meet you again. It's no coincidence that I'm your Juvie, Roar."

I rubbed my face hard, kneading my forehead, pulling my cheeks down, and then round to my temples. Holding firmly on to my temples, I looked at him and finally said, "Are you saying you got caught on purpose?"

"Of course I did. I had your bracelet that blocked my picoplant. How could I get caught whilst I had that?"

"How did you know I would be allocated you?" I tried to find holes in his story.

"Because I allocated myself to you."

"How?" I asked impatiently.

"The same way I reprogrammed Pipila's ankle traps when we were kids—I did my research. I learnt what I had to do to become an employee for Fellcorp. I studied hard to become Band A and land myself a position as a programmer. My job is to design, maintain, and upgrade all the software used to run this place."

"You did all that just to meet me?"

"My whole life I've spent planning the day I would meet you again. And it's all down to what I found under that trapdoor. So, what do you say? Worth the risk? Are we going out to play tonight? It'll be like old times."

"You're sick."

"Oh, I know. See you at seven?"

"Curfew starts at twenty hundred hours."

"Yeah, but dinner starts at *nineteen* hundred hours, and if you think you're leaving me in here again, you'll never find out what's under that trapdoor."

"Are you trying to blackmail me?"

Tayo got up off the bed and leant over into my ear suggestively. "If I were going to blackmail you, it would be for far more than just dinner duty."

"You're disgusting, Tayo," I said, laughing and pushing him away from my ear by his mouth. The dirty filth licked my hand. "*Ergh.*" I held my hand out in front of me. "There's something seriously wrong with you." And I wiped the saliva down his claret overalls.

⁂

The rest of that day was spent trying to cope with the anxiety. I hadn't completely decided if I was going to do it yet, but a part of me deep inside knew I really needed to.

The whole time in the Khakidemy, I used a machine called the Logician, an augreal (the same chairs used in History) that took you through a series of escape challenges. My choice of machine served two purposes—the first, keeping away from Pax, and the second, training in logic just in case I needed it later during Tayo's Lunatics Picnic in the woods.

"So, are we doing this?" Tayo asked when we returned to his cell after dinner.

"How are we going to do it without getting caught?"

"OK. So, I need you to get me an Enforcer Uniform. They still fold into themselves, right?"

"Yeah, down to a compact carry case."

"Would you look odd carrying one down this corridor?"

"Yes! I would look odd carrying one, full stop. Unless it's after Curfew Duty. If your whole plan counted on that, then we might as well stop while we're ahead."

"Relax, Roar, it doesn't. Pass me your Slate. I'm going to reprogram your picoplant so the plinth doesn't detect it's you."

"Reprogram it?" I leaned away from him slightly.

"I'm just changing your ID number to one I've already registered in the system. The machine won't issue you two suits, so if I don't change it, when you get a suit for me, it won't release another when you go for yours."

"I'm not sure about this, Tayo."

"It's seven fifteen, so the EU Changing Facility will be empty. All you need to do is get the suit before Pax drops Beth and Mai back to their cell. You won't be out of place walking in an EU. You'll just look keen and ready for duty. Just make sure the coast is clear before you walk back in here. You *can* do this, Roar."

"I don't know..."

"Take it one step at a time. Get the suit and come back here. If you change your mind, just take the suit back."

"Ummmh," I moaned, hesitantly handing over my Slate.

He took it, giving a reassuring nod.

Tayo was right; the EU Changing Facility was clear when I got there. I stepped up onto a plinth, ready for the suit to unfold itself around me. When I arrived back down Tayo's corridor, Pax walked my way, chaperoning Beth and Mai. With my shattered heart bursting out of my chest, I slowed down so he reached the Davoren Sisters' cell first. I didn't know what else to do. Tayo said he needed the suit before Pax arrived. *Is the plan foiled? Maybe I should turn back.* Before I had a chance to, Pax exited the sisters' cell, so I had to continue walking towards him. Fortunately, Pax didn't bat an eyelid, his mind being elsewhere, and then he was gone.

"Nice one, Roar," said Tayo, holding up a high five.

I ignored it and dropped my visor. "Pax has already dropped the Davoren Sisters back to J-16."

"Did he see you?" Tayo's high five closed to a fist.

"Yes!"

"Did he suspect anything?"

"No, I don't think so. He didn't even know it was me."

"That's fine, then." Tayo paused to think. "Better, in fact. We couldn't wait for Pax to drop the girls off first because we didn't know how long he was going to be and the EU Changing Facility would've had people in there. And obviously we didn't want him to see you walk back in here. But if he's gone and didn't suspect anything, then the rest of the plan will be easy."

"He will probably be in his room for the rest of the night now," I added, feeling calm enough to continue the plan and release the EU. Its components began retracting into itself, forming a compact rectangular carry case.

"Exactly—out of the way. That's the hard part done, Roar. Now you can get your suit with no trouble. Pass me your wrist."

It felt so surreal having Tayo scan *my* wrist. He reset the ID back to mine, and then turned the Slate on to his tattooed arm.

"That's not your picoplant wrist." I watched him scan the wrong arm.

"I've got a device in this arm. It's basically like a picoplant but not quite. It allows me to do everything my picoplant does when it's blocked by your bracelet, but it's untraceable. I need to activate it so I have full use of the EU's features."

Tayo came and took hold of my hand. My reflex reaction of avoiding his touch had completely vanished. For the first time I trusted him implicitly. I had to; my life was in his hands. Before removing my bracelet he held my gaze for a moment first. I think he became aware of his newly acquired trust.

Real picoplant blocked, he stood in front of the carry case, suiting himself up, and I handed him the taser gun. What dream was I in? Tayo stood before me in an Enforcer Uniform; this evening was getting weird.

"Check the coast is clear, and we can go for yours. I'll follow a few paces behind until you're dressed."

Once I dressed in my EU, we could now walk side by side without attracting any attention. Tayo was right about the hard part being over, and I began easing into the plan.

"Hey, beautiful." Tayo initiated a private chat.

"No, Tayo. Just no."

"There's no escaping me now. I'm right in your ear."

"I *can* mute you, Tayo."

"As if you would."

We exited out of Claret Quartz and rounded on reception. We were allowed out thirty minutes before Curfew started to give ourselves a head start putting distance between us and the institute. By twenty hundred hours the city had to be empty, and any stragglers were likely to be away from the centre, nearing their homes. These were our targets.

The Claret receptionist pressed the access button to allow us out. Everything was going smoothly, and I had the impression Tayo gave this plan a lot of thought.

"Hold the door," called a voice from behind us.

A cold chill slithered down my spine. "Tayo, that's Ryker!"

"It'll be fine," Tayo replied, unfazed.

"You two are eager today," said Ryker, catching up with us. "We're getting a head start, too. The further out you are, the more chance you have of catching one."

"We actually just enjoy being outside," I said, sorrow permeating my entire being wondering what Curfew Duty would be like now with Pax hating me.

"Oh, it's you two," said Ryker.

Out in the city, Tayo and I turned in the opposite direction to them both.

"Oh, I see how it is. You don't want to share the glory. May the best team win! *Serve, Honour, Protect, and Defend*," he yelled, quickening his pace and turning on his tracker. "Hold on a minute, Pax," he called out, walking away backwards. "Your picoplant is defective. You best go get that seen to."

"Yep. Good. Cheers, mate," said Tayo, giving Ryker a sarky thumbs-up.

"*Tayo.*" I switched to our private chat, watching Ryker creep away still looking back at us over his shoulder.

"What? The dude's a prick."

"You idiot! Firstly, do you mind not swearing in front of me? And secondly, you're supposed to be *Pax*. If Ryker suspects anything, we're done for. Oh god, what am I doing?"

"*Firstly*, are you really that precious?" he sniped. "And secondly, see why I can't stand Youngens? It's human beings they're exploiting. Good people who are trying their best to get home on time. We are hunted like animals and branded criminals, all for not being able to get indoors by eight o'clock. Who is Boulderfell to dictate what time I'm allowed out of my house?"

"Venair's ruler?"

"*Says who*? I am perfectly capable of deciding for myself what's immoral. Who am I harming by being outside during the night? *And then* he raises his horde of untouchable spoilt brats to uphold his laws, and shoot young kids in the back for making them look stupid."

"Alright, Tayo," I said sensitively. "I can see where you're coming from."

"I'm sorry, I know it's not your fault you're a Youngen." Tayo sighed. "It's actually mine."

"No it's not. Why would you say that?"

"If I'd have gotten you to safety when you were a baby, then things would've been different."

"Stop being so hard on yourself. Preventing a child from being raised in the institute is frowned upon. My parents died, adoption is contemptible, and being raised in the institute was inevitable."

"I just wish things could have been different, that's all."

When we reached the woodlands, we'd lost most of the sunlight to the canopy of leaves. Tayo picked up a path suffused with young, vibrant bluebells. The rich, earthy scent infused my helmet and soon subtle almond tones accompanied it. Then an orchard of blooming

Japanese apricot trees came into view. Masses of dainty pink flowers reclaimed the overhead space. Although Pax and I wandered the woodlands often, we had never ventured in so far. I had no idea of the ethereal beauty hidden deep within its depths.

"Wow, this place is beautiful," I said, gently touching a star-shaped flower.

"It's a bit longer this way, but I thought you would like it."

"I do."

"Come on, this way."

The common plant life returned, and we lost sight of the trail as we waded through stinging nettles up to my waist. I felt like I navigated through the remote outback, so far removed from the scenic woodlands I'd enjoyed earlier. This place hadn't been inhabited for years.

We arrived at a barrier of steel palisade fencing with sharp triple-pointed tops. *Danger of Death* signs hung on the fencing ominously, warning us at evenly spaced intervals. I held on to the fence posts with both hands, peering through to the other side. My armoured gloves didn't grip on to the 'W' profile well, and I wondered how we were going to get over the three-metre high spikes.

"Go on, over you go." Tayo bent down, holding his linked gloves out at knee height.

"*What*?"

Tayo laughed and unlinked his hands. "I'm just kidding," he said, giving the fence a tug. A five-post-wide gate swung open, flattening the overgrowth on the other side.

"You amaze me sometimes, Tayo. In more ways than one."

"Took me every night for a month to make this. I used to have a tunnel under it when I was really small, but they discovered it and filled it in. I'm guessing they thought it was a foxhole or something since it was so little, and luckily, I didn't arouse suspicion."

"I'm surprised it's not electric."

"Why? The fear of death from radiation poisoning not enough for you, Miss Aviary?"

"Miss Aviary?"

Tayo closed the gate behind me and continued on as if I never said anything. A short way in, I made out a house in the distance. I could see two floors and a lot of windows. A large white curved roof met the ground, covering the building like a flexed strip of plastic.

"Is this...my old house?" I asked, the thought just occurring to me.

"It is. You okay?"

I didn't answer. Truthfully, I wasn't, and I hadn't prepared myself for the reminder of my past life. I didn't exactly remember my parents, but I remembered what it felt like to be with them, and I knew I missed them.

"We are not going by the house, Roar. The trapdoor is over this way." Tayo began talking to ease the pressure so I didn't have to pretend I was okay. "My house is not far from here," he said, gazing out into the distance. "The houses in this part are expensive. People pay to be surrounded by nature. The land is pretty much free to roam, and there aren't any fences sectioning off gardens or separating neighbours.

"See the large window on the roof? That's how I used to break Curfew when I was a kid. As a teenager I'd just walk out the front door, but as a kid I used to climb out of my bedroom window and slide down the roof."

Tayo stopped and began feeling the ground with his foot. He turned to me and lifted his visor. Tayo's piercing-blue eyes awakened the memories inside me; this was the spot we both stood hand in hand thirteen years ago. It was the last time I ever saw my dad. 'Go with Tayo. Mummy and Daddy will be right behind you.'

Without saying anything, Tayo reached down and pulled up the perfectly concealed entrance. Inside it was pitch black, but the EU allowed me to see down a steep spiral staircase. As my head disappeared underground, the staircase straightened out, and with it, the smell of dirt grew weaker. Stranger still, the deeper I descended, the clearer the air felt to breathe.

Tayo pulled out a torch from under a step. He lit up the way, so I removed my visor. We had reached a dark, dank tunnel, and I could just about see the dead-end. The walls were narrow and the ceiling curved, giving me the impression we stood in an unused pipe.

"You've brought me down to see a…pipe?" I outwardly expressed the huge anti-climax.

Tayo sighed and looked up and down the tunnel. He carried on walking towards the dead-end, feeling the wall as if he were looking for something. Then he took off the EU and, with his head in his hands, slid down the wall.

"Tayo? What are we doing down here?" I asked. "Please tell me this wasn't a ploy to get out of the institute."

"Aurora, I wouldn't do that to you."

"Then what are we doing down here?"

He lifted his head out from his hands. "Do you trust me?"

"Less and less by the minute, Tayo."

"Suit down."

"Huh?"

"Take off the suit."

"You are unbelievable, Tayo. What the hell am I doing down here?"

"Please, Roar. Just try it."

Out of sheer exasperation, I released the suit. It clinked as it retracted into itself, coming to lay on the ground in a small carry case.

Bright rays spread outward from my entire body. At the same time, the pipe burst into life. A network of tunnels appeared around me, and the dead-end transformed into a magnificent door. The wave of panic drenched my veins as I anticipated Tayo's horrified reaction.

I was going to lose them both in less than twenty-four hours and I couldn't handle it.

Tayo stood up from his pit of despair and pulled me into his body just like he'd done this morning. "Come here, don't look so worried, Roar." He exhaled on the top of my head.

"You're not scared?"

"No, I'm not scared," he said gently into my hair.

"Oh, Tayo, I am."

CHAPTER TWELVE

TRAINED IN NINJA

What was happening to me? Descendants of the Puracordis Civilisation had been eradicated, and maleficium was said to no longer exist. Moreover, we always joked about it as if it were myth; nobody really believed it ever existed. Who *were* my parents? Both raised in the institute, so possibly orphans. Were they killed for using maleficium?

"What am I, Tayo?" I backed away in fear of hurting him.

"Hey, stop it." He edged closer.

"I'm dangerous, Tayo. Stay away from me."

"You couldn't keep me away from you before; what makes you think you can keep me away from you now? Hmm? Now, calm down."

"I can't control it. I don't even know if I can hide it. What if I hurt somebody?"

"Roar, we will learn. I will help you, whatever it takes."

"How did you know bringing me down here would...do *this*?"

"I didn't know for sure. I just hoped. The first time I came down here, the door was there, and then a few days later it was gone. Come, let me show you." Tayo walked me to the once dead-end.

No longer blocked by a concrete wall, the bottom of the tunnel had turned into an intricately ornamented door. Beautiful golden motifs decorated a red inlay. In the centre of the double doors, a golden tree trunk reached its branches outward around the frame.

At first glance, the branches appeared to be ladened with leaves, but after closer inspection, an array of picture carvings came to light. The more I looked, the more I saw: animals, hands, eyes, stars, spirals, and more, all fashioned the glorious allure.

"When that nanny—"

"Nanny Kimly," I interrupted.

"Whatever. When she took you away, you held your hand out to me." Tayo took hold of my hand and pulled up my jacket sleeve. "This is how I knew to bring you down here." He stroked my birthmark with his thumb. "I saw this." Then Tayo showed me one particular carving among the many—one of my birthmark.

I responded with an unintentional inhale. "No! Oh no, Tayo."

"I know." He pushed his lips together. "Crazy Kalmayan Kid."

"He knows!"

"Beware the angel with the devil's mark."

"It's a bit melodramatic—*devil's mark*?"

"They are overly dramatic, though, aren't they? With all their facial tattoos and shaved heads." He pulled my sleeve back over my birthmark. "We have some time before he is released to figure out what we are going to do."

"This isn't your problem, Tayo. Why burden yourself?"

"I don't know. You grew on me. If you were like the rest of the stiffs in the institute, maybe I wouldn't, but you're different." He shuffled from foot to foot. "I couldn't save you before. Maybe I can save you now."

I wandered around the pipe aimlessly, not really looking at anything, my attention taken by my thoughts. I needed to learn how to control myself, and fast. "You knew about me all this time?"

"I had my suspicions. I was intrigued more than anything: a three-year-old with a bracelet that blocked their picoplant; a cover up on the parents' death; your birthmark in these carvings; and all this disappearing days later."

"Do you know where all these tunnels lead?"

"No, there was only one tunnel here before."

"And the other side of this door?"

"Nope. I was hoping you could open it," he said, looking up at the impressive door, following the curved architrave with his eyes.

I placed my hand on the door and ran my fingers over the tree trunk. I pushed the edges, and probed for any hidden handles, but I came up empty handed. "Maybe when I learn how to make my skin do that *thing* it does?"

"No rush. I've got nine more months of doing nothing. Talking of which, ready to go back?"

"Oh. Yes."

"No diversions on the way home. We haven't got long."

When we climbed up through the trapdoor, darkness had descended. We power-walked our way out of the creepy woods, and once in the city, I inspected my picoplant tracker. White dots advanced on the institute from all directions; we were tailing right at the back.

"If we do this again, there's a glass fountain I want to show you not far from here," said Tayo, looking over his right shoulder.

"Can I be honest with you?" I interjected.

"Knowing you're Puracordis not proof enough for you? You need further convincing?" He tilted his head in my direction.

"No. Alright. I'll be honest with you—"

"I think I know what you are going to say," Tayo cut back in.

"I really don't think you do."

"Your drea—I mean, memory?" he mocked.

"OK. You do know what I am going to say. I thought you'd think more on the lines of *I'm never doing this again*, but anyway, I wouldn't remember anything if it wasn't for that recurring dream."

"Good to know you've been dreaming about me your whole life."

"I've been dreaming about a six-year-old boy, Tayo." I backhanded his EU with my glove. "In the dream, I see you staring up at a glass fountain before Enforcers come out of the institute."

"Yeah, that's what happened that night."

"How do I know that?"

"I've always felt something bigger was at play, something supernatural. Your father pushed up the trapdoor right under my feet, right where I stood. It's too coincidental."

I nodded in agreeance.

"Well, so far," Tayo continued, "it seems your powers consist of shining like a beacon and psychic dreams. Is there anything else that's happened in your life that you can't explain?"

"I don't think so." I tried to think on the spot. "When I was a kid, I was amused by my history instructor sitting in his chair. When I thought about how much funnier it would be if the lights flickered, they started to. But that's weak and probably just a coincidence."

"Well, we'll have to see if your magic is powered by thought."

"This black streak in my hair is weird, too."

"I've heard stress can do that, and you were really beside yourself this morning."

"I guess so...but overnight?"

"I don't know," he admitted.

As we neared the Claret reception, I felt a mixture of emotion, sadness at seeing an end to our excursion but also apprehension about getting Tayo out of his EU.

"How are we doing this, Tayo?"

"Right," he said slowly. "We have two chances to do this without getting caught. We pass by the detention centre, and if I can duck into my cell without anyone seeing, then I'll hide the suit until you can take it back. If we don't manage that, then we need to go into the EU Changing Facility together and pray it's empty."

"Are you kidding me? You had this whole plan worked out, and you're leaving the last, *most vital* part down to chance?"

"Mmm, I was just pleased you didn't ask me *before* we left the institute."

"*Ghurrr*, Tayo." I clenched my fists.

We made it to the reception and waited for the doors to be opened. "Come on, quickly," complained the receptionist. "You're late."

"Sorry, ma'am," we replied.

There was an entrance to Claret Quartz on either side of the reception desk, and Tayo promptly opened the west one. As we were on our way in, Navies were on their way out. But so far so good; there was nothing out of the ordinary to pique anyone's interest. The most unusual thing would probably be walking down Tayo's corridor still wearing our EUs instead of holding them.

I held my breath as Tayo's cell approached. We walked a clear corridor, and this part seemed to be going as smoothly as the rest of the plan. Tayo should be able to duck into his cell without detection. We were almost at J-14 when I heard the sound of a door sliding. A Second-year boy appeared a few cells ahead. I released my breath forcefully. We were going to have to try the Changing Facility. After passing the Second-year, I turned to give Tayo a disapproving look— not that he would have been able to see it through my visor, but he should know it wasn't good. But I ended up turning a full circle— Tayo was gone! The Second-year looked over his shoulder at me, and then peered into the Davoren Sisters' window. Seeing nothing out of the ordinary, he moved across to Tayo's window. We were done for. Tayo clearly entered his cell in eyeshot of this Navy.

Or so I thought. The Second-year scratched his head and continued on down the corridor. He didn't know what he saw, but that was too close. *I swear to god, the next time I see Tayo, he is not going to know what hit him.*

When I got to my bedroom, it didn't surprise me to see the interconnecting door closed. I had never wanted Pax so badly. Twenty-four hours without him (when we were usually in each other's pockets) had been really tough. I missed him so much; I missed him poking his head around the door when he was bored; I missed him pulling me into a headlock whenever he felt like it; and most of all, I missed how he made me feel whenever we were alone. I sat for a while, with my legs crossed, in front of the adjoining door, spinning my Promises ring around on my finger. A small cough from Pax pinched at my heart. It was distressing how emotional pain could be felt as physical pain.

That night, I had a dream like no other. It was as vivid as my recurring dream, and it left me wondering if it was another so-called psychic dream. In it I stood in an impressive room of colossal proportions, a room that could only be defined as a sacred space— such monumental architecture would only be for such a place. In the body of the room, an alley of white marble columns supported the highly decorated ceiling. Red, gold, and symmetry were a running theme, with coves around the high ceiling, and everything covered in carvings with a distinct similarity to the ones found on that door from last night.

I was drawn up a wide white-quartz walkway with golden trim, towards a deep-brown mahogany lectern. Perched on the slanted top was a large leather-bound book. It appeared antique but wasn't worn; its layers of embossed detailing were well cared for. Inset on the front, in the centre of an oval, was a brass embellishment of my birthmark. My fingers clutched around the hard-backed cover, and as I hauled it open, a blinding ray of light poured from its pages—and then I was awoken by Soami.

"Good morning, Miss Aviary. You have a last-minute alteration to your schedule today."

"What's the time?" I grumbled at her, perplexed by the pre-alarm wake-up call.

"Zero four thirty hours, Miss Aviary."

"Why are you waking me up?"

"Seioh Jennson requests an audience with Paxton and yourself at zero five thirty hours. He would like you down at breakfast before you attend this meeting."

Just then, there was a knock at the interconnecting door. If my internal organs weren't already in my throat, they were now.

"Come in." I tried to sound relaxed. In actuality, I was terrified of seeing him.

"Soami, lights on," ordered Pax. The bright lights switched themselves on at once. Pax stood by the corner sofa in his crumpled charcoal pyjamas, his blond-brown curls flattened against his forehead. I tried to tidy my own bedhead as I squinted through the dazzling room at him. "Morning." He brushed through the polite niceties. "Did you get that message from Soami?"

"Yeah, a meeting with Seioh Jennson."

"Any ideas?"

"Not a clue."

"Tut." He forcefully pushed air out through his nostrils. "Alright."

The feeling in my stomach promptly turned to annoyance at Pax's rudeness.

"Sorry, Aurora. I think this might have something to do with my visit with Lady Merla Liddicott yesterday."

My anger dispersed at his admission. I nodded quickly, stuck for words. He had actually gone to break the betrothal. My eyes blurred from the water building in them. "Alright, well, I need to get dressed," I prompted for him to leave.

"Sure. Sorry." He disappeared back in his room, closing the door behind him.

I let the tear fall from my eye. Without drying my face, I forced myself to get ready. It took me a while because I felt so drained, and I didn't expect it when I arrived at the Food Hall first. The empty room hummed from the stillness, and I took a seat in Claret Quartz. I don't know why I held my breath when Pax walked under the archway. I secretly waited in anticipation for Pax to choose a table. *Please sit with me.*

But Pax sat alone at a table in Navy Quartz. Every inch of me wanted to try and reach out to him, convince him I wasn't dangerous, but it was a pledge I couldn't know to be true, so I left him to eat in peace.

At zero five thirty hours, Pax and I waited outside Seioh Jennson's office to be called through. The occasional sound from doors opening made me observe the floor panels whilst I waited for boots to pass through my periphery. I wouldn't describe Seioh Jennson's invitation into his office as welcomed, but that air in the corridor was starting to feel thick.

Pax and I stood to attention in front of the black wheelie chairs waiting for permission to sit down.

"Sit." Seioh Jennson took a deep breath, knitted his fingers together, and surveyed us both with an unnerving expression. "I trust you both slept well?"

"Yes, Seioh," we lied.

"Now," he said, exhaling. "Are you aware you undertook an unauthorised Curfew Duty last night?"

Fear flooded my system so fast I almost brought up my breakfast. Pax opened and closed his mouth. Then his head turned slowly in my direction.

"It is not a difficult question, Mr. Fortis. Are you aware you undertook an unauthorised Curfew Duty last night?"

"No, Seioh." Pax peeled his eyes off me. "I was not aware *I* undertook an unauthorised Curfew Duty *last night*," he articulated each word with a lacerating clarity.

I felt the saliva thicken in the back of my throat. I swallowed hard, keeping my eyes locked forward.

"Are you aware that in doing so you committed an act of gross misconduct?"

Pax rubbed his eyes with his thumb and finger. "Yes…Seioh."

My body began trembling from the prolonged state of fight or flight.

"I trust, Mr. Fortis, you do not need to attend refresher training on the institute's code of conduct?"

"No, Seioh."

Seioh Jennson sniffed and rested his chin in his hand. "Without order, there is chaos, and without structure, there is instability. Carelessness will not be tolerated. Schedules must be adhered to for the safety of you and those around you. Do you understand?"

"Yes, Seioh," we replied.

"I'm putting you both on a restricted schedule for one week. No duties; no lessons; no training. I want you both maintaining the rooftop garden. I have also arranged for you to attend a daily counselling session with Lady Merla Liddicott, which is in regard to your enquiry yesterday.

"It has also been brought to my attention that, Paxton, your picoplant is defective, so I'm sending you to get it replaced immediately. If you can stay behind, I have arranged for you to be escorted to Vencen Hospital. That will be all from you, Aurora. You are dismissed."

I stood up reluctantly, not wanting to leave Pax alone in case he divulged all to Jennson whilst I was out of the room. I had resigned myself to the fact I was going to have to leave, but I paused by the open door where I had a thought. "Erm, Seioh, does that mean Juvie chaperone, too, or not?"

Pax closed his eyes. Clearly the answer was obvious, but it wasn't to me until just then.

"Is Juvie chaperone a duty?" Jennson responded.

"Yes, Seioh. Sorr—"

"And did I say no duties?" he interrupted me, instantly getting my back up.

"Yes, Seioh." I wasn't going to try and apologise again. He said nothing more, and dismissed me with a finger. *Oh, I have a finger I could dismiss you with, you…you lettuce.*

Later that day, whilst lying on my bed with Silliah, Pax arrived back from hospital. He came bulldozing through the adjoining door like a riled-up pitbull, his jacket slung over his shoulder, and his muscular abdomen just visible through his navy-blue vest. On his right arm, a bandage wrapped around his palm and wrist.

"If you two must do your duties together, can you at least wait until our schedules match up?" He unleashed the animal.

We both nodded briskly.

"Aurora, we have our meeting with Lady Liddicott."

I continued nodding.

Pax left the room as abruptly as he entered it.

"Do you think he realised he was shouting?" quipped a confounded Silliah. "And since when does he talk to you like that?"

"I deserved it," I admitted. The poor guy had his picoplant replaced for no reason, *and* he was now on a restricted schedule because of me.

"Trouble in paradise?" She raised a shapely eyebrow.

"Something like that."

"He doesn't believe the cheating rumours, does he?"

"Whoa—no. Nothing like that."

When I entered Lady Merla Liddicott's office, Pax already sat on the yellow sofa in the far corner. I scanned for Lady Liddicott but only Pax occupied the room, so I lowered myself down on the fuchsia-pink armchair and held the yellow cushion on my lap.

"Lady Liddicott has gone to get us a hot drink," said Pax. He sounded calmer than earlier, but I still sensed hostility.

"Umm…" I hesitated, not really feeling like I could speak my mind.

"I told her you don't like tea or coffee."

"Thank you."

"You need to tell Silliah to get her picoplant checked. Tell her to go in a few days so it's not obvious."

"You knew there was nothing wrong with your picoplant?"

"Yes, Aurora." His disappointment hung in the air. "What you and Silliah did last night was worse than gross misconduct. Do you realise how stupid that was?"

"I'm so sorry, Pax," I said, meaning it with every fibre of my being. Even though he hated me, he still covered for me.

"When are you going to learn that your actions have consequences?"

"I…I'm sorry," I whispered to hide the break in my voice.

"Just—" He stopped, giving a long sigh. "Just don't do it again."

The door slid open, and Lady Merla Liddicott wafted over holding two corrugated cardboard drink cups. She set them on the teal coffee table in front of the sofa.

"Good afternoon, Aurora." She stood over me expectantly. "So, unless you want to counsel Paxton and me, I think I'll have my chair."

"Oh." I shot up to my feet. I joined Pax on the sofa and gingerly sipped my…peppermint hot chocolate; Pax must have told her it was my favourite.

"Right then." Lady Liddicott settled down on her chair, placing a Fellcorp tablet on her lap. "I request that you both be honest and open in these meetings. Our methods are a little unorthodox but they are successful. I am an expert in psychology, and I am trained in the art of hearing what is not said. I've been doing this longer than the time you have both spent on this earth combined, and together we are going to remedy this situation.

"Paxton, when you were sixteen, you disclosed to Seioh Jennson that you had no interest participating in Unity and requested to be omitted. Naturally, you became a cause for concern subsequent to your match this year. So, you'd think it should come as no surprise to discover you wanted to end the betrothal. But it did come as a surprise.

"You see, I have orchestrated Promises Ceremonies for decades, and I have been witness to countless readings whereby the participants have dramatised for effect. I would say this to be the case for ninety-nine percent of the ceremonies. You two fell into the one percent."

Lady Merla Liddicott turned her tablet to face us and played our Promises Ceremony. I watched with a knot in my chest. I didn't know it then during the ceremony but I really would learn to love him in time. When the recording finished, I wiped a tear on the back of my finger before it had a chance to escape my eye. Pax sat with the arch of his bandaged hand covering his eyes.

"I'm going to give you two five minutes," said Lady Liddicott. She swiftly left the room.

"I can't do this, Aurora," Pax said faintly, keeping his eyes closed and holding the bridge of his nose. When he looked at me, his eyes were glassy.

"Then why are we doing this?" I shuffled closer to him.

"Don't." He flinched away.

Sensing his fear, I sat back in the corner of the sofa and remained there until Lady Merla Liddicott returned.

"I understand this is distressing for you both." Lady Liddicott arrived back to her chair. "However, we do need to continue. If at any time you need a break, just let me know, and I will leave the room.

"As I was saying before, it is a rare occurrence to be present at a ceremony such as yours, and this is reflected in the video's view count. Are you aware your ceremony is the most watched of this year? For many years, in fact."

We both shook our heads.

"Paxton, tell me, how did it feel watching that back?"

Pax gave a solemn shrug as he continued to trace his finger around the arm of the sofa.

"Your co-operation, please, Paxton."

"It's upsetting," Pax reluctantly obliged. "Because I care for Aurora; I just don't want to be betrothed."

"Would it hurt you if Aurora was betrothed to another?"

"Yes."

"Thank you for your honesty." She turned to me and commented on the tears streaming down my cheeks. "Aurora, I can see you are upset."

Her words alerted Pax, making him look up from his finger drawing. "Can we take a break?" he asked, impatience colouring his tone.

"Of course," Liddicott replied, promptly leaving the room.

"Hey." Pax came and enveloped my body. "Aurora, come on."

I heard the pain behind his voice. I buried my head into his shoulder to hide my face. A sterile scent from the hospital tainted his familiar natural smell. We didn't speak, but the gentle stroking on the back of my head soothed me, until Lady Liddicott returned.

"Can we finish up for today, please, ma'am?" Pax requested somewhat forcefully.

"Usually, as part of the process, it is not permitted, but yes. We will resume tomorrow at fifteen hundred hours."

⚅

On day two of our rehabilitation-slash-punishment, Seioh Jennson and Lady Merla Liddicott met Pax and me on the rooftop garden. The glass roof still covered the garden, but that was the extent of resemblance to the last time I stepped on it. The early morning sunlight gently awoke the city, and its birth imbued me with a sense of new beginnings. Even though Pax and I didn't speak after yesterday's counselling, I felt it'd been a step in the right direction.

"Good morning," greeted Seioh Jennson, standing in front of the usual colourful flower display. "Although this exercise is a consequence of your malpractice, it is also part of your counselling." Seioh Jennson held up an item. "Put your hands out."

"Uh, Seioh…"

"Yes, Paxton?"

"Please excuse me for talking out of turn, but is that really necessary?"

"Yes, Paxton. Speak out of turn again and you'll find yourself with more than just a tether."

"I'm sorry, Seioh."

Pax and I held out our hands, and Jennson secured handcuffs around my right hand and Pax's uninjured left. Between the two cuffs, a short rigid bar ensured it impossible to avoid physical contact from our hands and arms.

"Lady Merla Liddicott is only here to observe you both. She is not supervising. Paxton, I trust you remember what to do up here?"

"Yes, Seioh."

"You'll be working on the garden until the afternoon, take your lunch and Mando-sleep like normal, attend your counselling at fifteen hundred hours, and then remain in your room until dinner. Is that understood?"

"Yes, Seioh," we murmured.

Once Jennson left, Liddicott kept her distance, and Pax herded me around like a lost child. I had no idea what I was doing. I'd never maintained a garden in my life. He was pulling me around, gathering things up, dragging benches, and moving pots.

"How do you know what you are doing?" I asked Pax, slightly frustrated with feeling like dead wood.

"I didn't cope too well in Mustard. This was given to me as a form of discipline."

"Oh." His answer surprised me. "As much as you're good at your training, and as much as you follow the rules, you don't like it here all that much, do you?"

"Where would you want to be if you knew your parents were still alive, but the only thing keeping you apart was the fact you were born?"

I'll take that as a no...

As Pax bent down to pick up a large plastic tray, our hands touched and a spark flew between us. Pax squeezed his fist so tightly his knuckles lost colour.

"Jeez, Pax," I hissed covertly. "It was a static shock—relax." The idiot thought I used maleficium. "Will you give me something to do instead of dragging me around like a ragdoll?"

"What do you think I'm doing?" he reacted. "I'm getting it ready for you. It's not like I can send you on your way." He held up our cuffed hands. "I think it's you who needs to relax."

I assessed my surroundings and saw that Pax had indeed set up a workbench for us. Then we both snorted at how ridiculous we sounded.

"Now, sweethea—Aurora."

"I don't care what you call me, Pax."

"I'll pull out the daffodils and shake them off; you trim the roots and put the bulbs on that tray."

"Yes, sir."

"Tut, where is your off button?"

We exchanged sneers and set to work. For this, I was the one who needed two hands. Pax pulled the daffodils out one-handed and put them in the middle. He kept his cuffed hand malleably over with me so I could hold the bulb in one and trim the roots with the other.

The day passed quickly and quietly, and by that I mean we didn't speak much. But regardless, I enjoyed being in his company—he was still his thoughtful, considerate self. At lunch, we sat with everyone, and I'm sure nobody suspected a thing. Then, before we knew it, it was time for our counselling.

"Come in, come in. Take a seat," Lady Merla Liddicott welcomed us at the door. On the teal coffee table, two cups of hot chocolate were already waiting, so Pax and I assumed the same positions as yesterday. "Well, you both seem happier today. I believe yesterday was a success."

"I stopped it because Aurora was upset," Pax remarked.

"No, Paxton. I brought the session to a close because you consoled Aurora. It was a positive step forward. Now, remember, we need open minds for this to work, and I feel you are already holding a defensive position, Paxton.

"I didn't need to observe you today to know you're most protective of Aurora. This was evidence enough." Lady Liddicott held the tablet round to face us.

My tummy twinged at the thought of watching another video. I wasn't sure I wanted to see it.

Lady Liddicott played footage from the moment we were eliminated from the Parkour Games: we were in each other's arms, waiting for the annihilating touch from Theodred Dorchil. It was so painful revisiting memories from a time when we were happy. The first time I realised I had feelings for Pax was during this game. When I ran into him, immense relief radiated out through every pore on my skin. But truthfully, I think I first knew when he stepped out of the booth wearing his pitch-black picosuit. I remember shortly after, not wanting to open my hand to see the token because it meant leaving him.

"How did it feel watching that back?" Liddicott addressed Pax.

"I told you, I still care for Aurora."

"So, how did it feel?"

"Well, not good!"

"Although it is not an option, hypothetically speaking, at this stage would you still want to repudiate your betrothal?"

"Must you insist on upsetting Aurora?" Pax flicked me a sideways glance.

"Your co-operation, please, Paxton," Liddicott replied calmly.

"Yes."

"You would still—"

"Yes." He didn't let her finish.

His sharpness cut through me. These meetings were forcing us together, and I started to realise he would probably be ignoring me still if it weren't for them.

"Do you view Aurora as someone who needs protecting?"

Pax looked over at me. I kept my eyes down on my Promises ring. "No," he answered honestly.

"You are a complex case, Paxton. But with your help, I am ruling out a few possible reasons as to why you would want to see an end to the engagement."

Oh, if only you knew. This woman was trained in ninja, and I wouldn't draw an easy breath until I knew what she was capable of detecting.

CHAPTER THIRTEEN

UNHOLY

On the morning of day three, Pax and I were instructed to remain in our rooms before breakfast and wait for Seioh Jennson. Crouched on the platform steps around my bed, jogging my foot on the spot, I heard movement coming from next door. I took my finger out of my mouth and listened closely.

Seioh Jennson appeared at the interconnecting door. "In here, please, Miss Aviary."

"Yes, Seioh." I got to my feet and dubiously headed into Pax's room.

"Take a seat," Jennson instructed, shutting the adjoining door behind me.

He meant for me to sit on the corner sofa with Pax. My eyes swept over two china bowls and two glasses of water on the white coffee table. I surreptitiously assessed Pax's mood, all the while edging closer to my seat. Pax sat back with his hands on his lap. Catching my gaze, he greeted me with a very subtle wink—or was that a blink? Either way, it coincided with a faint smile, sending my belly in circles.

"Right then," began Jennson, standing behind the coffee table in his immaculate black suit. "Neither of you are to leave this room today—"

"*This* room?" I burped.

"Yes, Miss Aviary. *This* room. As in, Paxton's room. The only time you will leave *this* room is to attend your counselling session at fifteen hundred hours. Then you'll be straight back here, in *this* room, immediately after. Your food will be delivered to you. Should you require anything else, then Soami is on hand to inform me, and should I deem the request reasonable, I'll get it brought to you. Are my instructions clear?"

"Yes, Seioh," we chimed.

"No objections today, Paxton?"

"No, Seioh," said Pax, a little taken aback.

"Very well," Jennson replied, turning on his heel and leaving Pax and me alone together.

"Seioh Jennson has been a little off with me lately," said Pax, pulling his eyebrows together.

"Maybe I'm his favourite person, and he knows you're hurting me." I accidentally spat some venom.

"*You're* his favourite person?"

"That man hates me, I swear." I laughed, putting my feet up onto the coffee table.

"He doesn't normally talk to me the way he has been."

"It's because you went out on Curfew Duty when you weren't supposed to."

"Oi, you."

"Too early?" I scrunched my nose.

"Hmmm." It was a deep dismissive hum.

"Well, if I must stay in here, then I get the bed. You can stay on the sofa."

"Whatever." Pax picked up his bowl. "I wonder why they are keeping us cooped up?"

"Beats me. These counselling sessions are weird." I leant forward, taking up my bowl. "*Ergh.* What the hell is this?" I scooped up a spoonful of slimy grey slop and let it drip back into the bowl.

"It's Juvie food."

"What?" I did hear him; I just couldn't fathom why I was being given it.

"It's a balanced diet in a bowl."

"Why are they feeding us this?"

Pax pursed his lips, shrugged his shoulders, and hummed 'I don't know' without opening his mouth.

"Oh god, it's disgusting. And it's *cold*." I shuddered. "I can't eat this."

"Just eat it."

"No. I think I'm going to get myself something from the meal dispenser." I put my bowl on the table and left the sofa.

"Sit back down."

"No," I said, walking past him. Pax held out a straight arm at my waist to block me. I swerved my hips to avoid it.

"Sit back down before I make you sit back down."

"How are you going to make me when you're afraid to come anywhere near me?"

"I'm not afraid to come near you—*sit back down*."

"No. I think I'm going to get me a nice roast dinner," I teased him.

I almost reached the access button when Pax spun off the sofa, picked me up with a fireman's lift, and threw me down on the bed. I sat up on my elbows and smirked at him.

"A roast dinner? Really, Aurora? It's zero six hundred hours." He brought over my bowl of slop. "I'm pretty sure this is all we are getting, sweethea—" He stopped.

"Just call me sweetheart! I don't care."

"Take it," he requested when I gave the bowl a dirty look.

When I accepted the bowl, he turned for the sofa. I dipped my fingers in the gross pile of goo and flicked it across his back. Pax froze to the spot, feeling the cold specks land on the nape of his neck.

"Oh, no, you didn't." He turned on his heel slowly.

Before he got the bowl off me, I managed to grab a fistful and fling it at his face. He turned his head to avoid the incoming attack, but the grey goo splattered against his cheek, chin, and throat. Pax grabbed his own handful, restrained me in a headlock, and smeared the cold, wet slop down my face. Scraping the residue from over my eyes, I shoved it down the collar of his jacket. He managed to reach for the bowl and return the strike.

The noise from our laughter and (my) screaming attracted Seioh Jennson's attention. He entered the room as we were in full swing. We stood to attention at once, slop tangled in our hair, caked down our faces, and adorning our uniforms. Seioh Jennson took stock of the state we were in.

In an intense, silent minute, we stood painfully still, waiting for Jennson. His eyes closed. He shook his head. He gave a dismissive wave of the hand. Then he walked back out of the room. Pax and I couldn't believe our luck. We turned to each other with our mouths open before bursting out laughing.

We took turns to take a shower and spent the day lying around idly. I exiled Pax to the sofa, where he stayed, whilst I lorded it up on his bed wearing a pair of his pyjamas. More slop arrived at lunchtime, but I was still not hungry enough to eat the vile stuff. Pax told me he would force-feed it to me if I didn't eat at least half, so I stomached some to avoid a repeat of this morning.

As it neared our session with Lady Merla Liddicott, I had Soami ask Seioh Jennson if I could run next door to get a clean uniform from my wardrobe. Seconds later, I had a message from him on my Slate which simply said the word, 'yes.' After showing Pax I had permission to leave his room, he sat back down on the sofa and stopped guarding the access button. Then at fifteen hundred hours, we left together to see what Liddicott had in store for us today.

"Good afternoon, you two," greeted Lady Liddicott. "I have an exercise prepared for you if, Paxton, you could take a seat on the rug."

Today, there were no peppermint hot chocolates by the sofa, but a pot of ice cream on the floor beside two large yellow beanbags. The area for our exercise was on the floor where we sat shortly after the Unity results. However, today, instead of plastic chairs, there was a rectangular rug covered in yellow, teal, and fuchsia triangles.

"Aurora, head on over to the sofa. I'll meet you there in a moment," instructed Lady Liddicott. I sat down and watched her secure a less-than-impressed Pax to a beanbag on the floor. My hand found my mouth as I observed incredulously.

"Right, Aurora," Lady Liddicott spoke quietly. "This exercise is intended to be playful. The chocolate ice cream by the beanbag is Paxton's favourite. It is not available from the Food Hall and can only be enjoyed during the Unity festivities. All I want you to do is convince Paxton that you are going to feed him, but then deny him a single drop. It's that simple. You can eat as much ice cream as you wish, but under no circumstances are you to allow Paxton to consume any. Do you understand the rules?"

"Yes, ma'am. Eat ice cream; wind-up Pax."

"You are not to discuss any of these instructions with Paxton, understood?"

"Yes, ma'am."

When I joined Pax on the rug, he eyed me curiously. I saw his hands were handcuffed to loops on the sides of the beanbag.

"Kinky," I said with a giggle, crouching down on the floor.

"What the hell is this?"

"We're going to eat some ice cream," I said, picking up the beautifully rich dessert. The ice-encrusted top sparkled under the bright lights as I placed the tub onto my lap.

"Why do I need to be handcuffed to eat some ice cream?"

"So I can feed it to you."

"Oh, what?" He rolled his head backwards in a small circle.

"Your co-operation, please, Paxton," I imitated Lady Liddicott.

"You're lucky I like that ice cream."

"Oh, good."

I dug the spoon into the creamy chocoholic's dream. Perfectly melted, it oozed up over the side of the tub. I ran my tongue around the rim of velvety overspill. Pax watched me hungrily. Now I understood the reason for the slop. We were deprived, making the desire for this ice cream that much stronger. I took out a spoonful and licked the stray ribbon of chocolate syrup dripping over the edge. Pax's light-brown eyebrows furrowed briefly, and then the corners of his mouth curved into a knowing smile as he realised my wind-up.

I quickly changed tact, bringing the spoon up to his mouth. When he leant forward, I pulled the spoon away and sucked off the top layer with my lip. He cocked his head in disapproval. I steered the spoon back towards him to see if he was desperate enough to eat the ice cream that had already been in my mouth. This exercise was great, extremely contrived. Pax was indeed willing to eat my leftovers. I denied him again and helped myself to it. Pax's fists clenched and unclenched in his handcuffs. I took him another spoon and allowed the slippery dessert to fall into his lap.

"Oops."

"I swear to god, Aurora."

"Alright, no, I'll stop."

I peeled out another shell and crawled closer to him. He believed my lie and parted his lips to receive my offering—and then I ate it. After a few times, Pax wised up to my game and stopped playing. Now, when I brought him a helping, he no longer attempted to take it, so I sat happily eating it all to myself. He smouldered at me with a face laced with revenge and amusement.

As one last-ditch attempt to get him to accept the ice cream, I tried my own experiment. I wondered if Pax would do something under the guise of the exercise. I showed him I had some in my mouth and sat over his legs. Holding my parted mouth within reach of his, I waited. Pax's occupied eyes stared deep into mine. He leant in, paused, and then met my cold lips with a soft, relaxed tongue.

"Nicely done, Aurora," approved Lady Liddicott at the end of the exercise.

A charged energy accompanied our walk back to Pax's room. Truthfully, I was worried to what extent he might try to get me back. Upon the door to room 4-3-4 closing, Pax backed me up against the wall. He held under my chin as his eyes washed over my face, my lips, my neck. But his mind was still set, and knowing it was wrong to give me false hope, he retreated.

Before he made it away, I took his hand and encouraged him back. It was permission. I knew he hadn't changed his mind but at this point I didn't care. I had to disperse this energy and take what I needed. This time our lips found each other. His hands cupped my cheeks and my head rested against the wall.

Unlike last time, Pax pulled away first. He pushed his forehead against mine and kept a firm hold on the sides of my face. With his eyes still closed, he spoke in barely more than a whisper, "Oh, Aurora, I wish..." he said, stopping himself and choosing his words carefully. "I wish there was somewhere that didn't care."

He didn't look at me when he turned away, which was just as well, because my skin had a vivacious hue. At the flash of panic, my skin settled back down to its normal pale ivory.

※❀※

On day four, we were given the same instructions as the day before: stay put and eat slop. By fifteen hundred hours we were itching to get out of that suffocating room.

"Oh no, not again," grumbled Pax, entering Liddicott's office.

211

The room had been set up in exactly the same way as the day before. Even I couldn't be bothered with the exercise today. It was fun but soul destroying afterwards. Pax wouldn't be swayed, and these sessions were proving pointless. Lady Liddicott would never know the real reason why Pax didn't want anything to do with me. Even though being forced together was showing him I wasn't dangerous, that didn't change the fact I was still a death sentence for him.

Lady Liddicott secured Pax to the beanbag once again, but this time, she gave me some new rules. "Today, you are allowed to share the ice cream with Paxton. If you are able to convince him to eat it, then you can both go to the Khakidemy after for training, *but* you are not allowed to disclose this information, understood?"

Yes! Easy! Oh, thank god. We were getting really agitated being held captive in our room, and I really couldn't wait to work out.

I hurried over to the carpet and sat on my knees. The gorgeous dessert waited by the beanbag and I held it in my lap. Pax gave a heavy sigh. Ignoring his frustration, I gouged out a huge spoonful, took half of it myself, and held the rest out for Pax. He tightened his lips and shunned the spoon.

"Alright, I'll get you a fresh spoon," I said, thinking very carefully about what I was allowed to say. I guessed telling him I wasn't going to tease him was off the table. I offered a fresh sample. This time Pax shook his head. *Come on. This isn't a wind-up today.* "Pax. You are going to want to open your mouth." Was that crossing the line? I didn't care. I was desperate.

"You'll have to excuse me for a moment," interrupted Lady Liddicott. "I've got an urgent matter I need to attend to. Suspend the exercise until my return. I won't be long."

When Liddicott vacated the room, I rounded on Pax. "This isn't a wind-up today, I promise. If you eat the ice cream we get to go *train.*"

I didn't understand the look tainting his face. Why wasn't he happy?

"I've been told I'm not allowed to eat the ice cream," he said bluntly.

"What?"

"Mmm-hmm."

"But if you *do*, we get to go *train*."

Pax gave me a warning tilt of the head. "I'm not breaking the rules, Aurora."

"Please? It's just ice cream."

"I think I get the point of this exercise."

"Yeah, me too," I said quickly. "You eat ice cream…we get to go *train*."

"I'm not eating the ice cream, Aurora."

I made a ruffled growling noise in the back of my throat and threw myself up against my beanbag. Pax wore that all-too-familiar soft smile with raised eyebrows.

The door *whooshed* open and Liddicott returned. "Please accept my apologies and continue." She carried on past us and settled back into her fuchsia-pink armchair.

I tried turning up the heat and did everything I possibly could to get Pax to eat the ice cream. I tried (and failed miserably at) eating seductively; I begged discreetly in his ear; and I even tried spreading it on his lips for him to lick off—we weren't going to training. Today, Pax enjoyed watching me desperately trying to persuade him, whilst I was the one left frustrated.

"Now, tell me. Do you understand the reasons behind this exercise?" asked Liddicott at the end of the session.

"Yes, ma'am," answered Pax.

"*No*," I piped in.

"Care to explain, Paxton?" said Liddicott.

"You think I'm scared history might repeat itself. You're proving to me I'm strong-willed, and that I wouldn't give in to temptation like my parents did—no matter how hard Aurora tries. If it means breaking a rule, I'm not going to do it."

"Didn't you break the rules by telling me you weren't allowed to eat the ice cream?" I rebuked.

"No. You did. I had permission to tell you if you disclosed the rules of the game first." He cut me back down to size.

I slunk down in my seat and didn't mutter another word. Now I understood that tainted look on his face when I told him we could train; he was disappointed I broke the rules.

Lady Liddicott deduced it was fear coercing Pax to end the betrothal. She surmised he was afraid of physical contact—I'm assuming she saw him flinch when our hands touched up in the garden—and she blamed the reason on Pax's parents. When Liddicott asked Pax if this was correct, he agreed just so she would stop trying to figure out the actual reason. Our sessions with Lady Liddicott continued once a month after that, but purely as a way of keeping an eye on us. I supposed the counselling proved successful in the sense that I was allowed to interact with Pax at times, but our relationship didn't improve much more than that. He kept to himself and the interconnecting door remained closed.

After a week of not seeing Tayo, we were both happy to see each other again, but I'd not forgotten what he did in front of that Second-year Navy. When I walked into his cell on that morning, we had an impulsive hug before I twisted his arm behind his back and insisted he apologised. I knew how much he hated all this *'enforcery'* stuff, which made it that much funnier. The apology took a while, since he was unusually good at fighting pain, but I won—eventually.

⚮

When I woke up the next morning, I kept my eyes closed trying to suppress a draining sadness. I had been coping with Pax keeping his distance, but I already found this morning difficult. Without moving my body, I coaxed my eyes open and slowly blinked away the fatigue.

"A wave of black musical notes?" burst Pax, charging through our door.

And just like that, I was wide awake, my heart leaping out my chest. "Um. Good morning." My mouth twinkled. I surveyed him sideways, still not moving my head.

He perched on the edge of my bed and stroked the black streak of hair from my face. "Feeling up to it today?" he asked.

Absorbed by his touch, I pressed his hand against my forehead. *Ohh, I've missed this.* "A bit more than I was." I pulled his hand over my eyes, hiding behind it.

"What did you think?" he asked. "That I was going to allow you to be a sitting duck the whole game and not play?" He removed his hand from my face but still allowed me to hold on to it.

"Can't say I know what I thought, to be honest." I stared at my hand grasping on to his.

"Well, those electric shocks really hurt, so I'll always do my best to prevent you from getting it. So, what is it?"

"What is what?" I said, placing my eyes back on his.

"A wave of black musical notes."

"I don't know; it's not like I've had you training me this time."

"You *need* me to train you? Are you not capable?"

"Oh, sorry, Seioh." I dipped in my chin.

"It's *The Lost Device*." He covered my face with the duvet. "It gives you a high-pitched ringing in the ears."

I removed the duvet to an empty room. "And I can order my own breakfast," I shouted after him. "Fanks." That bit I mumbled under my breath. On the last game, he ordered my breakfast for me before I'd made it to the Food Hall, and I really didn't want him to this time. I found it easier to cope when Pax wasn't being nice to me. His kindness only made me miss him more.

On my way down to breakfast, countless pairs of my own sapphire-blue eyes stared back at me. *Smokin' Axe* made a comeback, and just like Brindan predicted, fans had gotten their hands on our video loop from the last TPG. The awful footage showed my hand awkwardly placed around Pax's waist and Pax's arm draped casually over my shoulder. He looked so handsome in his picosuit, and I really hated these sad reminders of our happier times.

In the Food Hall, the *whole* table wore our team badge—and that included Ryker and Pipila. They all thought it was hilarious that our combined beauty was the only premise for the fan club. Nobody, not even a *Boulderfell*, had supporters unless they showed potential of winning.

After Silliah plaited my hair, Pax, Ryker, Pipila, and I set off for the plain white door in the Khakidemy. Thankfully, my frenemy entourage didn't last much longer after that. Pax and I placed our hands on our booth, the edges celebrated our arrival by shining gold, and we disappeared through the glass double doors. Pax began unzipping his jacket as I untied my boot laces.

"I saw that," Pax said without looking at me.

"Saw what?"

"You know."

I did know, but I wasn't going to admit it. Pax had started undressing before I stepped up onto my plinth, initiating the partition wall. When Pax pulled his vest over the top of his head, I couldn't help but sneak a peek. Fed up with him always making the rules and deciding when he would interact with me, I went over to him.

"What are you doing, Aurora?" he asked, sounding more curious than serious.

"Nothing. That's what we do now, isn't it? Nothing?" I circled around him, running my fingers over the groove in his spine and across his stomach, admiring his shirtless torso until I stood in front of him. A quiver rippled through me as he reached out and stroked down the side of my neck with the back of his fingers.

"No, you're not allowed to touch me," I said, swiping his hand away. "You're breaking the rules."

"It's not the rules I'm worried about breaking."

"My heart is fine," I lied, and by fine I meant already broken. I stepped up onto his plinth with him. His hand came to hold on to my neck again. "No. You're breaking the rules," I repeated, pushing him off the plinth backwards.

He smiled and shook his head. "I'm not breaking any rules, Aurora." He grabbed my hips and picked me up.

Wrapping my legs around his waist, I stole a kiss as he carried me back over to my plinth. He wasn't ready to put me down straight away. He knew it wasn't right for us to do this and it needed to stop, but he made the most of the moment whilst it was here.

"Now behave." He pressed his lips to mine once more before turning away, leaving me on my plinth. I felt that familiar heat rising from the inside and I fought against it. Then I smugly smiled down at my skin not trying to guide aircrafts into landing.

A black picosuit, a pair of gloves, and some running trainers later, we were ready for our video loop. This footage consisted of me repeatedly shrugging Pax's arm off my shoulder until he hooked my head into a lock, holding me there until the recording ended.

When we stepped outside the booth, I heard the same music playing as last time, and it caused an echoic memory to pump adrenaline around my system. The music was the type that played in my head when our new Slates were issued, and I was running in slow motion to collect mine before a massive queue formed. Those melodic violins building to introduce those thundering drums—I daresay I felt excited.

"So, are we going to climb up again?" I asked Pax, resting my knee on the black sofa and holding around the pillar for balance.

"Hmm." He thought about it before saying, "Yeah, climb up again, I'd say, but our performance last time would have been scrutinised, so we don't want to be predictable. This time, climb up higher and meet me in the centre."

"Didn't you call that a war zone last time?"

"On the ground—yes. The massacre will be under us if we climb high enough."

Lady Joanne Maxhin began psyching us all up with, "Who's ready for the mid-year rematch?" Then after her speech, she called us through to the next room. The music starting blaring, and Pax kept hold of my hand as we flocked with the crowd.

We put our hands in the velvety black pouch together. This time, I took both tokens up in my hand and left him feeling around the empty bottom. He closed his eyes and scratched his eyebrow, warning me without saying a word. I quickly placed the token in his hand.

My purple token again, but this time with 'The Parkour Games, June, 2119' printed on it.

"Find me," I mouthed to him mockingly before turning for my cage.

Soon enough we were all divided. I had Theodred from *Sovereign Skill* in my cage again but no sign of Romilly. Before I had a good look around, the lights went out, the strobe lighting began flickering, and the screaming air raid siren sent my insides churning. Smoke rippled out through the archways, feet were being stomped around me, and then we were released.

I entered the archway with the bustling swarm. The chant that changed my mind-set last time erupted:

Unity united us,

You and I, unite us.

We will fight and we will fall,

Together we can do it all!

I will fight and I will fall,

I WILL FIGHT,

I WILL FALL,

And for you, I'll do it all!

Jumping, shouting, whistling, and skipping accompanied it. I wondered if Pax would be shouting it this time, since he no longer wanted to be united.

In the chaos, I tripped up in the middle of the stampede. I hit the floor, and at the same time, a fist punched me in the back of my head. The force sent my chin slamming into the solid floor, snapping my teeth together. It was dark and noisy. Disorientated, with an all-consuming pain tearing through my face, I sat on my heels, squeezing my chin in one hand and rubbing my skull with the other. As I checked myself for blood, a slender hand entered my sight, and Celeste helped me to my feet.

"Thank you," I yelled over the noise, aware I was squinting.

"You okay?"

"Yeah," I replied, brushing myself down.

"Your capsule is here. Have fun, darlin'."

I stood in my pod, still rubbing the back of my head, thinking to myself that at least I wasn't holding everyone up this time—but also thinking *ouch*. Soon, the ground moved from under my feet and our descent under the institute began.

"Five, four, three…two…*one*," announced that voice that came from nowhere.

The door revolved open, exposing the blinding light, but not wanting to waste any time, I assessed the obstacles above my head. Video loops decorated the outskirts of the arena, and I caught a glimpse of mine. I snorted in my throat; ours stood out for all the wrong reasons. Usually, the footage was either stale and stagnant from the camera-shy, or brooding and intimidating from the competitive. Ours was *hilarious*. I didn't know it at the time, but we were both smiling from ear to ear as I tormented Pax and he restrained me.

Finding myself lucky with the alley I started in this time, I reached out and touched both black walls at the same time. With my hands set firmly on the textured surfaces, I gripped on with my feet and began scaling the walls vertically, but I only managed a short way before I realised my camera hadn't followed me out of my pod. Jumping back down, I checked my darkened pod and spotted it lying lifeless in a small recess. The small beetle-looking thing remained inactive when I picked it up. *Do I just continue without a camera?* I guessed so and pocketed the tiny device.

When I turned around, Beignley Boulderfell gave me a start. Step by step, he stalked towards me along the left-side wall—on the right-side wall…*not* Romilly. Beignley crept forward with another girl, one I didn't recognise. She was about my height but noticeably older than me. Well, I thought to myself, *Unholy Reign* haven't united and no victory tunes have played yet, so…

I watched Beignley carefully. He had an uncanny resemblance to Ryker. They both had the same beetle-black eyes, and their brown hair carried the same style: a short back and sides cut with the long top sweeping up and off to the side.

Beignley straightened his spine out from his stalking pose and squared up to me. "Kneel down," he ordered, so close his breath touched my nose.

"Er, yeah, I don't think I'm going to do that." I rejected his suggestion.

"Go on, have a guess what Bounty I have on me this time."

"None. You haven't united."

He walked around me and breathed into my ear, "You would think that, wouldn't you?"

With my path now clear, I tried to walk away from him but the girl blocked my way ahead.

"Who's this?" I asked Beignley without taking my eyes off her. "Your Fell agent? Too scared to pick on a First-year on your own?"

"Kneel," she spat in my face. Even though her eyes were blue, she had a darkness rooted deep within them.

"Back off," I warned, getting prepared to call on my training. *It's two against one, but if I'm to go down, I'm to go down fighting.* She reached to make me kneel in front of her, but I pre-empted her move and performed an arm control technique, taking her down to the floor. I held her down with my knee in her back and checked on Boulderfell. What I expected was to defend myself from an attack; what I got was a circle of blue triangles spiralling my way. On impact, my picosuit shone with a blue aura, freezing my whole body solid. The girl crawled out from under my knee and repositioned my stiffened joints, giving them exactly what they wanted, and leaving me kneeling. I had a feeling the camera digging into my hip was the least of my worries.

"*Mere Trifle* would have turned your fingers to jelly," taunted Beignley, answering my question from the last game. "I did want to use that first for poetry but needs must. *In the Name of the Law* will do just fine. *Unholy Reign* had finished either first or second place for five years straight until you came along. This is what you get for cheating, you bitch!"

Beignley kicked me in the stomach at the same time his *Coward's Accomplice* kicked me in the kidneys. The air left my lungs, and I suffocated on the lack of oxygen. The pain in my front did not compare to the excruciating throbbing in my back. A few seconds later, the blue aura faded around my picosuit, and I collapsed on my side.

"Not in the face, Laucey," instructed Beignley. "It needs to look like she fell."

Trainers plunged into my stomach, my back, my ribs, all over, each blow snatching the air from my lungs. A sudden hot pain ignited inside my torso, and the shoes to my chest brought an unbearable amount of razor-sharpness. I tried to curl up needing the pain in my front to end, but the brutality jarred my body violently. I couldn't breathe. Unsure how much longer I could cope, I welcomed death, until unconsciousness relieved me.

CHAPTER FOURTEEN
IS IT CHEATING

I woke up in an acute panic, unable to control the noise coming out my mouth. It was almost like the air raid siren but if someone kept tapping pause and play continuously. The shallow breaths were a result of the immense pain I felt when breathing normally.

"Shh-shh-shh," reacted Pax, startled by my distressed waking state. He sprung out of the recliner and pulled me into him. "You're safe, you're safe, you're safe, you're safe."

Luckily, his arms wrapped around my head and not my battered body. The sound coming from me stopped, but my cry turned into an inconsolable sob brought on by the sudden security. The more my body trembled, the tighter Pax held on.

We were in the Recovery Centre, the place eliminated players were taken after passing out. Before round two, all bodies were removed and placed in a room full of black stretcher-like beds to regain consciousness. With the picosuit deactivated we *could* wake up, but everyone recovered at different rates, and since we needed our partners to gain access to our booths to get changed, comfy leather recliners were positioned by each stretcher.

"What happened to you? Did you fall?" he asked, feeling my trembling lessen.

"Erh-erh-erh-erh-erh-erh, I don't—I don't," my voice said, quivering. I didn't know what to say; all I knew was I needed to get out of there. I pushed forward onto my feet. "MMMUHHH," I yelled through a clenched jaw at the pain.

Pax instinctively caught my body. "Sit back down. No, sit. Aurora, I think you're really hurt. No. *Listen* to me," he said a little more forcefully when I tried to stand again.

"Pax, please. I need to get to my room."

"I think it's best you get checked over first."

"*Please.* There's nothing wrong with my feet," I begged, too panicked to listen.

Pax wasn't happy but still agreed, and he aided me to our booth to get changed. Every agonising step made me wince, but I tried to hide the pain on my face so Pax would let me continue. When I eventually arrived at my room, I sat down on the bed and covered my face to release the built-up anguish. I fell sideways into my pillow and continued to cry.

"Sweetheart, you're really worrying me." Pax crouched down to unlace my boots. "Did you fall?"

"Yes," I lied, knowing he would never stop worrying about me during another game if he knew the truth.

"I'm going to go get a nurse."

"Can you get Nanny Kimly?"

"OK." He carefully pulled off my boots and left.

A worrying sharpness cut through my ribs as I lay face down into my pillow, but the misery kept my head there.

When Pax returned, he was alone. "Nanny Kimly is not the on-call nurse, but she's coming as soon as she can."

I didn't answer, keeping my face turned into the dampened pillow. The mattress rocked from Pax joining me on the bed. I felt he was close, and knew he would allow me to burrow into him, but I didn't want to. I had too much physical pain to deal with, and I didn't need the emotional one to go with it. Instead, I reached out for his hand.

"Little Lady?" her voice came from the door.

"Nanny Ki—" I choked up. The sound of her sweet voice brought forth the child she once knew me to be. My body trembled from fighting back the torrent bursting through, and I pushed my eyes closed with my fingers as if doing so would stop the tears from coming.

"Paxton, could you give us a moment, please?" She could tell something was very wrong.

"Of course," he replied, leaving the room at once.

Nanny Kimly's soothing voice met my ears but the despair prevented me from hearing her words. Soon, she began carefully removing my jacket. "Oh dear." Her hand came to her mouth at the sight of my body. "You walked here from the Recovery Centre?"

"Yes."

"Tut, Little Lady." She frowned. "Do you have numbness or tingling in your legs?"

"No."

"In your groin?"

"No."

"It seems your picosuit armour has done its job," she said, examining my joints. "Does it hurt more to sit or lie down?"

"Lie down."

"To err on the side of caution, I'm going to arrange for you to be scanned. I suspect a fractured rib but nothing more. Next time, if you are hurt, you stay in the Recovery Centre until you are assessed, do you understand? They will scan you down there for internal damage and broken bones. You shouldn't have moved before you knew. Paxton says you fell. Now, are you going to tell me the truth, Little Lady?"

I carried on rubbing my eyes.

"Hmm?" she hummed, pulling my hand away. "If someone has done this to you, Aurora, you need to tell me. They won't get away with it."

"Even if it was a Boulderfell?" I asked rhetorically.

"Were there any witnesses?"

"No."

"So, it's just your word against theirs?"

"Yep."

We both knew what that meant. Accusing a Boulderfell without any proof was as good as provoking a hornet. They would mobilise the entire nest to sting at their defence. Provoke one…provoke them all.

My scan revealed a fractured rib but nothing else. They told me a restricted schedule would be unnecessary because ribs healed on their own, and my 'treatment' was to keep moving, cough normally, and carry out breathing exercises to prevent infection in my lungs. It all hurt like hell.

Pax stayed in my room after the nurse gave me the all-clear. On the day of TPG we had empty schedules, so he came to keep an eye on me.

"Shouldn't you be sitting up?" he asked me.

"Shouldn't you be hiding in your room?"

"I'm not doing this with you, Aurora. Do you want me to go next door?"

"No," I admitted. Deep down I was mad at him for what he was doing to me, and although I usually contained it well, when I wasn't feeling great, I struggled that much more.

"Well then, shush. Do you want to watch the games with me? It might help get your mind off things." Pax turned on his back and pulled his Slate out from his pocket. He unfolded it into a tablet and opened the platform used to watch the games. "Apparently, all the purple team cameras malfunctioned at the start of the game?"

"Yeah, mine didn't work."

"Sometimes there's a technical fault, but the game technicians rectify it soon enough. You can just continue without it. When they fix the issue, your camera will find you."

I had a feeling the camera issue wasn't a happy coincidence. *Unholy Reign* planned to jump me. Ryker said before, they were gunning for me. To pull it off, they would somehow have had to be in the pods either side of me to reach my alley as fast as they did. They would have also had to make sure they could get to me before I united with Pax, otherwise we could have eliminated them. So much thought had gone into such a cold-blooded attack, and it was those two who were the cheaters. How was it possible for Beignley to have Bounty without uniting with Romilly? The only thing they couldn't have known for sure was who got to beat me up. They left that purely to chance—a purple or yellow token. I'm assuming that punch in the back of the head wasn't accidental either.

"What happened to you?" I asked Pax.

"Do you want to see it?"

"No."

Pax nose laughed at my brutal honesty. "Alright. I made my way to you because your dot wasn't moving on my radar. I had a feeling something wasn't right, but before I reached you, *Unholy Reign* eliminated me."

"Oh. Almost like they knew where to find you."

"Yeah, I guess."

They knew Pax would be coming to me; they knew exactly where he would be.

We watched *Unholy Reign* win the mid-year rematch by using *In the Name of the Law* against Theodred from *Sovereign Skill*. Romilly sent out the attack, so chances are they both had that Bounty in their inventory ready for me.

※

"Aaay, you came for me," said a relieved Tayo when I picked him up that evening for dinner duty.

"Why so surprised?"

"Because you didn't have to. Oh, how far we've come," he said zestfully, punching the air sideways across his chest. "I didn't even have to beg this time. 'I've only come to change your bandages; You can sit back down,'" he mocked my words using a deep voice. "Now look!"

"Do you want me to just turn back around?"

"No! God no. And I know you would."

"Exactly. So how about you pipe down?"

"How did you do in your game?"

I shook my head with a curled lip.

"What? Not good?" he asked, wrinkles forming between his eyebrows.

"I got jumped by Beignley from *Unholy Reign*. I didn't leave my starting position. You can't tell anybody, though, Tayo."

"Why?" He sprung up from the bed and stood examining my face intently.

"They made it look like I fell, by kicking my...my..." Unable to finish the sentence, I fanned a hand down my torso.

"Let me see."

"No, Tayo." I gave the observer's window a glance.

Tayo took me by the hand and dragged me into the ensuite.

"Let me see," he repeated.

I gave a gentle huff and remained still, our gazes locked onto each other.

"Aurora."

I rolled my eyes and unzipped my jacket. Tayo gently lifted my vest, and his hand found his mouth in the same way Nanny Kimly's did.

"Holy crap, Roar."

"Mmm."

Tayo wrapped his arms around my shoulders and rested his chin on my head. "You realise what that's going to look like in a few days, right?"

"Like yours did. I had my picosuit armour on and they still fractured a rib."

I could tell by the movement on Tayo's jaw that he clenched his teeth. "I—and I would swear if you weren't so precious—*hate* those Boulderfell."

"You can't tell anybody, though, okay?"

"Who am I going to tell?"

Just as we were about to leave the ensuite, Tayo held his arm out to my chest, pushing me back inside.

"Tayo, have you seen Aurora?" It was Pax. I held my breath and listened.

"She came but realised she didn't have her Slate," Tayo answered. "That was a while ago, though. Maybe she's not coming to get me tonight?"

"Did you wash your hands?"

"Er…"

"I'm joking," Pax said, chortling. "Thanks. I'll check the Food Hall again."

"Whoa, Tayo. That was quick thinking," I said, coming out of the ensuite.

"I didn't think you two were talking?"

"We're not really. He's just been watching over me today because of…well, this." I pointed to my stomach again.

"Why won't you practice your magic, Roar?"

"Because I don't want it," I said flatly, trying to pass him.

He blocked my path to the door. "But you might've been able to use it today and protected yourself. What if they come for you again next time?"

I groaned at him. I knew what he was saying was right, but I wasn't ready to admit it. "Can you just drop it?"

"No, Aurora. I won't. I'm worried about you. Please let me help you with it. It's who you are. Why try and ignore it?"

"You really aren't going to shut up, are you?"

"No. If it means you'll listen to me, then no. I'll keep on until it drives you crazy."

"You're already driving me crazy." I tried to pass again.

He stepped in my way, bringing his eyes lower to mine. "Please, Roar."

"How? I have no idea how to use it. It didn't come with an instruction manual."

"You don't need one. You use it without one. All I'm saying is embrace it and at least *try*."

"Argh. Okay, *fine*."

"Yes!"

⁂

My magic schooling began immediately, but I didn't have much to show for it. The only thing I could do was rattle objects for a while, supposedly with my mind, but unless I intended to shake Beignley to death, I needed to keep trying.

It was Pax's birthday at the end of June, and it crushed me not being able to celebrate with him, but I did sneak in and leave a peppermint hot chocolate on his bedside table for him to wake up to. Oddly, he was nowhere to be seen recently, and I had no idea where he kept disappearing to. Stranger still, Pipila kept leaving the table at the same time as him, and I wouldn't see either of them unless it was meal time, or unless Pax and I had a duty.

Today, on the thirty-first of July, it was my seventeenth birthday, and Nanny Kimly was the first in my room this morning.

"I'm probably not going to see you today," she said, perching on my bed. "So I wanted to come wish you happy birthday before I missed it."

"Thanks, Nanny Kimly."

"Here, I want to show you something." Nanny Kimly took out her Slate and showed me a 3D walkthrough of a bedroom unlike any you'd find in the institute. The room was cosy yet modern with an indulgent fur rug snuggling the feet of a cushion-dressed king bed. The bed actually *faced* a display screen, and to the west of the screen, a wall-length window looked out at a glistening, crystal-clear lake. Surrounding its banks, a barricade of trees offered privacy.

"What is it?" I asked. "Well, I know it's a room, but why are you showing me?"

"This is a room in a house I've started renting for my retirement. I know you're having a few complications with Paxton, and this room is yours if you ever need some time away, *or* if you ever accidentally stay past Curfew listening to all those stories about your parents."

I didn't know what overwhelmed me more: the really kind and thoughtful gesture; hearing her acknowledge my difficulties with Pax; or her mentioning my birth parents for the first time. "Nanny Kimly, I…I don't know what to say."

"It wasn't supposed to make you upset." She gave a watery-eyed smile, wiping away my tear.

"I'm not upset," I said in a broken voice. "It's so nice." And then I wiped the tears rolling down her cheeks. We both gave a sniffly laugh at our silly crying. "Thank you; it's amazing. I really love you, Nanny Kimly."

"I love you too, Little Lady. I know it's a while yet before you leave—"

"And you! You're only fifty."

"Which means…I can retire anytime I want now."

"But you're not going to, are you?"

Nanny Kimly laughed. "I'll see you through a few more years. Don't you worry."

"Don't you scare me like that."

Pax knocking on the adjoining door interrupted our moment, and Nanny Kimly placed a hand on my knee. "I'll leave you two to it. Happy birthday, Little Lady."

"Thanks again, Nanny," I said, before calling out to let Pax in.

Nanny Kimly and Pax wished each other a good morning, and then Pax passed me a green takeaway drink cup.

"Happy birthday..." He leant over, stroked my hair, and kissed me on the forehead.

"Thanks," I replied, taking a sip of my peppermint hot chocolate.

We stared at each other, masking our sadness with a soft smile. I couldn't remember the last time I had spoken to him. Suddenly, Silliah came falling through my door, red in the face and panting. Seconds later, Brindan arrived.

"What are you running from?" I asked Silliah.

"This idiot." She pointed an extended thumb towards Brindan. "He was trying to get in here first to wish you happy birthday, but you're *my* best friend." She eyed him with a fake scorn.

Brindan grabbed Silliah by the slack in her jacket and held a hand over her mouth. "Happy birthday, Aurora," he said quickly.

"Thanks," I answered, giving Silliah a quick look.

"No! I was supposed to say that first," she mumbled under his hand.

"Typical woman," jibed Brindan. "Talking too much and you missed your chance."

"Happy birthday, Aurora," said Silliah, shrugging Brindan off. "Here you go."

She handed me a small square box wrapped in rose-gold wrapping paper with a gold floral pattern and a golden bow. I unwrapped it to find a long woven-rope bracelet identical to the one I had given to Tayo for his birthday back in April. I'd never told her I lost my old one. She must've just assumed since I no longer wore it.

"I know how much you liked your old one," said Silliah. "I couldn't find those black stones but I'll keep looking."

"Thank you, Silliah. I love it," I said, leaning forward to give her a hug.

"Breakfast?" prompted Brindan.

"Well, I need to get washed and dressed." I gestured down at my charcoal pyjamas. "Meet you down there?"

After another hug from Silliah, I watched her and Brindan fight their way out of my bedroom door. Then after a quick shower, I rushed to see Tayo. I had something I really needed to show him.

"Happy birthday, my little Roar," he greeted me at the door.

"Kiss me again, and I'll punch you in the mouth."

"I kissed your *hand*," Tayo said, overwrought.

"Exactly. Do it again, and I'll punch you in the mouth." I couldn't hide my smile anymore.

"Grr. You had me there," he said, swinging his arm to hook my neck. "I just can't tell with you."

I jumped back to avoid his grasp. "You know I could have you on your back." I laughed, avoiding another of his attempts.

"I'd rather you on your back. I prefer being the one on top."

His reply caught me off guard, and he yanked me into the ensuite.

"That's…not what I meant," I spoke in an unintentional whisper, staring up into his piercing-blue eyes.

Still keeping hold of my lapel, Tayo's eyes brushed over my lips. The familiar rush of heat burned from under my skin, and I concentrated hard on dispersing it.

"I'm not sure you would punch me in the mouth." He paused briefly in careful consideration, before leaning in closer.

"I…wouldn't risk it."

Tayo's mouth curved, but he still didn't move, the cogs still ticking over. His smile grew larger but he let go, sidestepping to look outside. I released my breath. My legs jittered, and I inhaled deeply to calm myself.

"The coast is clear, Roar," he said with a new kind of smile.

"Right," was all I could manage. Back in the cell, I tried to compose myself and forget what just happened…but I couldn't. What I had to show him would have to wait until later.

We walked to the Food Hall with a strange, awkward energy. As I sat eating, I kept glancing over at him. He had the sleeves to his claret overalls folded up around his elbows, showing his tattooed arm. Could a guy have attractive arms? I was being weird.

"You alright?" asked Silliah with high eyebrows. She flicked a look towards Tayo.

"Yeah!" Clart, too much. "Yeah," I said with a cough. Oh no. Silliah was so good at detecting this stuff. Think, Aurora! "Where's Natashly?"

"She was released three weeks ago."

"Oh, I didn't notice."

"It's really sad when they go. You don't think about it, but we spend so much time with them, it's only natural you start to *bond.*" She tilted her head forward, giving me an intentional stare.

Oh no. She knows.

"Crazy Kalmayan Kid is alright," interjected Hilly. Thank you, thank you, thank you. Oh, thank you, Hilly, with all your intrusiveness.

Silliah repositioned herself in her chair, letting me off the hook. "When's he going?"

"Erm, January sometime," replied Hilly. "He was a bit strange at first, but he is really sweet."

"Hmmm, sweet," repeated Silliah, looking back at me. "What about Tayo?"

What a cow.

"January, too." I gave her an unconvincing warning stare, trying to hide my smile. Then we had a private text conversation on our Slates:

'OMG, YOU FANCY TAYO!'

'No. Really, I don't. He is an arrogant jackass.'

'I don't blame you. He is so fit!'

'I don't fancy him. I'm betrothed...'

'No harm in looking.' She included a winking face.

'I'm going now.'

'Say hello to Tayo for me.'

Standing up, I put my Slate away and took my tray to Tayo, still unable to look him in the eyes. The time in the Food Hall was supposed to have made things better, but Silliah had made it so much worse, and now I'd forgotten how to be normal.

"You can stop being weird now, Roar," said Tayo back in his cell.

"I'm not being weird."

"Right, okay. Well, I'm going to be normal, and you see if you can catch up."

My eyes narrowed at him, and I casually jumped up on the counter opposite his bed. "I'm not bei—"

"Shhhh. So, have you thought about what we are doing about the Kalmayan Kid?" he asked, lowering onto the bed and resting back on his hands.

"I can't think of anything except to extend his sentence. But I couldn't do that; it's too mean."

"It might be the only thing to keep you safe."

"I'm thinking about extending your sentence."

"Why?" He sat up with a straight back.

"You've only got five more months," I said, staring down at my hand doing an awkward finger crawl by my side. "And when you go, I'm never going to see you again."

"I told you back in the day you were going to miss me once I was gone."

"I never thought I would, and I mean never. But you're the only one who knows about me." I quit my silly finger dance and looked over at him. "What am I going to do when you're gone?"

"Well, not extend my sentence, whatever you do." Tayo stood up. "If I cuddle you, are you going to start being weird again?"

"I wasn't be-hmm-mm-mm." My words were muffled by Tayo smothering my head in his overalls until I shut up.

"You will be fine without me, Roar. I'll make sure of it. Who knows, I might see you out on Curfew Duty."

"Oh no, don't you dare."

"What was this for if it wasn't permission?" Tayo reached into his pocket and put on my old golden bracelet I'd given to him for his birthday. I figured he had been wearing it since the Lunatics Picnic, anyway, and I knew what it meant to him—it was his freedom.

"Oh, that reminds me. Look!" I remembered I wanted to show him something. Collecting my thoughts, I waved an open hand over his arm.

The bracelet disappeared, fading out of sight.

"Holy sh—sorry," he apologised for almost swearing. "Whoa, Roar. When…how…what the hell?"

"I had that dream again; you know the one where I open that leather book?"

"Yeah?"

"Then I woke up and knew how to do it."

"That's incredible! Wow. I'm so proud of you, Roar. What is it you do to do it?"

"I don't really know," I slowly admitted, looking down at the invisible bracelet.

"Maybe if you can figure it out, you'll be able to do other stuff."

"I just tell it what I want. I mean, I don't say it, I just think it and not in words either. I don't know; it's hard to explain. I kind of imagine it."

"Oh, Roar." He squeezed me really hard.

"Ouch! Body. Rib. Ow."

"Sorry. It's been ages. It's still hurting?"

"Only when you squeeze me like that."

"Oh. Sorry. Um, so, can I have my bracelet back, please?"

"Nah. I don't think so."

Tayo didn't like where this was going; I could see it written all over his face.

"You're either going to give it back," he said, stroking his fingertips up my thigh, "or I'm going to make it weird until you give it back."

"Whoa-you-can-have-it-back." I sat up rigidly and grabbed hold of his hand to stop the swirling feeling around my body.

"That's what I thought you said." He held out his wrist. After I returned the bracelet, he gave a sarky smirk. "Thank you."

"Oh, shut up." I flicked the back of my fingers over my thigh, shunning the tingling.

"Anyway," continued Tayo. "I know it's your birthday, and I couldn't exactly do much for you whilst in here, but..."

He turned to his bed and pulled out a piece of paper from under his pillow. I felt myself frown as I registered its familiarity. He gave me a sketch of a...me?

"Is that...?"

"It is," he answered before I even needed to finish.

"When I was a baby?"

"Yes."

"How? Have you got an old photo of me in here somewhere?"

"No, Roar." He didn't like the strange accusation.

"You drew this from memory?"

The realistic drawing was of my tired little face looking off to the side, the curls to my white hair nestled around my chubby cheeks, and my old unicorn-print pyjamas just visible on my shoulders.

"Yes, my little Roar. Happy birthday."

The next day, after a criminology lesson on my own, I headed to Tayo for lunch. To avoid Na-Nutta, I took the corridor between Navy Quartz and Khaki Quartz. As I turned in, I almost bumped into Pipila. Altering my course, I ignored her as I normally would, but Pipila stepped back into my path.

"What?" I said when she intentionally blocked my second stride to pass her.

Up until this point we were usually invisible to each other, but she clearly desired my attention today. Finally when her needs were met, she stepped out of the way. I rolled my eyes at her pointless attempt to intimidate me. Thinking the idiot realised she'd failed, I continued on my way.

"You might be betrothed," she called out, "but he enjoys me more."

If I knew exactly what that meant, I would have had her right here in this corridor, but my uncertainty kept my fists by my side. She ended the encounter by winking at me over her shoulder. I took a few steps back to see if wherever she headed was about to make her comment clear. Then I saw my world come crashing to a devastating end. He wouldn't...

Pipila walked through a Khakidemy door being held open by Pax. My paranoia would've probably been contained if it wasn't for his guilt-ridden face. What the hell were they doing? I couldn't un-see it. Is it cheating if the person has expressed a desire to repudiate? Is this what the rest of my time here was going to look like? Watching the person I lov—really care about, and my enemy sneaking around right under my nose?

I didn't remember moving my legs again but found myself sitting on a table in Claret Quartz.

"Aurora? We're over here. Hello? Aurora?" A touch on my shoulder brought me back to Earth. "You okay?" It was Silliah.

"Yeah."

"Come on. We're over here."

Next, my legs carried me to another seat. I was with the Fanciable Four, Silliah, and Brindan. Words fell out of my mouth, "Pipila and Pax." All six pairs of eyes hit the floor, the table, and anywhere but on me. "What?" I demanded for an explanation. The eyes moved on to other inanimate objects around the room. Silliah's found mine. "What are you not telling me?"

She stood up and took my hand. "Come on. Not here."

We marched round to Silliah's room. Probably a wise decision it wasn't mine, in case Pax returned to 4-3-4, causing my hands to incidentally find his throat. Her bedroom was small, exactly like the one I spent a few days in before I united.

"We thought you knew." Silliah encouraged me to sit down with her on the bed.

"Knew what?"

"About Pax and Pipila."

"Silliah, why would I know that? Are they... Do they...?" I couldn't speak; the idea tore out my heart. "Do they like each other?"

Silliah's face showed one of confusion. "Hang on. You actually don't know?"

"Know what?"

"Aurora, there is a way to end a betrothal. That's what those two have been doing together."

"What way? Having an affair can end a betrothal?"

"What? No. Whoa, Aurora. No, not an affair."

"Then what?"

"By getting a first-place spot on the Colosseum score boards."

"I don't get it. How does that end a betrothal?"

"If you get a top spot, you are given an invitation. There's one thing Seioh Boulderfell cares more about than repopulating his city with offspring raised by 'his children' and that's Serve, Honour, Protect, and Defend."

"It's an invitation to become a Fell agent?"

"It's an invitation to leave here and enrol at the Boulderfell Institute for Fell Agents where you train to become one. I'm sorry, Aurora. I thought you knew."

"I know he doesn't want to be united. I just didn't know there was a way not to be."

"Brindan says it's because of what Pax's parents did. I think Pax likes you too much and doesn't trust himself."

"Hmm." I didn't want to lie to her so I didn't say anything. "What? And Pipila wants to leave, too?"

"Yeeeah, but Brindan doesn't know if Ryker knows, so best keeping that to yourself."

CHAPTER FIFTEEN

GONE

Silliah rejoined the others in the Food Hall whilst I headed to see Tayo in a sort of daze. It really shouldn't have come as a shock to me; Pax made his intentions clear from the start. But he was my Pax, and he was leaving.

"Hey, Roar, I've been thinking…"

I wonder how Pax is doing on the scoreboards. He is quite good already, and if he has been training hard recently, it may only be a matter of time before I lose him. I'll have to go check after lunch.

"Roar, are you listening?"

"Sorry. What?"

"What's the matter with you?"

"Nothing."

"Roar." He came and sat up on the surface with me. "I know you. You do this whole 'I'm fine' and I'm all like 'no you're not,' and we do that a few times, but I don't relent, and then you end up telling me. So now, cut the BS and tell me what's wrong."

"Pax found a way of ending the betrothal."

"Oh."

"Hmm."

"How do you feel?"

"Numb."

Tayo held my hand beside our legs and let out a long sigh. "I hate what he is doing to you."

"I'm not exactly thrilled," I said, aware Tayo's grip tightened as he spoke. I had also learnt that when he sighed like that, it was usually his way of internalising his feelings so they didn't show outwardly.

"Did you two...you know?"

"Did we?" I asked, unsure.

"Did you sleep together?"

"*No*. Young Enforcers aren't allowed to...you know...do *that* whilst enlisted here."

"Really?" His eyes burned into the side of my head.

"Nooo." I couldn't look at him, keeping my eyes on the blank white wall opposite.

"Why?"

"Because Boulderfell doesn't want us having children before we've been discharged."

"There is contraception for that, you know?"

"I don't know, Tayo. I guess he doesn't want that distracting us all. It's actually illegal."

"You're kidding. That is *extremely* weird. So, does that mean you are all—"

"Yes."

"Until you're thirty?"

"Yes."

"Wow." Tayo gave a short awkward laugh. "What would happen if you were to?"

"Dishonourable discharge with a thirty-year prison sentence. If you get pregnant, then you are made to have the baby so it can be raised here. Did I not tell you about Pax? His parents are in Max."

Tayo's fingers under my palm twitched. "Aurora." Tayo calling me by my real name made me look at him. "Tell me you realise how messed up that is?"

I held my shoulders up to my ears. "I can't do anything about it, Tayo."

"But you know it's fuc—"

I shot him a look.

"—messed up?" he continued. "You know that Boulderfell guy is a right bloody weirdo?"

I knew he was being serious but I couldn't help but laugh. "Tayo."

"I'm being ser—"

"I know. I get it. What do you want me to say? Fine, it's weird, but I would be homeless if it weren't for him."

"No, you wouldn't."

"*Anyway*, what were you saying earlier?"

Tayo tutted at my change of subject but he let it drop. "Fine. I was thinking about what we could do with that Kalmayan Kid."

"Oh right, and?"

"You know what you did with my bracelet; do you think you could do it with your birthmark?"

"I can try, but he has already seen it. How's it going to help the situation?"

"If you can make it disappear, then all you would have to do is convince the boy you drew it on yourself and get him to wipe it off. Explain to him you found the symbol on the internet and you didn't know what it meant."

"Oh my god, Tayo. That is genius." I pulled my hand out from under his and waved it over my birthmark. Nothing happened...so I tried again.

Nothing.

I hitched up Tayo's sleeve and tried the bracelet.

Again, nothing.

"Maybe your powers are linked to your emotions. You were quite happy yesterday, but you've had some crap news today."

"Yeah, maybe. I'll keep trying. Come on. Let's go to the Food Hall." I jumped off the counter, and Tayo held out his wrist for me to scan.

"Are you going to stop staring at me today?"

"*Ohhh*, get over yourself, Tayo," I jibed, hiding how mortified I was that he'd noticed.

Tayo slid off the counter, scooped me into his side, and kissed my hair before pushing me past the door frame so he could exit the cell first. He poked his tongue out at me from the other side of the observer's window. I quickly grabbed my Slate and turned up his ankle trap, bringing him to a sudden stop.

"Do that again," I said on tiptoes, leaning into his ear, "and you'll really wish you hadn't." Then I carried on in the opposite direction, leaving him rooted to the spot.

"Er, ma'am?" he called after me, gesturing at the trap.

"Get a move on," I ordered him. Tayo stared back, trying to gauge if I was joking or not. I brought the weight down a tiny bit so he could move but only by using a lot of effort. Then I turned the corner, leaving him there, and poking my tongue out at him before I disappeared.

By the time he reached the Food Hall, I'd already finished, and I gave him my tray before he even walked under the archway. Tayo sucked on his bottom lip, trying desperately to control his reaction in front of the Food Hall full of Navies. I laughed to myself as I walked back the other way towards Claret Quartz, but then, after I'd amused myself, I released his trap so he could catch up.

"You think you're so clever," he said from up close behind my back.

"Stay a few paces behind but keep following me."

"What?"

"Seioh Jennson is up ahead. I want to talk to him."

I ran to catch up with Jennson about to turn the corner towards Claret Quartz.

"Seioh," I said, jogging to keep up with his speed walk.

"Yes, Miss Aviary—and ask me your question without starting it with *erm*."

"Yes, Seioh. Erm, Oh!" I came to a stop. Jennson continued power walking as though I never existed. After kicking myself, I ran to try again. "Seioh."

"Yes, Miss Aviary." The whole time he kept his eyes on where he was going.

"I was wondering…am I earning any Worths yet?"

"Yes, Miss Aviary, since yesterday. Check your account."

"Thank you, Seioh." I stopped jogging and watched Jennson turn into Mustard Quartz.

Tayo caught up with me and intentionally bumped into my shoulder. "You are funny."

"You heard that?" I asked, cringing.

"'Ask me your question without starting it with *erm*.' 'Yes, Seioh… ERM'!"

"If we weren't in the open right now, I'd have you—oh, never mind."

"Yeah, good idea. Wouldn't want you being weird again."

"Did you like your walk to the Food Hall? Would you like to do it again?"

"No, ma'am." Tayo actually looked worried.

"Well then."

I smirked. Tayo scowled. But I wasn't mean, and I took him back to his cell without a weighted trap.

After a day spent living in my distracted head, trying to digest the fact Pax was leaving, when evening came, he weighed heavily on my mind. I could hear him in his room, and every little noise caused me to stare at our door. I put my attention back on my Slate until a cough sent me fixating again. *That's enough*, I told myself. But it was no use, so I made myself go and take a shower.

The steam billowed out of the glass door, and I took a seat in front of a row of jets allowing them to pummel down my spine. The force sent the water splitting in half, creating a soothing mist around my face. With the rainfall shower massaging my legs, I swayed my head over a jet to knead the soft tissue on the back of my neck. Then I drew a heart in the condensation on the door…and cursed at myself. *Dammit.*

A while later, I dried my hair and put on my standard issue underwear—an all-white T-shirt bra and briefs—after I decided a visit to Silliah was a good idea. When I opened my wardrobe for a Navy uniform, I saw an item scrunched up in the bottom corner. It was Pax's pyjama top from the day we had our food fight. I held it out in front of me as the bittersweet memory played in my head. I slipped my arms in it and traced the 'PF' embroidery with my middle finger. *He is…my Pax.*

Losing the battle, I wandered over to our adjoining door and listened. He was only on the other side of this wall, but yet to me, he felt so far away.

Turn around, Aurora.

I pushed the access button.

He lay on the bed, mood lighting set to a sapphire blue, and his attention taken away from the Slate in his hands. I stood still in the doorway unsure of what I was doing. Pax's eyes fell upon his initials on the shirt, and then lowered to my bare legs. He watched me cross the room. Neither of us spoke.

I climbed to sit astride him, and he lifted his arm, bringing his hand to rest on my outer thigh. Those troubled amber eyes searched mine. When the unbuttoned shirt gaped open, Pax sat up to pull his own shirt off over his head. He ran his fingers underneath my collar and allowed the pyjama top to slip off my shoulders. Our bodies touching, we were skin on skin for the first time. He watched as he ran the back of his fingers all the way down my arms. Then he pushed his fingertips up my spine, coming to hold on underneath my hair. When he kissed my shoulders, I breathed deeply into his neck, fighting the temptation to kiss him back. Why was my body trembling?

The affection becoming too much to bear, I pushed him to lay back down and placed my ear over his conflicted heart. We composed ourselves here for a while as I listened to his heartbeat steadying. With his fingers running up and down my back in a gentle rhythm, my eyes closed. His natural scent calmed me.

"Why do you want to leave me?" I asked, keeping my eyes closed and my head on his heart.

I…don't, I heard him say faintly.

"You don't?"

"Huh?"

"You said you don't?" I repeated, hearing his heart starting to race again, so much so, it made me sit up to see him.

Pax's arm came over to cover his face. "No, Aurora. I didn't *say* that; I *thought* it."

"What? Ah-Ah-I'm sorry. I'm really, *really* sorry. I didn't mean to do…to do…that. I'll never do it again." I tried to apologise for invading his privacy, but Pax didn't respond. "I'm sorry for coming in here. I think it's about time I start…healing."

Pax kept his eyes covered and nodded. That was all the confirmation I needed, so I pulled my Promises ring off my finger, left it on his chest, and ran from the room.

⚝

In the time that passed, my heart didn't heal. I didn't know how to make it start recovering. How could I when I saw his face every day? That being said, I was trying to help myself, and I hadn't stepped foot into his room since. The only thing keeping us together was our meal times and the odd duty. The rest of the time he trained in the Khakidemy with Pipila, during which he'd managed to procure a twentieth position on the Flexon Pro scoreboard. Now all that was left was watching him climb up the ranks, one by one, until he was gone from my life forever.

Tayo seemed to be the only person who could get me to forget here and there. We'd been practicing making my birthmark disappear, and I was getting pretty good at it, but I could only make it invisible for a short time before it came back of its own accord.

"What do you think?" Tayo asked. "Fifteen minutes enough time for you?"

"I'd rather longer, but it's taken three months to get this far."

"Fifteen minutes can be enough for some girls."

"What?" I asked, completely lost, and watched Tayo laugh to himself like I wasn't in the room. "Laughing at your own jokes again, Tayo?"

He laughed more. "Well, if I don't laugh at them, who will?"

"Certainly not me." I glowered at him until he calmed down.

"Right, so are you doing this?" He leant forward off the bed and dragged the chair I sat on towards him.

"I suppose."

"Do you have Silliah's thing?"

"Eyeliner."

Tayo held out his hand. "Give it here, then."

I took Silliah's brown eyeliner pencil out from my trouser leg cargo pocket and passed it to Tayo. He removed the lid and brought my hand to rest on his knee. I curled my fingers around his thumb, and he lifted his eyes to mine.

"What have you gone all quiet for?"

I shrugged.

"What's up?" He surveyed me.

"I don't want you to leave, Tayo." My eyes began to sting.

"Come here; come with me." He stood up off the bed and led me into the ensuite to hold me in his arms. His hand scrunched the back of my neck. "I've got two more months yet."

"It's just going so quick."

"I know." He breathed the words into my hair.

"Please let me extend your sentence?"

Tayo swallowed and his breathing grew heavier. Then after a minute he said, "Alright."

"*Alright*?" I pulled out of the hug.

"Yes. Alright."

"But, do you—oh no, I can't do that to you."

"Start sneaking me some decent food, and I'll stay longer if you need me to."

"You really would do that for me, wouldn't you?"

"Yes, Roar."

"Well, I'm not doing that to you."

"You do what you need to do, okay?"

"Maybe six more months?" I half joked. "But I think what I need to do first is go and see the Kalmaya—what is his name?"

"Poynter."

"Right." I took a deep breath to prepare myself. "It's getting late, so I'm going to have to let you know how it goes in the morning."

After Tayo drew over my birthmark with Silliah's eyeliner pencil, I located Poynter's cell. Pressing my back up against the wall to J-87, I steadied my nerves. Tayo left a tiny section of my birthmark visible so I could tell it was definitely gone. I focused my mind and waved my hand over the drawing.

It didn't work; I could still see it there. It must've been because I was too nervous. So, I closed my eyes and thought about the time Pax bit my neck when we were play fighting. I let the stimulating feeling develop throughout my body. Reopening my eyes, I gave the invisible thing another go.

It didn't work. The memory had a sadness ladened in it, and I needed to try something else. Closing my eyes again, I remembered the time I twisted Tayo's arm behind his back to make him apologise. My mouth curved into an easy smile at the memory, and I gave the magic another try.

Again, nothing.

Fine. I had something else I could use but I was putting it off. The memory I thought about was Tayo yanking me into the ensuite and telling me he didn't think I would punch him in the mouth if he kissed me. I remembered the strange tension, those piercing-blue eyes, and the heat rising under my skin.

I reopened my eyes and could feel the animated energy accumulating in every cell. I waved my hand over once again and imagined the birthmark disappearing. Thanks, Tayo. I smiled to myself after I looked down at the drawing without its underlay. It worked. *Okay, fifteen minutes. Here goes nothing.*

When I opened J-87, the lights switched themselves on. The sleepy boy, already startled by the rude awakening, was sent into a panic at the sight of my face.

"Hey, it's okay. Poynter, I'm not going to hurt you."

Terror entangled the boy's eyes. Knowing I had to play this one very carefully, I crouched down by the door. I saw the tattoos on the left side of his face and forehead clearly for the first time, thick black lines, dots, triangles, thinner lines jutting around, creating small symbols. It was possibly another language, but not one I'd ever seen. Poynter huddled into the corner, pulling the white duvet up to his chin.

I tried to keep my voice soft. "I just want to talk to you."

His body visibly trembled, but he was paralysed with fear. When the boy didn't speak, I sat down on the floor properly. This was going to take longer than I expected, and time was not something I had an abundance of. I began by having a one-way conversation with myself. "What is it you are so scared of? We haven't met before, have we?" All the while, Poynter's expression remained the same: totally petrified. I stretched my arms out above my head and Poynter's eyes followed my wrist. I cringed at my conspicuousness, but I really needed to get this plan moving. "You don't like my drawing, do you?" I could tell he listened, because he seemed confused, and I continued having a conversation with myself. "What does it mean to you?" I held up Tayo's artwork.

"It's," Poynter finally spoke. "It's—"

That was all I got from him.

"I found it on the internet," I explained. "It's supposed to mean balance. That's why it looks a little bit like the number eight." *I'm lying to an eight-year-old boy—I'm going to hell.*

Poynter's countenance changed, and he slowly shook his head. "That's not what that is."

I pushed my back against the wall, sliding up to my feet. As I did so, Poynter scurried further into the corner.

"I'm not going to hurt you, I swear. I'm just going to sit down on the chair." I spun the chair around to face the bed and lowered onto it. "What does this symbol mean, then?"

Poynter shook his head again.

"It's not real." I held my hand out to him. "It's a drawing."

Poynter lifted his head up as if to get a better look. "A drawing?"

"Yeah. What did you think it was?"

"You weren't born with it?" The duvet began gradually coming away from under his chin.

"Born with it? No. Look." I rubbed some of it away. So far so good; no real birthmark showing underneath. Then I held my wrist out for Poynter. "See for yourself. You're allowed to touch me. You have my permission."

Poynter dropped the duvet and leant over on his knees. He used his index finger to smudge the eyeliner and then sat back on his legs. "I wouldn't draw that on yourself," he spoke, seemingly more confident.

"Why not?" I asked, investigating what my birthmark really meant.

"It's the mark of the devil."

Oh, of course, that old chestnut: 'Beware the angel with the devil's mark.' "How can an angel be wearing a devil's mark?"

"It's the mark of the Guidal. It is said among my people that when this symbol returns, the bearer will summon the darkness."

"The Guy Doll?"

"No, the Guidal."

"What's the Guidal?"

"Puracordis."

"Puracordis? Do they even exist?"

"Yes."

One-worded answers; the joys of conversing with an eight-year-old. "How do you know they exist?"

Poynter shrugged.

My head hurt.

So, my birthmark is the mark of 'the Guidal,' who's said to 'summon the darkness.' What does that even mean? He was right about one thing, though: I was Puracordis.

I leant back in the chair, trying to act naturally. "So this 'Guidal,' other than being Puracordis, what is it?"

"The person who's going to summon the darkness."

"And that's it?"

"That's all I know. It is why we hunt Puracordis: to find the Guidal. Our queen is trying to stop the evil."

"Queen?" I repeated, rubbing my forehead. Just then, out the corner of my eye, I saw my birthmark reappearing underneath the smudged eyeliner—and at the most inopportune moment possible! I pulled my sleeve down and pretended my Slate vibrated.

"Sorry, Poynter." I stared down at my blank screen. "I've got to go, but I'll come see you again tomorrow, if that's alright?"

"Yes, ma'am."

I think he liked having someone to talk to on the subject. I presumed nobody else here gave that kind of talk the time of day. I left the cell with a smile; Tayo's plan worked. He could be so calculated, it scared me. Even though tonight's scheming proved successful, I was still none the wiser on how an angel could bear a devil's mark. Surely it wasn't an evil symbol. It was on the door in the pipe and on the leather book in my dream. Perhaps the evil they spoke of was maleficium.

I had so much I needed to share with Tayo, it made my night's sleep restless. Of all the information I learnt from Poynter, one thing would punch me in the gut at the returning thought. If I was the Guidal, then I was the reason they hunted Puracordis—which meant the Kalmayans were looking for *me*. I realised now the significance of Tayo's Lunatics Picnic. If he hadn't been able to convince me to go, I wouldn't have known that Poynter was aware of me. The boy would have been released in two months, and then the Kalmayans would've been knocking at my door. I shuddered to think what might've become of me—and Pax, for that matter. A disturbingly accurate death sentence came to mind.

The alarm didn't need to wake me in the morning. I was already up, ready, and waiting. After cleaning the eyeliner from my wrist, I sat practising my magic. I couldn't afford the risk of having such an obvious giveaway being on display. It was now even more critical I mastered this invisibility lark. After waiting fifteen minutes and watching my birthmark reappear, I timed how long it took before I was able to make it go again. I ended the stopwatch at seven minutes. *Hmm, could be worse; seven minutes there, fifteen minutes not.*

With Tayo on the brain, I bounded to J-14. Outside, the mornings were once again dark. The trees had cleansed themselves of their rusty coloured leaves and the roadways were decorated in them.

Halfway down Tayo's corridor, an impending realisation caused my body to go into shutdown. I slowed down; a protection mechanism kicked in, prolonging the devastating reality from tearing me apart. Tayo's cell door was *open*.

Apprehensively, I peered into the observer's window. *He could be in the ensuite.* Until I knew the truth, it wasn't real, and that ignorance was my only preservation right now, but there was only so long denial could protect me. I passed the threshold into Tayo's empty cell.

The bed was slept in and crinkled. The wardrobe by the door was empty. A pair of dirty white plimsoles lay at the foot of the bed. I whipped out my Slate to check my schedule. Then my knees buckled, and I collapsed onto the bed. I was no longer a Juvie chaperone to J-14. Tayo had been granted early release.

The oxygen was sucked from the room and I couldn't breathe. Taking up Tayo's pillow, I held it to my face. My wet cheeks stuck to the cotton, and I repressed the need to scream into it. He was…my best friend. I didn't even get to say goodbye.

Soon, I could breathe through the short, jerky breaths juddering my upper body. How long I sat there for, I didn't know. A figure drifting past the door dragged me back into the room. It took a step backwards, returning to stand in the doorway. Then it entered the cell and sat on the bed next to me. A hand wearing a Promises ring touched my leg. I looked up.

"Don't, Pax." I pushed his hand off my leg.

"Aurora—"

"Have you changed your mind?" I interrupted, pulling my closed fist to my chest when he reached for my hand.

"Aurora—"

"Exactly. So then *don't*. Stop pretending you care about me."

Pax closed his mouth and made an indignant airy noise at the back of his throat. I could see his clenched teeth through his strong jaw.

"Can you just go?"

"Aurora," he said with an exasperated undertone.

"No. There's nothing you can say to me that will make me feel better. If you won't go, then I will." I didn't finish my sentence before heading towards the door.

"They are in a holding room waiting for Curfew to end," he said quickly.

I stopped in the doorway. "They?"

"Curfew ends in three minutes. Walk and talk?"

"Fine." I resigned myself to the fact I would need to go with him.

"We need to hurry. They will probably be waiting in the Claret reception already."

"Tayo had two more months yet." A pain tore across my chest, but the sadness quickly turned to resentment at our time together being taken from us early.

"His sentence was extended by an Enforcer. After their initial sentence, it's up to Seioh Jennson to release them. The Kalmayan Kid is leaving too. Seioh usually allows Juvies to complete their whole sentence, but Maigen passed her Worths exam yesterday." Pax cleared his throat. "The girls are leaving today."

"Oh." I could tell he, too, battled with his emotions.

"You know, after your first Juvie leaves, you learn to not get attached. But I've had the Davoren Sisters for two and a half years. After that long, I guess you can't help but grow fond of someone. Each time they left before, I knew they were coming back. It's different this time."

I couldn't believe how stupid I was for letting myself get so attached to Tayo. Juvies are not one of us. They all leave at some point. Pax was right: I would never make that mistake again.

Pax held open the Claret Quartz doors, and I exited in time to see the reception doors part. Standing in front of them, looking like a united front, was Beth, Mai, Poynter, and Tayo.

The sisters must have been imprisoned in the summer, because they both had short sleeve T-shirts on. Bethoney had clearly grown quite a bit since then. Her blue jeans swung above her ankles, but the hem around the bottoms was frayed. I assumed she'd probably worn them when they were too big; given their Worths situation, they were probably Maigen's hand-me-downs.

Poynter was cloaked in some kind of long tan wrap with a hood. His baggy brown trousers cuffed in around his ankles, and the excess material meant his growth spurt went unnoticed.

Tayo was...*oh*. I had only ever seen him in claret overalls (or topless with shorts). Ironically, he now sported an impeccable, well-tailored, *navy-blue* suit. A buttonless side split, a small straight collar, the slim fitted jacket made him unrecognisable. His black shoes were polished, and everything about him conveyed Band A. Under his left sleeve, a silver and gold watch joined my old golden bracelet. He'd styled his hair, but I was pleased to see he used product to make it look intentionally messy. Tayo was no longer my jackass of a Juvie—he was a *young man*.

As he stepped off to leave, I coughed to get his attention. All four of them turned to look but I only saw Tayo. His smile reached his piercing-blue eyes as they locked on to mine. My throat cramped from suppressing the agony building inside me. A few steps later, I lost him to the morning darkness, and he was...gone.

CHAPTER SIXTEEN

NOBODY EXCEPT YOU

I wondered if the human body ever dried up of tears, because the amount I'd shed in the last week was abnormal. I didn't remember much of the past seven days because I wasn't there to live it. Where I was exactly, I wasn't sure, but I would imagine it was spent in the deepest, darkest corners of my mind.

Waking up in the mornings just wasn't the same anymore. For the past eight months (after 'Nothing will ever come between us. You're Puracordis? Goodbye!'), the first person I would talk to, the first person I would see was now *gone*. I didn't know how to be a First-year without him.

I wished I never took it for granted. I wished I could have spent more time with him. 'You know I hate it when you leave me in here.' I heard his words distinctly in my head. I did know, but I did it on purpose. If I could go back, I would never leave him in his cell during meal times again.

"Aurora?" There was Pax again, pretending he gave a shit.

"Get out, Pax."

"You've told me to get out every day for a week. Has it worked? No."

My body shifted as his weight rocked the mattress. I kept my eyes securely closed. "I forgot you get a kick out of seeing me upset."

"Are you getting up?" he asked as if I hadn't said anything.

"Get out."

This morning was going exactly the same way as the past six... or was it seven? I had no idea anymore. The duvet slipped off my face, and I flung my arm over my red-rimmed eyes. Once again, Pax scooped my limp body up in the air. I'd stopped fighting—it was no use. Every day he would carry me to the ensuite, threaten to get me undressed if I didn't, and then wait on the other side of the partition wall in the small walkway. I would leave the ensuite dressed for another Tayo-less day, and ready for my shadow to follow me to the Food Hall.

On a table in Navy Quartz, I didn't waste any time in falling forward onto my arms. Everyone blamed my behaviour on Pax. They thought I was upset because he was leaving. He'd climbed three spaces in a week and now held the seventeenth position for the Flexon. At this rate, he'd be gone partway through next year.

This morning, Ryker came and squeezed my shoulders like he'd done every day this week. Brindan kissed my head. Silliah and the Fanciable Four hugged my back. Then they all sat and conversed like I wasn't in the room.

I covered my ears to dampen Hilly's shrill voice, "The Kalmayan Kid has been gone a week today."

"Still missing him?" I think that was Shola.

"I miss his little smile in the mornings," Hilly replied with a brightness in her voice.

I heard the sound of metal on china as Silliah put her spoon down and said, "I had no idea it was like this."

"Oh, I'm not talking to my next Juvie," butted in Hilly.

Silliah laughed. "Took the words right out of my mouth."

"Oh my god," burped Hilly. Even my curiosity piqued. "Did... anyone...see...*Tayo* in that suit?"

Hearing his name sent me spiralling back down into my dark, dark...*dark* abyss. I couldn't do this. I was on my feet and out of the room quicker than Pax was on the Flexon. The door I found myself outside was one I'd only been behind a handful of times. My knuckles tapped on the door.

"Come in," called Seioh Jennson.

My fingers found the access button, my legs carried me inside, and my body keeled over onto the black leather sofa. Seioh Jennson continued working on his computer and didn't acknowledge my arrival. He didn't speak and neither did I. Lying on my front with my arm draping to the floor, I stared at the inside of my eyelids until I found peace in my dreams.

Seioh Jennson left the room. Seioh Jennson entered the room. The tapping of Jennson's typing lulled me back to sleep.

"Little Lady?" Nanny Kimly spoke softly. "It's time for dinner, darling." She knelt on the floor, bringing her eyes level with mine.

I blinked the office back into focus. Seioh Jennson was no longer in the room.

"Nanny Kimly, I don't want to do this anymore."

"You don't want to do what?" she asked, her head tipping to the side.

"I don't want to be here. I don't want to train. I don't want to go to lessons. I don't want another Juvie."

"Oh, Little Lady." She put her hand to my cheek. "Go and get in bed, I'll bring you some dinner, and we can talk, okay?"

Without speaking, I slithered off the sofa.

Nanny Kimly met me back in my room with a bowl of casserole on a white tray. I had already changed into my pyjamas and tucked myself up in bed, setting the mood lighting to a piercing blue.

"You slept on Seioh Jennson's sofa all day?" quizzed Nanny Kimly, holding an amused but confused smile.

"I honestly didn't know where else to go. If I had come in here, he would've only come and got me up."

"Yes. You are probably right. Now, are you going to tell me what this is all about? Why do I get the feeling this is about more than just Paxton?"

I shrugged.

"Am I right?"

I shrugged again.

"Juvies come and go, Little Lady." She guessed it in one. "You will learn to not grow attached to them."

"You don't understand," I said, dipping my spoon in and out of the gravy, giving it more attention than necessary.

"Oh, but I do, Little Lady."

I peeled my eyes away from my casserole. What did she know?

"Don't think I didn't recognise who he was."

My chest tightened, and I put my full attention back on my dinner. "Who he was?"

"Yes, Little Lady." She gave me one of her you-can-drop-the-act looks. "Mr. Tessan had a brief visit here once. He was too young to be a Juvie that time, but he wasn't averse to breaking Curfew then, and evidently, he didn't grow out of it."

"I didn't know you recognised him. Why didn't you say anything? I asked you about Tayo at the start of First-year and you wouldn't tell me about him."

"I know a great many things, Aurora. Not all of which I can tell you whilst you're enlisted here. I've told you before, it's best to keep the questions to a minimum."

She'd been telling me my whole life to stop asking questions about my old life. I realised now it was because she knew my parents were ex-Enforcers.

"I know you're not allowed to talk about them, Nanny Kimly, but I wouldn't tell anybody, you know?"

"I've learnt no good comes of it."

"Are you talking about Pax?"

"He isn't supposed to know about his parents."

"Nanny Kimly, it's not your fault. What he is doing to me has nothing to do with you telling him about his parents."

"Even if that is so, it has affected him in other ways."

"Regardless, he had a right to know." I still tried to assure her.

"He struggled in Mustard after, and I learnt my lesson. No good comes from talking about past lives." She gazed towards Pax's room, her hazel eyes losing focus. "Right, Little Lady." Her eyes sharpened back on mine. "I've got rounds I need to do. Are you going to be okay?"

"Yeah, I'll be fine. Thank you, Nanny."

"And regarding Tayo, you'll feel better with time, I promise."

Tayo...

My mind wandered back there.

※

"Good morning, Miss Aviary," greeted Soami the next day. "You have a last-minute alteration to your schedule today."

The last time Soami said that sentence was after Tayo's Lunatics Picnic, when Seioh Jennson requested a meeting. The memory caused me to break out into a sweat, and I was grateful when Pax pulled the duvet off my face.

"Aurora?"

"Get out, Pax."

"Are you getting up?" he asked, taking a seat on the bed.

"Don't you get bored with being so self-righteous all the time?"

He ignored my comment. "Where's your Slate? You have a last minute—"

"*I know.* She was talking to me, not you."

He must have found my Slate on the bed because he said, "Yours is the same as mine. We've been put on a restricted schedule. You didn't go on an unauthorised Curfew Duty again, did you?"

"No, Pax. I didn't."

"Alright, just checking. Come on. We've got a meeting with Seioh Jennson."

I took no notice of him and kept my arm over my face. But when I felt Pax stand up from the bed, I knew what was coming, so I rolled to the other side and got myself up for the first time this week. I didn't look behind me as I entered the ensuite.

When I exited, I hoped Pax had gotten the message and had gone to the Food Hall already, but that was wishful thinking. I forgot to take a Navy uniform in the ensuite with me, and he stood waiting in the walkway holding one out to me. Taking it without a thank you, I shut the door in his face.

The second time I came out, Pax wouldn't let me pass him. He dragged me into his chest, and I instantly burst into tears. Why? I had no idea. It was easier being mad at Pax, but I didn't want to hate him anymore.

"I know you're mad at me," he said, stroking my hair. "Just please let me help you."

"I can't." I pulled away.

At breakfast my head found my arms; Ryker massaged my shoulders; Brindan kissed my hair; and Silliah hugged my back. All the while, Pax still sat next to me. I don't think anyone knew what to make of the situation, but nevertheless, they all handled it like it was normal.

When Pax and I reached Seioh Jennson's office, the door opened before we could knock, and Jennson requested we follow him up the elevator to the first floor. Our destination? The rooftop garden.

As the glass doors parted, a strong wind gusted through, caressing my entire body. The roof had been retracted and the unexpected morning breeze refreshed me. I hadn't felt like this in days, and it was as if the invigorating breeze swept by and lifted me from the abyss. The sun on the horizon boastfully doused the sky in a mixture of rosy glows and silvery wisps worthy of a display screen. Pax and I stood enchanted by the sunrise. I could almost feel the broken parts of me starting to heal.

When we turned around, Seioh Jennson was nowhere to be seen. Pax shrugged at me and slung his arm over my shoulder. I rested my head against his, and even though it was chilly, we didn't move until the blazing rays forced us to look away. Pax then activated the roof, returning the garden back to how I was accustomed, and we spent the day gardening. Pax taught me how to sow seeds. He was surprised to see we were planting food, since previously, he had only ever grown flowers. We watered them using the rainwater collected by the harvesting system, and then we watched the sunset before returning to our rooms. It was too early for dinner, and the restricted schedule gave us nothing better to do than wait around.

⚜

"Good morning, Miss Aviary," greeted Soami the next morning. "You have a last-minute alteration to your schedule today."

Oh, not again. I felt around for my Slate to see what it was, but before I found it, the interconnecting door opened.

"Aurora?"

Today, I didn't answer.

"Aurora? Have you seen our schedule?"

Pax swiped the duvet off my face. I remained quiet and still, my eyes closed.

"What are you doing?" Pax asked, laughing. I could hear the confusion in his voice. "If this is another attempt to get me to leave you alone, it's not going to work."

I carried on playing dead.

Pax tickled under my ribs, instantly causing my body to convulse, and I instinctively grabbed for his hand, ending the irritating, painful sensation that for some unknown reason made me laugh, not cry. I guarded my ribs with my elbows and continued to stay motionless, fists clenched just in case.

"Are you waiting for me to pick you up today?" asked a still none-the-wiser Pax. He didn't wait for a response and scooped me up. "What are you like?"

Pax carried me into the ensuite. When he put me down, I thought about lying on the bathroom floor to see how far I could push him, but I decided against it and instead opted for standing with an impassive expression.

"Aurora," warned Pax, starting to gather what was happening. "Are you really doing this?"

I stared at him enigmatically. *Go on,* I thought, *get me undressed then.*

"Really, Aurora?" He gave me one more chance to get myself ready for the shower. "Why do you insist on testing me?" Pax stepped into me and reached for the top button of my pyjama shirt. He lingered with his fingers pinched around the button and sighed. Then he undid it and slowly slid his fingers down to the next one. The shirt parted slightly, and when Pax saw I had no underwear on underneath, his eyes came up to meet mine. He searched my face to see how serious I was. I maintained my impassive stare, so Pax continued to make his way down the buttons until the very last one was unfastened. He circled around to stand behind me, gathered my hair to the centre of my back, tucked his fingers under the collar, and slid the top off my shoulders.

"Stop-I'm-joking-I'm-joking," I said, giggling, and snatched my pyjama top closed.

Pax rolled his eyes. "You're in a better mood today."

"Get out." I restored the habit from the past week but this time with a smirk.

"Ah, that's more like it."

"What's the last-minute alteration to our schedule?" I asked.

"We have training after gardening today, at fifteen hundred hours."

"Hm, that's not so bad."

In the Food Hall, I didn't have my head on the table today. Pax was right; I did feel better. Maybe it was the gardening; maybe it was spending time with Pax; maybe it was talking with Nanny Kimly; or perhaps, maybe it was knowing that if I really couldn't be on form, I wasn't going to be forced. When I hit rock bottom, Seioh Jennson allowed me to sleep on his sofa. I mean, I wasn't going to try that again, but it made me feel like the people here were human, and we were seen as human, too.

This morning, Ryker came and dug his thumbs into my trapezius. "Look who's stopped feeling sorry for themselves."

I immediately grabbed his hand and twisted it into a wrist lock.

"Ouch! Yep! Okay, definitely feeling better."

Why is it when I stand up to Ryker, the table falls completely still? I let go of his hand, only for him to slap me on the side of my head. I glared at him as he walked around the tables to the seat opposite me. Brindan stroked my hair, then circled the tables to take his seat opposite Pax. Silliah still hugged me, but she kissed my cheek today and then sat beside me.

"Feeling better today?" Tyga hugged me, then sat next to Ryker.

"Yes. I suppose I am," I replied, still a little surprised myself.

His light-brown eyes flicked sideways at Pax and a repugnant look overcame his boyish face. *Oh…he doesn't like Pax?* Or maybe he didn't like what Pax was doing to me. I was annoyed that Pax couldn't accept the fact I was Puracordis, but in the same breath, I couldn't blame him either. It wasn't really Pax's fault. But I couldn't explain that to Tyga.

"Good. I'm pleased," said Tyga, taking his eyes off Pax. "When are you training next? I am *so close* to beating your score on the Flexon."

"Oh right." I smiled. "Have you been waiting to tell me that, or something?"

"Only for like a *week*."

"Erm, I'm pretty sure I've beaten my score since that time you watched."

"Dammit. Well, you're going to have to show me. I've been trying all year to get ninety-two."

"What can you get?"

His face creased. "Seventy-nine."

"Not too far off."

"Yeah, but it suddenly gets really hard after sixty. How these Third-years get over one hundred, I have no idea."

"I can have a go later; I've got training with everyone today."

Later that day, after gardening with Pax, I changed into my training clothes, and entered the Colosseum with Silliah and the Fanciable Four. I couldn't help but see how Pax was doing on the scoreboards: he still held the seventeenth position with one hundred and eighty-two. It got harder at certain stages, and one hundred and eighty was apparently one of them. He would need one hundred and eighty-four to get sixteenth. But it was a long way off first place, Saulwyn Field with two hundred and thirty.

All six of us gathered around the Flexon Pro, and everyone took their turn—none of them managing past sixty except Tyga. "Eighty-one. Impressive work, Mr. T Cicero," praised Soami.

"OK," Tyga jumped off the machine. "That definitely gets harder past eighty. Did you see how quickly that changed?"

"I think it does," I agreed, nodding. "Eighty-one is still amazing."

Lady Joanne Maxhin seemed to think so, too, because she awarded Tyga one hundred Worths. When she walked away, Tyga encouraged me to take my turn.

Stepping onto the black foam pads, my mind wandered somewhere else. I found that I didn't really need to concentrate so hard anymore, and it was easier when I just allowed my body to do the work. When I tried too hard, for some reason I did worse. Relaxing was the best way. My movements became fluid and effortless. I lost all sense of time and all sense of myself. That was why I found that electric drone sound so irritating. It would wrench me back to reality.

"One hundred and sixty-one," called out Soami. "A new leaderboard entry. Congratulations, Miss Aviary."

Holographic confetti exploded above our heads, immersing the whole room in an ocean of glittering shrapnel. The multitude of pieces fluttered gracefully, mimicking the catching of a breeze. I watched one float its way downward, twinkling as it twisted and turned, then fading out of sight before reaching head height. At the same time as the confetti bomb, all the text displayed on the scoreboards broke down into a thousand pixels, and came together in one large swarm. This huge mass whizzed around the Colosseum walls, passing through each board in turn. Once the pixels reached the Flexon Pro scoreboard, they wrote my name at the twentieth position, then returned back to their original places.

After my achievement was recorded, the room of Navies turned to give their commendation. The room was so loud I could hardly hear Lady Joanne Maxhin speak, "What did I tell you, huh? Did I not say we would be seeing you on the scoreboards in no time? I'm awarding you five thousand Worths for being the only First-year I have ever seen up on those walls. I'm proud of you, Aurora."

"Thank you, ma'am."

"Holy clart, Aurora," shouted Tyga. "I've got no chance. How do you do that?"

"I just relax and don't try too hard."

"Let me try," he said, jumping back up on the machine.

Just then, I heard a voice in my head. I knew it came from inside my head because I started to recognise that slight echo-like quality to it.

Whoa, you might want to steady on there, little witch.

I spun on the spot for him. I knew whose voice it belonged to, but where was he? After a full circle, I locked eyes with Pax. He was standing up against the side of the next machine along, his eyebrows raised and wearing a thin smile. Did he want me to hear that?

I tried to speak back to him telepathically: *Just because I'm almost as good as you, I've got to be cheating?*

Pax heard me and responded: *You were turning before the pad had even lit up...just saying.* He pushed off the machine and turned away.

So he did intend for me to hear him. Was I turning too early? I couldn't tell. I would have to watch out for that next time.

"Get out the way. I ain't being knocked off the scoreboard by a First-year," said a fully-grown man, charging straight at me. He looked behind him, making sure Pax wasn't looking, and then he pushed me aside.

I lunged at the sore loser. "Do you wanna try that aga—" I was yanked backwards, a hand covering my mouth. Brindan's face appeared against mine.

"Go on," barged in Ryker. "Push her again and see what happens."

The man held his hands up to Ryker. "Alright, bro. I didn't realise who she was."

"Like hell you didn't. Now apologise."

With his blue eyes wide, the man looked over at me. "Sorry, Aurora." He slowly backed away.

When he was gone, I rounded on Ryker, but it seemed Ryker did the same to me.

"I don't need you to fight my battles for me, Ryker." I got my words out first.

Ryker's eyes were darker than usual. "Do you want to be standing at that chute again? Because that's exactly where you would've been headed if you had touched him."

"What the hell do you care?"

"I don't. Oh, whatever, you stupid bitch," said Ryker, taking off.

I didn't watch him go because I took off, too.

"*Arrgggh!*" I growled at myself, storming through the changing room doors.

What the hell was wrong with me? Ryker was right; I would've been punished again. That's if I'm not still going to be. I didn't have to touch Pipila on my first day, but Jennson still made me wear my Mustard uniform. *What have I done?*

"Come in," responded Seioh Jennson.

I pushed the access button, and without waiting for permission to sit, I slumped into the black chair in front of his desk. "Seioh Jennson, I did it again," I confessed, covering my face with both hands.

"Where's your Navy uniform, Miss Aviary?"

"It's in my locker, Seioh."

"Okay. Let me rephrase my question. Why aren't you wearing your Navy uniform, Miss Aviary?"

"Because…I lost my temper again."

"It is against the institute's code of conduct to not be wearing your Navy uniform, Miss Aviary."

"But, Seioh, I los—"

"Are you still in my office not wearing your Navy uniform?"

"Yes, Seioh." And I had no intention of moving. That was until he peeled his cold blue eyes away from the computer and gave me that death stare. I huffed loudly and left the office. *Whatever.*

I didn't bother going to the Khakidemy for my Navy uniform, and I didn't bother going back to see Jennson either. Instead, I went straight to bed. *Come and get me up if you care so much.*

I settled in bed, fully clothed, and I immediately started drifting in and out of consciousness. I was mentally exhausted and felt as if I could sleep for years. That was until I heard a noise. My eyes sprung open and my ears pricked.

"Pssst." I heard it again. The top of my head tingled, and I held still like an alerted deer. "Pssst, Roar, don't freak out."

What the hell. Was that in my head? "Tayo?" I felt stupid asking the empty room.

A familiar laugh sent my heart fluttering.

"Hey, my little Roar."

My eyes darted around the room. "Where are you?"

There was a quiet *shoosh* noise and movement on my periphery. Then out of my wardrobe stepped...

"Tayo!" I gasped, my feet finding the floor and setting off his way. Tayo held out his arms, literally having no choice but to catch me. My legs clung on around his waist, and with the force of impact he spun around. I squeezed him with such vigour; I never wanted to let him go. My jackass of a Juvie! I buried my head into his neck. So many questions, but they could wait.

Soon, Tayo loosened his grip around my lower back, and lowered my feet to the floor. He dried my cheeks with his sleeve, and we stood reacquainting ourselves with each other's faces.

"I've missed you, my little Roar."

"Oh, you have no idea." I pushed my face into his chest. "How did you get in here?" I asked, standing back to see his face.

"I am going to tell you, but only after I've done this." He placed both hands on the sides of my face, and then his lips came to mine. Tayo's mouth touched my mouth. *I'm kissing my jackass of a Juvie.* The thought shouldn't be doing what it was doing. My skin reflected my thoughts, but I didn't have to suppress the glow in front of Tayo. He pulled back and squeezed my cheeks a little harder. "Because after I tell you, you will want to punch me in the mouth."

"We...probably shouldn't do that again," I whispered breathlessly.

"No, okay. We *probably* won't." He pressed his lips to mine again and at the same time pushed me backwards. "Probably," he repeated with a kiss, stepping into me again so I had to tread back.

I couldn't help but smile. "Tayo."

He continued walking me back to the bed. Keeping his face close to mine, he stroked my glowing cheek. My heels hit the platform step and Tayo gently laid me down.

"Tayo." I was still smiling. My insides were squirming.

"Ohh, you're usually so quick off the mark with your training." He climbed on top of me. "What's going on?" He pinned my arms above my head and brushed his lips over my neck.

Overcome with a dizzying rush, I tried to sound convincing. "I could stop you."

"Oh, I know you could." He worked his lips lower…but then he stopped.

I pulled him back in to me.

"Tell me I can, and I'll continue," he said, leaning back and denying my kiss.

"Tayo," I moaned, pulling at his lapel.

"No. Tell me I can kiss you, and I'll continue."

"Okay," I mouthed silently.

"Okay what?" He turned his ear to me.

"You can."

"That's all I needed to know," he said, climbing off me.

My mouth dropped open. "You did not just do that."

"You do that thing where you think if you don't say 'yes,' then you're somehow less responsible for your actions. So, I was just making sure I had your permission."

I sat up and diffused my glowing skin. "And *you* do that thing where you take what you want without me actually saying yes."

"Oh, you do like talking nonsense, don't you? I got you to say yes."

"Only after—"

"Shhh."

"No. You—"

"Shush." He blocked me off again, but this time crawling back to me.

"Will you—"

He kissed me mid-sentence.

"You are so annoy—" I slowly gave up once his lips came to mine again.

Once he detected I'd yielded, he sat back, leaning on his hands. "You are so beautiful."

"Stop it." I had to check my arms to see if the burning in my cheeks was due to magic—it wasn't.

"What are you wearing?" Tayo waved a pointed finger in an 'S' motion.

I looked down at my black padded knees and green vest. "Oh, my Khakidemy training clothes—long story. It's weird not seeing you in claret."

Today, Tayo dressed in all-black. His trousers looked almost like my combats but his ones had a low crutch and excess material collating around his knees. His black jacket was made of leather but with fabric cuffs, collar, and hood.

"What is this?" I smirked at him. "Your ninja outfit for when you break into girls' bedrooms?"

"Hmm, about that..." He analysed his trousers, an unmistakable guilty look on his face.

"Are you about to tell me why I would want to punch you in the mouth?"

He nodded with that grimace I'd seen before. He exhaled and rubbed his palm side to side over his forehead.

"Tayo?"

Holding on to his forehead, he looked back up at me. "Remember when you asked me if I knew where the tunnels under the trapdoor led to?"

"Yeah..."

Tayo walked across the room. "One leads to your wardrobe." He lifted up a floor panel inside.

"Holy crap. That's how you got in here?" I stared down a small ladder.

Tayo nodded.

At the same time, I had an alarming thought. "Tayo, did you know that tunnel led to this room?"

He let go of the floor panel, held the sides of his face with both hands and nodded again.

"Tayo." I closed my eyes. "Did you allocate me my room?"

He didn't respond.

"Did you allocate me this *Unity* room? This room I couldn't have been allocated unless I was *united*?"

He still didn't answer, but he didn't need to—I already knew.

"Tayo, did I match with Pax?"

"Yes. I swear."

"But you were going to match me if I didn't unite?"

Tears grew in his eyes. "I'm so sorry, Aurora."

"*Were you going to match me if I didn't find a match?*"

"Yes."

My fingers shook as I covered my mouth. I felt sick.

"I didn't know you then, Roar."

I couldn't talk. I just wanted Tayo out of my bedroom. Unity was a lifelong commitment, an arranged marriage, and Tayo was going to pair me up with some random boy.

"I wouldn't do it now I know you." He kept his gaze down on his black trainers. "God, I would *not* do it now."

"You were going to unite me with somebody I didn't match with." My stomach turned over as it sunk in. A tear fell down his cheek, and I turned my back to him.

"I would have chosen your closest match."

I spun back on him. "And that makes it okay?"

"No. No, it doesn't. Roar, I'm so sorry."

"That was too far, Tayo. Your whole plan of getting caught on purpose, allocating me as your chaperone, jogging my memory about the bracelet, and convincing me to go see the door, all that was calculated but within reason—matching me was going too far. That was never your decision to make."

"I know…" He hung his head, his black fringe covering his eyes.

"You lied to me when I asked if you knew where the tunnels led to."

"No. You asked if I knew where *all* the tunnels led. I didn't know. There was only this one tunnel before."

"Tut. Fine, you weren't exactly forthcoming with the truth."

"It's been killing me, Roar, every day. I knew you would work it out once I told you about the tunnel, and I never found a good time for you to be mad at me, not as a Juvie."

"Can you just go, Tayo."

"Please, Aurora."

"Go!"

"OK." He nodded briskly, taken aback. "OK, but I'm going away for a few weeks, Roar. Please take my details so you can contact me if you want to." Tayo held his hand out for my Slate. "Please."

Suddenly, the sound of my room's access button being pressed flooded my body with adrenaline. I grabbed hold of Tayo's arm and forced my energy into making him invisible. My life depended on it.

"Oooh, not quite quick enough there, Little Lady."

"Na-Na-Nanny Kimly." The blood drained from my upper body, making my fingers tingle and my legs feel dense.

"Highly advanced conjuring, and without the incantation to aid you. Now, question is—how long can you hold him invisible for?"

"Er-er-er, ah-ah-I…" I was frozen, brain-dead, and jittering.

She tilted her head impatiently. "Bring him back, Aurora."

Something I never had trouble with was uncloaking something. I would just need to want it and nothing else. But I didn't *want* to bring Tayo back.

Turns out I didn't need to; within a minute, he came back on his own.

"Leave us, please, Mr. Tessan," Nanny Kimly addressed Tayo.

Tayo's face was as gaunt as mine. He didn't want to go, I could tell. There was a question on both our minds: was Nanny Kimly likely to get me arrested for being Puracordis?

"Aurora is safe. Please leave us."

I nodded to Tayo, and he reached for my hand, taking me to the wardrobe with him.

"You sure?" he asked in a low voice, his hooded eyes holding steady on mine.

"Yes. I think so. Yeah." I was still deciding for myself. "I'll be fine."

"Give me your Slate." He took my Slate from me and held it against his fake picoplant, transferring his details and adding himself as a contact. "Message me later, Roar, please."

"Alright," I agreed, his confession from earlier no longer my main concern.

"And, Mr. Tessan," interrupted Nanny Kimly. "You'll do well to remember that Aurora is betrothed."

"Yeah, to somebo—"

"Don't, Tayo." I grabbed his arm to stop him back chatting Nanny Kimly. "Just go."

Tayo leant in and kissed the side of my head. Then he lifted the floor panel and descended under the wardrobe. The self-closing panel lowered slowly after him.

"And you'll do well to remember that also, Little Lady."

"Pax is leaving, Nanny Kimly. He doesn't want anything to do with me."

"Until that time." She gave me a stern look.

I changed the subject to address the elephant in the room. "Nanny Kimly, I know it's a death sentence, but it's not something I chose, it's just something I am."

I sat on the bed with her and she took hold of my hands. Then she turned my wrist up and stroked my birthmark. "I know, Little Lady. I've always known. I've just been waiting until you were ready to tell me." Then Nanny Kimly did something that made me prickle from head to toe. She made her skin glow like mine!

"Nanny Kimly! Yuh-yuh-you're—"

"Shhh."

"Sorry. You're *Puracordis*?" I whispered, feeling my soul dance.

"No, Little Lady. I am not Puracordis; we are *all* Puracordis."

"All...?"

"Every child is born with the ability to conjure. The reason we are unable to is because of a chemical in the water. Nobody can conjure on Cryxstalide—nobody except you."

ACKNOWLEDGEMENTS

In this acknowledgment section, I would really like to thank the people who were there from the very beginning. I would like to first and foremost thank my favourite English teacher, Mr. Cummings, for instilling in me your passion for English. Not only that, you also taught me how to be tidy by ensuring every lesson we knew that "everything has a home and everything is in its place". It really stuck with me, and I repeat it whenever I'm home organising. I don't think you'll ever read this, but if this young adult, magical realism book somehow finds its way into your hands, then this thank you is to you.

I would like to thank every single author who inspired me to write. Whenever I would hear of someone being an author, I would be in awe. I literally thought writing a book was a superpower and something you knew you were born to do, which definitely wasn't me, so this leads me on to my third acknowledgment. My third thank you is for the motivational speakers who made me realise authors were not born knowing how to write a book, they do not have superpowers, and I was capable if I put in the hard work. Thank you to my Motivational Speeches podcast on Spotify and to Oprah Winfrey, Will Smith, and Ester Hicks. Thank you to my best friend Holly Salmon for introducing me to Ester.

Lastly, I would like to thank all my beta readers. Without your input my manuscript would still be just that...a manuscript. As you read this book, you will probably be able to spot your suggestions and improvements. Thank you to Hannah and Joely for being my very first non-family readers. Thank you to Andrea Husler, Tan

Ponk, Michelle Mitchell, Alea Cross, Daljit Aulakh, Marcel Jones, Suzie O'Sullivan, Nicole Kempis, Maduike Somadina, Avinash Ashu, Isabelle V, Shalini G, and Lillian. All of you helped make my dream a reality, so I sincerely thank you. And finally, to Entrada Publishing for giving my manuscript a home.

Lightning Source UK Ltd.
Milton Keynes UK
UKHW021322070422
401221UK00008B/203

9 781614 339366